Tiger Mates

A Romantic Caper Novel

Amrish Shah

PARTRIDGE
A Penguin Random House Company

ISBN: Hardcover 978-1-4828-3661-5
Softcover 978-1-4828-3662-2
eBook 978-1-4828-3660-8

Print information available on the last page.

To order additional copies of this book, contact
Partridge India
000 800 10062 62
orders.india@partridgepublishing.com

www.partridgepublishing.com/india

Tiger Mates

Contents

Acknowledgement vii
Prologue ix
Chapter 1 1
Chapter 2 11
Chapter 3 18
Chapter 4 33
Chapter 5 43
Chapter 6 54
Chapter 7 66
Chapter 8 76
Chapter 9 86
Chapter 10 96
Chapter 11 103
Chapter 12 111
Chapter 13 120
Chapter 14 132
Chapter 15 141

Chapter 16 149
Chapter 17 158
Chapter 18 168
Chapter 19 177
Chapter 20 186
Chapter 21 196
Chapter 22 204
Chapter 23 214
Chapter 24 225
Chapter 25 237
Chapter 26 247
Chapter 27 257
Chapter 28 267
Chapter 29 284
Chapter 30 297
Chapter 31 304

ACKNOWLEDGEMENT

A note of Salute to all the children who are being nurtured in the midst of violence, chaos, poverty, hunger across the world. With strength and love they fight battles everyday of their lives. Even if their bodies are scarred or bruised- their souls remain intact. Armed with belief and labour they overcome their sorrows and transform to be the ambassadors of joy, of resilience. Thus they experience the Truth. They are the real Tiger Mates.

AUTHOR'S NOTE:

The cosmos has figured out its Truth. You are the mystery.

Be Specific in the way you observe the world; in the way you experience your universe.

You are born with freewill to choose- how you want to feel life, how you want to love.

And that is how you will discover the secret to who you are, why you were born!

Prologue

I am as innocent as a toddler in a rose garden. I can't decide for anybody, which rose to pick. They call me Fate. I didn't place the thorns either. I don't setup life. I only give people choices. In an ocean filled with life, whether to swim, fight, dodge, rescue or simply stay afloat, it's all about a choice. These choices make their own individual choices. And those choices then make their own. Soon a tree of choices started by an individual flourishes. Do the branches bear leaves, flowers, fruits, wild berries or poison ivy is the perpetual quest that keeps the human race spinning the wheel of time... The sweet irony being nobody surely knows- where it all began or when it does all end. Just like the universe.

In this vast space, filled with breathing memories, with odours, encounters, records on pages of time, I find nestled like a dove, this is my haven. Let me pull out a juicy tale from my tree of life. I am fate, destiny, different languages have different names to describe me but deep down I exist, always and everywhere, people can run and hide but can't escape my grip. I sit and watch them trying to convince themselves that they can make their own destiny, they can but don't know how! I watch and smile, I stand and look, as if behind an ice glass. They err and fall into a black hole of Karma cause they are simply human in flesh and blood or atleast they think they are, till they discover the ultimate truth.

As Fate my job is to tell stories or rather collect them. I run my long and pointy finger on a yellow map of India: Chhattisgarh, Bihar, and Jharkhand... The map has been pinned up and down so many walls that by now its four corners are lost, devoured by time, pins and hands. I think, I have always been convinced, that powerful stories must be respected, in the lifetime of a storyteller one may only get one or two, three if he is extremely lucky. And because they are the stories that shape our future, our world, we must pay respect to them and honour them. In my case I have the liberty of being immortal and so are my stories. It's the story of two souls that were meant to be together. However first they needed to overcome their inner demons and then conquer love. Our two lead characters, two heroes, engage in a journey, a geographic journey, of course, but also one within themselves. *The journey inwards is a long one but most rewarding. Who can love anybody, without experiencing what love is?*

A woman in search for her truth, man-seeking adventure with a hidden mission. Do you see this line here? Come closer, yes, like this, rub your nose on the canvas, smell the dust of adventure, love and thrill that evaporates from my map. Do you see this area? This is the part of the red corridor area- Bastar, Dantewada, Kanker in Chhattisgarh. The Maoists, the Naxals have run it, owned it rather, for many years. They have nurtured internal terror. If terror from the outside can be fought by guarding all the frontiers on land, air and sea, how can one fight intestine terror, terror that is tirelessly thriving right within the heart of India? Like a full blown cancer the Naxals... the Maoists... are desperate to destroy the entire nation, slowly and steadily. Currently their rampant terror is the most lethal threat to the very social fabric of the country of India...

And this is where the story takes place.

What's my role in all this? I am an artist, I set up the stage, give people the chance to play the game as they like, I don't know how it's going to end, and on second thoughts maybe I do. I am fate. There will be breathless moments, uncertainties, bridges to build, bridges to destroy. Fear, revenge, greed, torment, lament, love and hatred and in the end there will be resolution. Resolution is when the all the dots get connected. Resolution throws light on the meaning, or meaninglessness of action and inaction.

Chapter 1

This story starts at many different times, where we are now is the empty room of an old school near Kanker, by the river Turu, in Chhattisgarh. It's the middle of a suffocating day, the room is empty and rundown: the ceiling has collapsed in one corner and the once white walls are now covered in mold and a few plants grow on the floor, breaking through the concrete floor. The power of nature in India takes back, sooner or later, like nature does anywhere in the globe; what men have tried to tear away: this is the true India, that of the overpowering and crude nature, the India of the small cities and of the wide forests, the contemporary India, the brutal India that takes rather than give and which is for this characteristic, the home of the Indian pirates. The Naxals, the gang of red terror…

In this tiny and rustic room the Turu Dalam Unit has met today, camouflaged and ready as always to initiate any action. They are standing around a carton box over which there are several sheets of paper, they are planning the next assault to a convoy. The men speak all at the same time, creating a cacophony of sounds and screams; one wants to act straight away and the other one wants to wait. They all wear the same outfit: camouflage gear, red band around their left arm and red beret, both the arm band and the beret have an emblem of a Chinese dagger sewn to them, the symbol of their revolution.

Madhav cannot quite distinguish the faces from where he is hiding, he has followed them here and is standing around a corner, but outside this small room there's the jungle, if he is seen the only thing he can do is run and hope they won't catch him.

He is a feisty man in his thirties, with pockmarks of poverty on his innocent face. In a region that offered nothing to honest people, he got caught smuggling goods and was offered by the police the option to become an informer instead of going to jail. He wasn't excited about it, and when they sent him home to give him a night to think it over, he also considered running, but then he looked at his blind wife- Neema cooking, at his coughing mother helping her and at his immobile father sitting on the doorstep, playing with his three year old son. If he escaped he had to do it alone, what would become of them? How would they manage to even obtain stale rice or contaminated water? Would the police take revenge on the blind Neema? Or his dying father? His ailing mother? His innocent son?

Madhav evaluated the situation: prison meant no money and being beaten up regularly, besides jails are full of the Naxals' small fish, they would know in a minute what he was there for and they would find a way to enlist him. He hated the Naxals, they had taken over his country, his state, his city, without asking, they had just snatched it. They said they acted on behalf of the people but never really consulted with the people on what they wanted. And he, Madhav, didn't want them. He wanted a free India where he or his family could get on a train or bus without fearing to be attacked by these dacoits!

So the decision came easy, between Naxal and informer he didn't like either, but the one he disliked the least was certainly the spy.

Of course he had considered the risk, and right now the risk seemed more real than ever and sent a cold frisson down his spine, but at the time he imagined something more adventurous than just sneaking after people and listening to them. It seemed more appealing, he also dreamt for a minute of something he had once seen in a movie... would they give him a gun?

Nothing of the kind, as it turned out the next day at the police station. He went to negotiate and was welcomed by a policeman who rolled around his wrist a pair of handcuffs and told him "Ah, Madhav, finally!!! We were unsure if we should come to your house, maybe your wife could have offered us something to drink..." and the grin on his face convinced Madhav to take whatever they offered and agree to whatever they asked for as long as he could stay out of jail and close to his wife. Ofcourse he too had a choice but that choice meant throwing his wife in front of the wolves. When he left the police station, after they had shown him for hours the photos and the organogram of the regional Naxal unit in Kanker, the ill-famed Turu Dalam, he was gutted. He realized the police are often not different than thugs and he knew at once, in the evening breeze, that he had signed his death toll. The Naxals are everywhere, they know who he is and what he does and if they let him live it's only because they either want something from him or because they think they will be able to use him in some way. His fears were appeased after a few months, when he collected some information about the Turu Unit and shared it with the police with no repercussions. He had started to live like he did before, at peace, not snapping at every sound of the night and without the nightmares that had haunted him in the first few weeks. He was sleeping with his wife in his arms with no fears.

Today in the midday heat, with his shirt glued to his back, he has a sad foreshadowing: the forest is thick, there are trees, plants, animals, he might have a chance; but the thought is wiped out by the knowledge that these people, the Naxals survive in the forest, it's their haven, they know every tree, every monkey, and every ant. If he tries to escape, they'll catch him. Following them here was a stupid idea, it's not far from the main road but there's no way he can get out of it alive now... He just thought that if he had information of some interest to report Sub-Inspector Pillai would give him something more than the pittance he usually gets for a leak. He also is well aware that if anything happens to him, his son would not be able to survive for a long time because his family is rendered useless by the cruelty of the cycle of karma. A blind wife, and dying parents in the most tormented region of the country, life could not have been more challenging for this father who wants to see his son-Raghav prosper with sufficient food, shelter and education.

While he is pondering, worry and sorrow mix in his veins poisoning his reasoning, he fails to look below his feet. As fate would have it, he accidentally steps on a dry stick that breaks with a groaning noise, which apparently echoes as far as Mumbai.

For only a second it looks like the gang hasn't heard it, focused as they were on the conversation. Madhav doesn't dare moving, or breathing for that matter, he nearly breathes a sigh of relief when he hears the heavy steps of one of the younger gang members walking in his direction.

He only allows his brain a fraction of a second to think *"If he comes any closer he'll see me and I have less time to run, the possibilities of him coming closer without seeing me are too slim as the space is so limited.... Run Madhav run"!* And before the nerves can take the impulse from his brain to his legs, he sprints like a prey.

Of course the hullabaloo he makes attracts more attention and makes the young guy, who had walked to the window incidentally, only to light a cigarette, run after him, all the others, alerted by the jump over the window of their comrade, join him in the manhunt. *Fear is far more cruel than fate.*

Madhav knows this forest pretty well, he has gallivanted here against his parents' will when he was a teenager, he has come here as a youth and has followed these people for months now. He runs and surprises himself knowing exactly where to go, without getting misled by the changing lights and the rich nature that seems to change the face of the forest at every turn. He dashes like an arrow but hears that behind him they are approaching: he estimates that two of them are already in front of him and one is behind, from his calculation one is also on his right hand side but quite far away, he is not to worry about him. But the two in front might realize any minute he is not ahead of them and turn back. He is trapped in between.

Madhav runs to the only side which, according to his calculations -and right now he is not too sure he can trust his rationality and projections-, is free and runs past the two.

He hasn't heard them shooting yet, he has seen sophisticated guns in the room so he knows they have them, but he also thinks that maybe, if he's very lucky, they have been taken by surprise and chase him, leaving their weapons behind. While he runs he also assumes that to be so fast they must have had machetes with them, to cut through the bush, and a chill runs down his spine. Death by machete is not something he looks forward to. As a child these trees have nurtured him and now he doesn't want them to get splashed with his blood. This forest must have protected my forefathers from hunger and poverty but they mustn't have seen so much of blood and gore as they see today.

Behind him, even if he doesn't know, is the boss of this small gang, not so important in the strategic ranks of the organization but one of the first ones to join the Unit, the founder, even. A madman, with a determination to make it to the top, now with his eyes wide open and white foam at the side of his mouth that makes him look like a forest predator. With the amount of hostility in his heart, he could put a hyena to shame.

The look in his eyes is scary, his eyes call for blood, and if Madhav could see them he would behave like a scared animal: he would stop running hoping that the lack of motion would convince the jackal of a false alarm.

But Madhav doesn't see those cannibal eyes and he runs for his life until he sees a clearing: the road, and an abandoned the petrol station. He knows that this petrol station has a payphone and this could be his lucky day.

Of course now they know who he is so if he makes it he will have to rush home, collect his family and catch the first train, any train, or bus, any bus, to anywhere.

But right now, with his shirt glued to his back and chest by a fair amount of sweat, his legs ripped apart by the millions of thorns he had to step on to run through the woods, his eyes stinging under the veil of salty sweat, all he can think of is that phone. The payphone is his passport to safety.

He will call the police, the gang will run away and he will plan the rest as he goes. He will reunite with his family.

A sense of inner peace reigns over him. His body is still running and shivering and his hands do shake like leaves in a storm, but in his brain everything is calm. Like it often happens a minute of two before one's death.

He runs through the clearing and doesn't hear any shooting *Ha, Ha! They have forgotten the guns after all!* He goes to the phone, sure that none of the gang members have seen him. He knows that if they are still in the woods it's harder for him to see them than vice versa but right now this is the only option he has. He reaches the phone, dials the emergency number and waits until some bored policeman picks up at the other end of the line.

"Hallooo?" sings the guy into the phone.

"Hello, its Madhav, pass me Anand saab, now!"

"Madhav who?"

"Anand saab... please..." implores Madhav who can by now hear heavy steps approaching behind him.

It's a minute, he lifts his trembling eyes from the wall he was facing, hoping that without looking at it the world could be shut out of his life for a few minutes but his light green eyes meet those of Kedar, the lunatic leader of this small group.

Kedar has run after him, like a predator, with the veins in his eyes growing redder by the minute, he has smelt him, found him across the woods, and now he is ready to kill. His nostrils vibrate as he inhales Madhav's sweat, the intense black eyes and the trembling of his nostrils make Madhav think for a second that he is not going to shoot but rather cry. What Madhav doesn't know is that Kedar has been waiting for this opportunity for a long long time. They had thought there was a mole in their group, then a friendly policeman told them that there was no mole, it was an informer, someone who lingered around them and sold their secrets to the cops.

It was enough for Kedar, he paid the policeman for the information and set off looking for the spy. He had suspected of Madhav, but the guy looked to useless and harmless that Kedar dropped him shortly after.

Today Kedar wants to kill Madhav for having spied on them but also, and mostly, for having walked on his ego, for having played a fool of him, for having outsmarted him.

Madhav looks into his eyes still holding the phone. On the other side the voice of Anand cries out Madhav's name but Madhav is paralysed, he could tell him that Kedar is right in front of him, that anything happens to him it's Kedar's fault, that...

But all he can hear is the sound of vultures that fly over them. *How do they even know there's going to be blood... These animals are crazy!* Thinks Madhav despite himself. He doesn't realise that he has been shot a while ago. The blood from his thighs is inviting the blood thirsty vultures. He tries to revisit his family in the confines of his memories but fails. He finds himself in a dark narrow space. He can't think, let alone speak. It's all pitch black for him.

One of the boys of the gang looks at the street and sees a government truck coming, it will be here in two minutes and if they don't hurry up they could be in trouble. He shoots at Madhav but misses him, he does it on purpose, Madhav thinks, probably to draw his boss' attention.

On the other side of the phone Anand screams "Madhav, Goddamn it!!! Are you alright, who is shooting? Talk to me!!!"

Madhav is frozen to eternity. He imagines a black cloud swallowing him like hell has arrived on this very earth. Through the dark matter he sees his helpless family followed by his doting son Raghav crying out of for him on the other side. But before he can hear the echo of the word 'Baba' shooting out of his reverie, Kedar groans like a sick hyena. He blinks twice, as if he has been woken up suddenly, he lifts his arm and point his gun at Madhav. He blinks again, those thick black irises make him look like a madman, he shifts his head to the left and without a word shoots in his head at point-blank. Kedar inhales the smell of blood to soothe his nerves.

Madhav's fragments of skull and soft brains are sprayed on the wall behind him and a smear of blood stains Kedar's right cheek. Madhav is still standing, his hand slowly lets the phone go and the voice of Anand falls into a void. The look on Madhav's face is puzzled, as if he didn't expect it to happen, he has a broken smile on his face, as if to say "such a shame to die on such a beautiful day" and his sweaty back, against the stained wall leaves a streak of blood as he slowly falls on the ground.

The vultures descend as the gang disappears into the woods again, leaving no trace of its presence other than a half smiling corpse and a hanging phone from which a far away voice fades into oblivion. Amidst an artistic splatter of blood and flesh, Madhav's dead eyes are frozen with a singular thought- "Why was I brought into this world?"

Chapter 2

The small river flows quietly into an even calmer lake, the sun shines and birds fly after one another like they do every day. A solitary man is fishing on the lake bank, he has a rather simple fishing rod, which he keeps fixing, he is not young and, like all ageing people, his sight is short. He throws the line in the water and as soon as the bait, a small and chubby worm twitching on his hook, touches the water it creates a series of concentric circles that hypnotize the fisherman.

What is there to fish in this stream? Nothing, probably, but something like a foreshadowing brought the fisherman right here this morning. He now sees an eagle fly over the water, *fishing my catch?* he thinks, and the perfect balance of this majestic bird, so close to the water and yet so light in the air, convinces him that she must be a sign, the symbol of something that is happening, that is about to happen, that he is about to witness.

He pulls the rod back a couple of times, checks the hook to see if the fish have eaten the bait and takes new worms from the ground grunting at the smart fish of this tiny lake.

At his third or fourth attempt he sees in the distance bubbles coming up from the still water, the fishing rod moves gently at first and then more and more anxiously, exactly as if a life, or rather the end of it, was attached to it.

The eagle flies over it, so close its wings touch the water leaving a long track. It looks at the prey but decides not to take it. The man runs towards the fishing rod and holds it firmly in his hands, he pulls, struggling at first and then more easily. His movements flow, he takes the big fish in his hand and decides to keep it, when they are too small he puts them back in the water, but today the catch is good and this fish will feed his family.

As he packs his things, ready to go home, the fish still twitching in the plastic bag, he sees the water of the lake, calm and still until a minute before, moving. The water vibrates under a sound, a distant hammering noise. *It's like seeing the water in a glass when you hit the table*, he thinks. The small waves move in one direction as if the movement that generates them came from the centre of the earth. It's a very different pattern than that of the circles.

On the bridge connecting the two sides of the lake an official convoy appears from the woods. There's a police jeep, the car of a clearly influential man, and another police jeep closing the line.

The man stares at them holding his meagre catch, his thin trousers rolled around his slim calves.

"This is where our money goes" murmurs the man to himself "In this country you better not pay taxes otherwise that's exactly where the money goes... escorts, entourage and bribes for these rogue politicians..."

He doesn't know that in the car there really is a politician who, unaware of where he is and blindly trusting his police escorts, talks nonchalantly on the phone. He wears a grey suit, so tight around his fat waist that he finds it hard to breathe. His stiff collarless jacket is choking him but he wants to show these peasants what an affluent man looks like. He will steal their votes, rob them of their rights and hopefully stay their representative for the rest of his life. The man stops digging his nose, wags his finger, also choked in a heavy gold ring, to ask his assistant to pour another drink.

The fat politician always has a bottle of scotch in the car, in Delhi, he wants one and even more when he comes to these remote areas, "Drinking is the only way out of it, for God's sake!" he says to his friends at the club every time he goes back home. He dresses in grey, with a black Indian fur cap on his head. From a distance he looks a little like Jawaharlal Nehru, architect of the nation, that's what he wants to look like: he wants the people to look at him and suddenly be reminded of some greater ideals. His own ideals are far more pecuniary: history teaches that people can be squeezed, even when you think there's not a drop of blood left in them, they surprise you by paying one more tiny tax, and the circle continues. The man is the one who will represent these commoners in the Parliament (besides, do peasants really care about being represented at all?) and in exchange for their voice heard in Delhi he is determined to get something back. Something big, possibly.

He is on the phone "Relax Yadav ji, you know very well the Central Government wilfully chooses to turn a blind eye. We're the big guns in this region. You keep the cash registers ringing; I'll keep the votes coming. Why worry?" and he lets out a hearty laugh as he slurps the remaining scotch in his glass and gestures his assistant for more.

At the same time, in the same convoy but on one of the jeeps, Senior Inspector Mahajan is also talking on the phone. He is relaxed, the drive was so far uneventful and there's no reason why it shouldn't end like this. Anil is on the phone with his younger brother, planning what to do during his upcoming holiday. He has raised his brother after their parents died. An uncle who was supposed to take care of them took better care of their money, deriving from the sale of their beautiful tea estate in Shimla, and sent them straight to boarding school, "to receive a better education". The quality of their studies was good indeed, as they both managed to get good jobs straight after school, but during the school years they had been forced -although they had been doing it willingly- to be one for the other as they were each other's only family left.

Anil was more inclined to study, his little brother was a little lazier, but even though fights over what to do were not rare, the two brothers loved each other dearly and spent most of their time together. After school they found jobs in different places but still managed to go on holiday together and organize little hiking trips around the country. The time they spent on the hills together had brought them so close that even death cannot separate them.

Anil is smiling, his leg wrapped in the multi pocketed khaki trousers sits on the front of the car as he is not driving and, because the drive was so smooth so far, he has no reason to believe things will be any different further on. He is relaxed, he is happy to be talking to his little brother and to have a professional crew he can trust. Less happy of having to deal with one of those thugs, the politicians, the legalized thieves that raid the country in search of votes, money or God knows what.

But this is a glorious day and he has decided that he is not going to let this guy spoil it.

He listens to his brother complaining about some job he has been assigned, apparently it's more physical than he expected and he has been bragging for a while on how bad he got beaten up last night before he could finally catch the guy they were after. Anil smiles "Bro... bruises will make a man out of you. I didn't become a cop sleeping on heat packs. Hey listen, I've applied for the Diwali leave..." His brother interrupts him, he is asking him something that makes him crack up, as he chokes on his own laughter he answers "Fine, fine... I'll see what I can do. Oh yeah, one more thing..."

But there's no time to think, to act, not even to speak and to laugh anymore. In one huge blast nothing is like before, everything is erased from this spot in the district of Kanker. From now on instead of a lake, a bridge, trees, there will only be a hole.

Among the flames that wrap the world around Anil's eyes, he sees the car they were escorting: the driver was blown up with the front of the car and in the back a sinister scene appears: the assistant is burning still holding the bottle firmly while the politician died with a grin on his face and his phone melted to his ear. Anil looks down at himself and sees only flames: the smell of burned flesh is unbearable and he would want to have the strength to see if there are survivors and if he can do anything for anyone, but his body is too weak. His lungs are filling with the black smoke and his legs are glued to the seat of the car. He knows there is no way out for him and the only thing he is sincerely sorry for is that his brother had to witness it from far away, frustrated and fearing the worse, unable to do anything or alert anybody. Anil didn't want to depart from this world leaving behind the trail of his dying voice that will disturb his brother for the rest of his life.

Among the bushes Anil sees the silhouettes of people, dressed in military clothes and sporting stars on their arms and berets. Naxals. He wonders how long they had been watching them for, he remembers that, when planning this trip, he had thought of the chance of them blowing the bridge. But as far as he was told the politician they were escorting wasn't that important and the fact that everything went smoothly had cheered him up. *How could I be so stupid?* He thinks *Of course there was no one around, they had planned to blow up the bridge, how could I not think about it? Was there a mole among us?*

But he is so powerless, all his strength is abandoning him and the smell of burnt petrol and flesh is overwhelming. He closes his eyes and as his eyelids melt on his cheek. He dies wearing a sad smile.

What will be of his brother, so excited of his new job as a cop?

The soil keeps burning, the parts of the bridge that collapsed into the little lake brought down gas from the cars and right now, between the two broken ends of an iron smile -the bridge- little fire islands light the still water of the lake.

The fisherman looks at the scene from afar, he has never seen anything like this, violence -yes, Naxal booby traps- of course, but this is beyond anything he has ever seen. He sees Anil looking around and then dying slowly, and right now he sees a guy looking around for survivors and shooting a couple of times through the flames.

The man shakes his head, these people have brought their quest for justice and an economically balanced world to a different, wrong level, and this is not what he had hoped for when he, many years ago, had looked at them with interest.

He knows that the people who are now going back to the bushes have seen him, he was the only person in the whole habitat and stuck out like an archaic character with his fishing rod and plastic bag full of fish, but he also knows that they think he's no threat, he is too scared to run to the police and tell them what he has seen. He looks at himself with rage, he would love to prove them wrong and go straight to the police station, with his pants rolled up and his fishing rod on his shoulder, but they are right. He is a coward, or maybe too old, or just aware of what happens to the families of those who dare to speak.

They are right: he will go home, trying to avoid people on the way and if someone passing by should stop and ask him what happened in that direction he will answer "Nothing, I heard a blast, maybe a car accident". He will go home, give his wife the fish to cook and go smoke outside. Would he tell her? She is the only person he loves on this planet and he could drop the conversation during lunch. Or not...

CHAPTER 3

Every choice that you make opens up a new world of opportunities. Thus every individual walks into a world created by his or her own self, which is fate. Like a matchstick, passion ignites a thought. Like rings of fire, the desired thought blazes the trail and thrusts you to your desired destiny. As fate I place these rings in different directions. It is for the individuals to make their own choices in order to arrive at a destination. The chosen destiny is the journey of the soul. Every being is the sum total of the choices that they make in the gamut of situations that crop up consistently. As fate I throw in the situation, as a being, you make the choice.

The story continues, and because a storyteller can skip a few years, we are now at the present time: five years have passed since the bridge blast, since the death of Inspector Mahajan. We are in Pokhara, Nepal, it's the middle of the winter and people hurry from one house, shop or bar to the other: it's freezing cold and the light outside grows dimmer by the minute very early in the afternoon. The wind whistles while pushing the body of rain, when it calms down, only for a few hours, the rain falls vertically and soaks every building in Pokhara giving it a pleasant, nearly Christmas-like look. In the town, where sounds and colours are numbed by the thick rainfall, small people, all wrapped up in their rain coats hurry from one place to the other.

This is one of the feet of the Himalayas and people come here to climb up: the city is full of hippy looking European climbers, of semi-professional climbers, their noses constantly white with sunblock and those funny sunglasses with coloured lenses.

There are also, of course, locals. They run around all day trying to gather all the necessary goods for the climbers who have hired them, they can find anything even if, apparently, the supplies are so limited.

The Sherpas are the backbone of the economy of this little city: they provide an income and act as translators between foreign climbers and the local shop owners or hotel managers. They are wrapped in their thick parkas and they walk up and down as cheerful goats, they always smile, always have a solution for every problem, and for many climbers meeting a good Sherpa is as important as being fit for the climb. They are often anonymous people but absolutely indispensable for a successful trip.

All Sherpa's and climbers meet at sundown at the local bar. Those who have just come down from the mountain have the veteran role and tell stories of every little event, those who are about to leave listen carefully and think *Oh, I wouldn't have made that mistake* or *That must have been nice, but I'll push myself even further* in a never-ending competition among climbers. The true climbers are always looking for surpassing their own capacities.

They know that the mind does play games, sometimes by setting preconceived limits but the inner wisdom will guide a climber to newer heights and perhaps unexplored territories. Strangely this holds true for non-climbers too. In a corner the Sherpa's drink tea and look at them, they probably laugh about those over prepared, over dressed, over experienced climbers from the west. The Sherpa's were born on these mountains, know and respect them like they were part of their tribes and it's hard for them to see climbing as a competition or a sport rather than just a mere fact of life. The Sherpa's climb because they are born to climb, they were meant to climb. They know when something becomes your lifelong passion, you don't compete, and you just do it. Untill your last breath. *You live in your shoes, you die in your shoes. And you go to heaven. Everyday.*

The bar is made of wood and stones, there's a huge crackling fire in a stone chimney which disperses in the air a pleasant smell of resin and dry wood, the lights are dim and the environment warm and cosy. There is a map of the region stuck to the wall, a few tables with decks of cards and chessboards and a pool table, dusty and which has evidently not been used in a few weeks. Behind the bar is Rajesh, a big and hairy Indian who has crossed the border with Nepal and no one knows for sure why he has set his home here. He is a little intimidating but overall a good man, none of the patrons know his past but they all know that this bar, where he works for a Chinese family, is for sure his future. There are some stories in life one can never know and Rajesh is one of them. Not just a character but also a mystery unsolved. However his eyes do a lot of talking.

He appears to be man who deserted his family and his country because he was falsely implicated in a crime that he didn't commit but that's just an assumption. Eyes can be deceptive and so can be stories. Rajesh drinks with the nicer guests and throws out with his bare hands those who cause trouble and in this cold Far East he is exactly what you would expect a tavern owner to look like.

At one of the tables a lonely man is playing an ancient Indian dice game on his own. Strangely there isn't any board on the table. The man with his back facing to the rest is shuffling three pieces of rectangular dice as if he was playing with his fate with his own hands. The calm eyes swear with desire to master his own fate. He looks like a guy so smart, he could conceal his great loss in the glow of the dark rum. Fortitude. Dressed in a pair of worn out denim trousers and a multi-pocket shirt with a waistcoat on top of it, he plays *Pachisi* by moving pieces of peanuts on the table and drinks in silence, as if he were having a very intense conversation with someone sitting in front of him who only he can see. Being a handsome man, although clearly distracted, there's something in the curve of his eyes that goes down, as if he has a moving story to tell or rather to hide. But the intense look in his light brown eyes, framed by his long black lashes confuses women, who seldom see his sorrow and more often only manage to see his irresistible lure. Often the expression on his face sends confusing signals to his observers. Is it the charming face or the leave me alone, I am cool attitude?

An old juke box is spitting out music played by a Nepali rock band, a couple of girls linger around it, it's pretty clear that they are waiting for someone to dance with them and to spend the night with, a place in this bar, in the heart of Pokhara, doesn't come for free, and they must make it worth their while. A group of boys is looking at them but, as always, boys are only brave when they are together and although they would all want to go each one pushes the guy next to him to go first.

The man sitting at the table, comfortable in his own company is Neil. He keeps rolling the dice, his hands are thin and long, the skin on his knuckles slightly lighter than that on the rest of his hand. He is lifting his glass to drink the last of his dark rum when he suddenly comes to a halt.

In the background the TV set that had spitted out commercials of face wash and fruit juices, packed with Indian Bollywood stars has interrupted the carousel of colours and music to hand out the evening news.

The music of the jukebox stops and no one puts coins in the slot for another round: everyone wants to hear what's happening in the world. The world out there, that is so remote for whoever lives here, and yet so present and vividly pictured by the tourists. The first news is about the Maoist terrorist groups in India, everyone seems to lose interest a little bit. Everyone but one.

Neil Mahajan sharpens his ears and listens to every word the anchor says and, with even deeper attention, to the politician talking. The charismatic face of the politician is staring into the visiting press reporters from every possible news agency complimented by a hyperactive battery of photographers. The shutterbugs trigger off with a speed apparently faster than the bullets that ring in the doomed land of these terror struck states within the heart of India.

"After the latest kidnapping of the District Collector where he was brutally beaten up and returned back to his village, I stand here in attention. It is my solemn promise to bring stability to my home State of Chhattisgarh. We will not be defeated, nor will we live in fear. Chhattisgarh will improve on infrastructure, power and water supply. We will build hospitals and schools. I will personally be inaugurating our first new school building in a couple of weeks. To maintain aerial security, from now on there will be IAF helicopters hovering above us. More training and resources will go into setting up combined paramilitary forces by the states of Chhattisgarh, Orissa, West Bengal, Andhra Pradesh and other affected states. Let those who harbour evils in their heart know that we will not give into them. We will combat Red Terror".

A wave of applause breaks through the audience at the press meet and Neil, who was still holding his glass in mid-air, finally downs it, thinking he has heard the same speech too many times to believe any word of it. The voices have changes, sometimes, the tone, or the words, sometimes there have been tears and sometimes rage but this speech is like all others: a pile of rubbish. Promises cannot bring a dead man back. Lovers break promises and get separated but if the Government promises the citizens of safety and security and fail then people die, families break apart beyond repair, beyond life.

If the politicians meant what they say, his brother may still be alive.

The sound of the explosion, a blast from the past literally reverberates in Neil's most painful memory. If Neil had a choice to erase one thing out of his memory, he would erase the sound of that life taking blast. That noise of the devils thunderous laughter is like an evil curse for a lifetime. Neil is instantaneously transported to his last phone-call to his brother. Sometimes he imagines his brother whispering in his ears "Neil my brother I miss you bro". Behind his back Neil hears soft steps, the feet of a woman, of a splendid one, unluckily in love with him. Xian, a beautiful girl in her mid-twenties walks behind him, for a moment he is strangled by her flowery perfume, a scent that is not common in nature at this time of year. It's a springy, tangy perfume that she wears "to remind herself of the summer", as she says. For Neil she is the warmest colour so far. Her presence makes Neil feel wanted.

Her traits are Chinese and she is delicate as a flower, even though inside her burns a fire that he perceives although not quite understands. He is aware that the fire may kill his innermost passion, his goal, his very purpose but that is only when he discovers it. Right now he is simply searching.

Xian has just arrived at work, she has worked in this bar since she was a teenager, it's her family owned bar, now handled by her solo. The well-lit bar is located at the crossroad of all the possible traffic between China, India and Nepal. She hands him another glass of golden rum.

"Looking good handsome! This is for you my bulls' eye"

"Ahhh thanks Xian, what would I do without you?"

She looks at him with her almond eyes, yellow irises that so many times have scared the people of the village, her makeup, despite being almost heavy, doesn't look cheap on her. Her piercing look makes him shiver, although he knows he is here on an assignment, he cannot fall for her because of his job and most of all because she's a girl, she has the right to a happy life. But once again she stabs him with her sharp tongue.

"No babes, the true question is what would Neil do with me?" and she smiles. Her smile is rather innocent, she has just eaten a candy and her lips are stained of a cherry red that makes her look younger and more cheeky at the same time.

"That smile of yours will get someone killed one day, young lady!"

"And why not you?"

"Coz I have no time for death yet, my love" and he downs the remains of his glass of rum, she smiles, more softly this time, less aggressive.

"Then make room for love... lots of crazy love, stop wandering..." and all of a sudden she's nearly shy, the fair skin on her cheeks turns pink as she blushes.

Neil sees that she's provoking him, her look forces him to take a step back: she's only a girl. And yet her confidence and the way she moves lead him to believe that she's not as innocent as she would want him, and the world, to believe. There's a lot more to Xian, but Neil still doesn't know what and he's also not sure whether he should know. He looks at her, without an empathetic look trying to make her feel like the beautiful woman that she is, and kisses her on the cheeks.

"Not all who wander are aimless, my love…" She regains control over her blush and her actions and cuts through with another sharp question.

"Really? So what's your big aim in your wanderlust life, Cris Columbus?"

Neil looks at the TV again, it has been muted and the music from the old jukebox invades the room while images run on the screen. People move their mouth but no sound is produced, the face of the CM of Chhattisgarh is shown again, Neil looks at it and then turns to Xian who is still waiting for an answer "Only time will tell".

The politician is short and chubby, he is wearing the typical Chhattisgarhi hand-woven jacket to prove that he's a man of the people, even if the rings in his fingers betray a wealth that most Chhattisgarhi's could not even dream of. His thick eyebrows curve and straighten, moving as black waves under the expressions of his face. His black eyes pierce through the camera, he's evidently a person who is used to carve words, embellish them, until lies are knitted into truths.

Right then, cutting off their conversation, a short and thin Chinese waiter approaches Xian. He looks a lot younger than he really is and seems to be shy around her: he is obviously secretly in love with her, with her strong and piercing character and yet her sweet look, she snaps, like all women whose sparkling conversation is being interrupted by a nuisance.

The little guy manages to stammer, "T-the R-Russian guy at table four is asking for Chinese pizza... I don't know, I think he wants to talk to you..."

Xian looks annoyed, she knows she has to go back to work but she ever hardly gets the chance to speak to Neil and wouldn't want to stop now... but business is calling...

"Ok, give him Momos, tell him they are on the house and I'll be with him in a minute!"

"O-ok!" and the young Chinese guy trots off.

Before saying goodbye to Neil she looks furtively around and takes a small parcel from under the bar, she puts her hand, palm down, on the bar and lets Neil stroke it.

"A little something for the road" she whispers as he holds her tiny hand between his huge ones and takes the parcel she had hidden between her palm and the table.

The contact with Neil's rough and cold skin makes her shiver. Only his touch, or one of his looks, is enough for her to stop thinking. And passing this small packet to him is the most thrilling thing she remembers doing, not so much for its secrecy as for the deep, long, intense contact she has had with him.

"Please don't refrain from speaking Chinese, it looks very sexy on you...someday lady I would love to hear you groan in Chinese" Neil signs off with a flirtatious remark to keep her thoughts percolate. She hadn't even realized that she had spoken Chinese a minute ago with the waiter. She blushes and hides her face in her hands.

This cheerful instant is interrupted only by a foreigner entering the room. Xian changes expression and even though all other patrons still see a smiling girl, Neil knows something has changed: she's a professional and her message is hidden between two very small wrinkles on her face, hidden to everyone but him. Xian sees a Thai man with a cap walk in and sit at a corner table next to the jukebox. It appears that this exclusive table is kept for patrons who come to Nepal for an agenda other than tourism. The table has little light falling on it and so remote in the corner that nobody can ever hear the conversations that take place there. It's almost like a soundproof cabin in the middle of chaos. Xian doesn't stop smiling but says: "Don't turn around just now. He is here. Table nine...Santa Claus" and lets out a hearty laugh in pretence as if he had just made a very funny joke and takes a block of notes to go and take the Russian guy's order.

Neil polishes off his drink, turns around slowly, like any guy sitting at the bar whose favourite waitress has just gone back to work and, with the pretext of looking at her, checks the room. He sees a Thai guy sitting at the table indicated by Xian. His not so casual attire gives him away, he is obviously not a climber and not a hippy travelling around India to seek enlightenment. He looks like what he is, a business man, in a sense, and does nothing to hide it. However as a distraction he wears a cap with the words 'Santa Claus' embroidered in thick font. Neil smiles and walks towards the table, without waiting to be invited he sits down. The guy doesn't look impressed, or scared, or simply shocked. He has a half smile on his face, sits with his arms down and lifts his chin slightly to take a look at him.

For only a moment Neil thinks that the arms below the table are suspicious, is he armed? He himself came unarmed and if this guy has a gun, things could turn ugly. But then he reassures himself; he has no reason to make things difficult. He's here for something he wants and has arranged to have, like Neil himself. Its plain business.

And businessmen don't kill businessmen.

"I was waiting for John..." he says while sitting down, hoping that leaving a sentence pending would push the guy to finish it.

"He got held up in Bangkok, no big deal, he sent me" Neil is getting irritated by this guy's attitude and by his idiotic grin.

"Well, let him know I don't like middlemen" *Don't show him you are upset you idiot!* He thinks to himself, *this guy has nerves of steel, don't show him you have weaknesses or he'll use them against you!*

"Relax my friend, John sent me and I have what you want, I'm sure you have something for him too"

The foreigner hands Neil a brown paper bag "High quality stuff..."

"We'll see about that..."

"Where is stuff for John?"

Neil takes his backpack, takes a look around to check if no one is watching them and extracts a few small parcels, rough diamonds.

"This only a few, John wants more"

"Yes, my friend, John will have more when John shows up. I'm here in ten days, same place same time, it's up to him, if he doesn't come the deal is off"

The foreigner looks disappointed, for the first time since they talk in an expression different from a placid grin changes his features.

"My friend, aren't you forgetting something?"

The foreigner dives his hand in a deep pocket and hands him a roll of banknotes.

"Thai Bahts? John knows I only take US Dollars..."

"Well, my friend, John ain't here. If you don't want Baht, you give money back!"

"Oh, about bloody time you spoke like a man! I'm Neil!"

"And I'm Peter" says the foreigner, finally more relaxed, sitting back down.

"Anything else I can interest you in?" says Neil as he pulls out a small package where a bunch of marijuana is tightly wrapped and rolls a joint.

Peter leans forward, without paying much attention to the joint Neil is lighting voluptuously, he looks around to check if anyone might be overhearing their conversation and says, "You know why I'm really here. We both know what I want"

"Say it," challenges him Neil.

But Peter is too used to being careful and weighing every word. He takes out his cell-phone and flicks through a few pictures until he lands on a close up of a beautiful gem. Almost a fifty-carat Alexandrite. Neil coughs on the smoke.

He expected something less risky, drugs, women, maybe... but this...

"Name your price," says Peter with his flat, expressionless face.

"To hell with that man, this is not happening" says Neil, petrified by the realization that this guy is mad, in the first place, but also not John's middleman, he is a partner or possibly even a competitor, or his boss.

Neil has stumbled on a big shot; he wasn't prepared for it and is not too sure what to do. His eyes wander around the room and land on the TV where images of the burning forests of Chhattisgarh are still rolling on the screen. For a minute he feels lost: India, Nepal, the Naxals, money, Xian, a gigantic Alexandrite... His reverie is interrupted by the soft voice of this stranger, heavily drenched in his Thai accent "We both know that this magical, colour changing gem is in your Goddamn jungle. The question is: who else knows? Who else wants it? What are they prepared to do to have it?"

And his words mix with those of the CM of Chhattisgarh, someone has turned the volume up and at once the bar is filled with words.

"This kidnapping is the last our State is going to suffer, we are done enduring pain, we are freeing ourselves, and we start today. Madhu... an honest government employee is back home now with a missing thumb that the Maoist chopped off but we will not take such atrocities lying down!" Neil feels sick for a second: broken promises, and broken bodies. Both the CM and Peter refer to Justice with condor, knowing better than anyone that there is no justice, neither here nor anywhere else and most of all not in this job. What does this guy have on him? Because if he pulls the right strings Neil is going to go straight to jail as soon as he sets foot back in India. Is Peter going to *force him to* get the stone? Or is he just politely suggesting a transaction?

"Look dude, I don't know what John or whoever told about me... but I'm a good guy, yeah some weed every now and then, a couple of little stones but a big stone like that, you need a big fish for that!"

"Let's not play games Neil, I know more about you that you'd want anyone to know. But I'm a gentleman, a businessman. If you can't do it... be a man to say it upfront…don't be an impotent talker like this prick politician…so what if you are a small time smuggler, think big"

Neil's pride is pricked, it's not that he *can't*, it's that it's frigging nuts to even try...

"Ok, here, can't is a big word..."

"Can't or won't makes no difference as far as I'm concerned. I want that gem and I am prepared to pay for it up to quarter of a million dollars. And I'm not going to stop before anything. I know you are a relatively small fish, but I thought that because you are sneaky, fast as a tiger, smart as a panther, able to disappear like a snake... well I thought you might have been a good fit for the job. But really, no hard feelings. I'll keep doing small business with you..."

The man pauses to take in Neil's eyes, his brain abandoned him when he heard the sentence- 'quarter of a million dollars, which, from his perspective is good: Neil is enticed with the thought of money. Everyone has a price, Neil is reckless at times, but that gem is entirely worth it.

"So you are telling me that I get into that shithole of a jungle, inhabited by terrorists and regularly bombed by cops, get the bloody stone and you give me quarter million bucks, just like that?"

"Well, listen to yourself, it's not "just like that", you could lose your life in a second holding it. It's a lot of hard work, and work must be paid for. Fairly, don't you agree?"

"Maybe it is a lot of work... almost a battle"

"So?"

"I don't know, I'll let you know next time, I need to figure out..."

"No problem my friend, I know some day you will find it, let's drink to it!"

But by this point words that don't make sense anymore to Neil. Or make too much sense. Like the Alexandrite the colour of Neil's face is changing from blue to red.

Chapter 4

At the same time as Neil and Peter negotiate on their future in Nepal, Debraj Roy, Kedar's counsellor in the Turu Dalam, the Red Terror gang of Kanker, watches the same news on their Chinese television set. Debraj is a man in his fifties, he smells of experience from head to toe and is the head of a gang composed of very diverse militants. Sometimes he looks at them when they are all together and has mixed feelings: he feels like the father of some of them, the really young ones, who seem not to have fully understood the philosophy of the movement, the ideas behind it. But really what are they? Sometimes he fears the theory, the ideas, the power of it have faded away.

He is intelligent to comprehend that when evil takes over a noble cause, things move in the opposite direction. But then his ego doesn't let him recognise the defeat that he is suffering from, a defeat of his purpose- to give justice to the bastardised people of Chhattisgarh. Standing atop the surveillance tower, Debraj looks at his troop and sees poor people hoping in a revolution that will give them what they weren't born with. When he left his life, a promising career as a university professor, many years ago, the idea behind the Naxals was to bring a communist revolution to India, to bring equality in a society based on castes and economic disparities. To reform the political system.

Debraj usually clad in a vintage 'world war two' military jacket, had set out to be a Martyr, his inspiration being Subhash Chandra Bose. He wanted to become the contemporary version of a daring intelligent militant reformer. A perfect combination of brain and brawn was his formula for rebellion. Overpower the government with might and sight. The idea was itself revolutionary for the world and all the more for India.

But revolutions need resources and many battalions, like his own, and sadly most of them were transformed in mere "suppliers": thugs who stole, pillaged, and ravaged to finance the survival of the movement. A movement that survived, the revolution is today far to come and the whole movement revolves around how much they can steal and ravage in order to keep the soldiers fed. People in the villages know that the only way to be spared is to join and so the "revolutionary movement of the Naxals" grows by the day, but it's not ideas that are brought in to speed the pace of the revolution as much as hungry mouths and empty bellies longing to be filled. They still live in the jungle and dress in camouflage gear, they still wear the red bands around their arms and the red berets with stars. But to Debraj Roy all this had lost significance as he keeps hearing, night after night, the youth of his movement wishing for houses and cars and money.

The revolution against wealth needed wealth to survive and its heroes were the ones who hoped that the revolution itself would have brought them more wealth. Greed and lust to a man is like his wife and the other his mistress. He can't survive without either for a long time.

As they watch the news Surya, one of the gang members, says "I'm not sure about this one" referring to the CM of Chhattisgarh.

"What do you mean *not sure*?" enquires Debraj, curious about this statement.

"He looks more genuine than others. He seems committed..." Debraj looks at him, a long stern look that makes the lieutenant look away, uncomfortable at being judged so closely by his chief.

"Commitment has to be unconditional, Surya. Do you think he would be sounding this committed if he were not in the CM's seat? Powerful speeches are scripted daily by skilled writers just so these Ministers can read them out to a blind nation that is hungry for a positive change. The truth is that people want change but very seldom are prepared to work hard and make sacrifices to obtain it. This is what we do: we are the ones who dare to bring change about... unconditionally. We fight if we need to fight, we put our lives on the line, every day, knowing that we might lose them any day. And to do it with no hidden agenda, with no desire to be elected or become rich, makes it effective. If we were in the Parliament or in a political party we would be forced to make alliances, agree to something or to please someone, and the first time you do it, first and maybe only time, it makes you a slave for ever. An agreement is the first step towards bondage: we fight for the people and fight amongst them because we don't want to hear one day "Yes, you did something good but at what price? You are now corrupt like everyone else!" Some might not agree with our methods but no one can claim that we have sold our souls to the power".

The troop nods in agreement.

Everybody knows, Debraj in the first place- this is only true in theory, and that many members of the movement have used their proximity to the people and their image to obtain things. His own men have abused their militant prowess right under his nose. Maybe he even knows.

He himself doesn't have a crystal clear record of activities, but this is the way it goes, those who are pure at heart die young and become martyrs. Whoever comes after tries to make the best of what they have. The truth is that he, like Kedar, has grabbed what he could, using his position only to gain more power. But by now power has gone to his brain, it has drenched it and misshaped it. Debraj speaks but only of what he once thought was right, his actions don't reflect his teachings anymore. A part of Debraj's mind reverberates with another tune, a different stream of thoughts: so how different is he from the politicians and how different they are from him.

His train of thought is interrupted by a radio call.

A young boy hands Debraj the Chinese radio set: Debraj wears the heavy headphones and grabs the microphone; he listens attentively and then gives his orders in a dry and imperative tone.

"When? No, no more. Unreliable. This time it's Purba's responsibility, it's her job" And closes the conversation before anything can emerge from the other side. He does catch the worried and astonished glances that the rest of his crew exchange, especially the younger ones. They have heard him mentioning Purba, a woman, he said "Her responsibility, her job" A woman?

He notices and wonders whether he should just let go, life can't be this hard, always having to explain each and every decision... But then remembers that if someone didn't take the time with him he would be as baffled as they are now.

"She knows she can't let me down. I trust her." He says with gusto. He wouldn't want to sound like he's justifying himself but the tone betrays him. He hands the radio set back to the skinny boy.

The skinny boy looks even more mystified than others and can't help himself, words slip out of his mouth and Debraj can tell that as he says "Dai, Purba?" he is already regretting it. "So?" Debraj says, trying to sound as natural as he can -although he is a guerrilla leader, a bushman, not an actor!

"Dai, she's a woman. How can you trust her with such a huge load of ammunition? What if she blows the operation?" One of them voices his doubts.

Debraj looks at their concerned faces with his grey and old eyes. Irony. He takes a minute before answering; he takes a long breath holding in a gulp of the hideous sugar wine they distil in the forest.

If he were to answer with a speech on gender equality the war would end without them. Also, he can't get angry at them because they are boys whose only image of women has been that of their mothers, cooking, cleaning, and going to the market.

Him, instead... When the movement started, in Chairman Mao's speeches there was a scent of equality, of justice, that no one was ever able to repeat. He weights the situation and decides to leave them with a statement they might or might not understand but which will give them something to think about.

He gulps one last sip and says “Oh guys, there are still so many things you have to learn about women...” and walks away leaving them puzzled both about his decision to send Purba ahead and with that last sentence. What is he sleeping with her?

A few minutes later, in another part of the jungle, a tribal man is running. His upper body is bare and he is just wearing a handmade fabric wrapped around his waist. His body signals that he is terrified to the core of his soul. He is out of breath, being chased but the most cruel and sharp of predators: another man. Or so he thinks. He stops, turns around to see if he is still being followed, the greenery behind him is still, if they are after him they are far away.

The man bends down and ties a small jute bag to his wrist, his life depends on its content and losing it would mean death. Suddenly, as he is kneeling down, a snake comes hissing close to him, he doesn’t want to move, as he knows only too well that those monsters are still looking for him. The jungle is a mother, it’s made to protect, and like some predators these ones only spot a prey if it moves. He is like a wild rabbit, if he stays very still the forest will close behind him and temporarily swallow his body, hiding it from the world.

He takes a stone and throws it at the snake, that is left unimpressed but at the same time decides that this little man is too much food for him and too dangerous too. The snake leaves, hissing and sliding away, and the bushman sits still until he hears noises right behind him.

The jungle hasn’t protected him today, its oily, shiny leaves have not shielded him from his predator, and they have offered him to death. The man now feels almost like the forest itself has put him on a plate, ready to be served for the meal.

He springs up on his agile knees and speeds again, he hears them close, too close, they have seen branches and leaves moving and now there's no place to hide: either he keeps on running or he's dead. In the background he hears shootings, unsure if they are aimed at him or if simply someone shot in the air to attract the attention of his companions.

The bushman is more afraid of the unknown that of the risk it bears: he has seen a pair of legs, a red band wrapped around the left leg, just below the knee, and a pair of boots. Rather small boots. He doesn't know how many they are and if he can trade something for his life, he will deal later with what comes after.

The firing continues, someone has a shotgun and shoots in the air dry and prolonged shots that sound like the cracking of wood in the fire. A massive log in a gigantic fire.

He runs and runs and at the end of the forest he comes across a clearing. Nowhere to hide.

He runs to the cliff to see how deep it is and his bare feet collapse into the mud: there a small river next to him, just a stream of water that falls for several metres into the big river down the cliff. He evaluates his situation: if he jumps the risk of dying is high and that of losing his small parcel is even higher, if he stays...

Before he can finish thinking of all the possibilities a sharp and warm pain makes him fall backwards. His heart skips a beat and his legs feel soft, only one does actually. As he falls to his knees and then, pierced by the intense pain, to his back, he sees blood flowing profusely from his right knee.

His breath trips between his teeth, he is uncomfortable with his calves and feet bent behind his back, but unable to move. The shot was precise enough to make him fall in such a position as to choke on his own breath and yet keep him alive for a little bit. Were they planning to save him?

For a moment his eyes light up. He even manages to smile as he hears steps approaching and sees a face. A woman's face.

He smiles as in his experience women are those who nurture, who take care of the wounded. He smiles but the smile freezes on his lips as he notices that the dusky woman he is looking at is also the one who shot him. Long legs, red band wrapped just below the left knee, clearly an old wound, and boots, those small boots.

Purba approaches, her long black hair is tight in a low bun right above her neck, her camouflage gear is a little worn out and the colours are faded but she is evidently a leader. The mole on her cheek gives her a sophisticated air; the funny thing is that she looks like she has just been resuscitated from a renaissance painting and yet the uniform looks perfect on her, as if she hadn't ever worn anything else.

Purba is the leader of the Naag Dalam, the group formed only by women of the Maoist movement of Chhattisgarh…The Maoist serpents, as they are referred.

And she wears this name like a second skin: she is sharper, more precise, more cruel and rational than any man in the movement, she leads her women with pride. Training with her is worse than training with any other commander but she picks her soldiers with care, making sure that by the end of the training their oath of loyalty is not only to the movement but also to themselves. They learn to understand their needs and their tastes, they learn more about themselves and are finally free from the weight of a man making decisions for them. They are grateful to her and by the end of their training they become members of a family. A family with guns and guts.

Other commanders have had runaways, including Debraj. Purba never had one, ever.

Today she walks to the scared man with a strange look on her face, he can't quite understand it, and he assumes it's a look of pity, but he can't really tell.

She kneels down next to him like a mother would in front of her child, unties the jute bag from his limb, she opens it carefully and extracts a dry and hard clot of earth. She weighs it in her hand and, holding it tight, dips her hand in the stream next to her to clean it. Then she wipes it with the trembling man's loincloth.

A massive, rough and dusty stone appears. Alexandrite, reddish-purple coloured... A rough gem of about 50 carats. What she was looking for. No one knows she's here, this is her private job, moonlighting as she would like to put it and she must think carefully of her next move. Men have taken everything away from her: her family, her virginity, her home: now it's her turn to take everything back. True, Debraj gave her a chance, but Purba knows better than anyone that nowadays Debraj is only a faint shadow of what he used to be, his ideals have melted in a glass of sweet wine. No, this is an executive decision: this gem will buy her a place of honour in the Turu Dalam, she could buy out the entire gang, she could buy every single politician in Chhattisgarh and finally be the one and only leader. But then there is power play within the Maoists. What if they dispose her off after the securing the prized possession? There's too much at stake to tell Debraj and Kedar about the finding, and she is sure, her own loyal serpents will not give her out.

The tribal man detects a hint of a smile on her face and nearly sighs of relief. He may be able to reunite with his family finally. So what if he couldn't secure the stone that he stole from another tribal, who was the original finder. After all it's the jungle out there and the law of the jungle is- devil eats devil. His tobacco-stained teeth make him look like a smiling alien with a ray of hope. But before he can catch a couple of deep breaths, Purba's eyes, shiny until a few seconds before, are back to the clear and cold cut they had when she shot him.

She lifts something from behind her and shoots him again, twice, in the head.

She puts the stone in one of her pockets and closes it carefully as two of her serpent militants throw the body down the cliff into the river. The tribal man falls with a splash and for a moment, before the current washes his body away, the water turns red. Purba reads his last thoughts-Devil eats Devil. Somewhere in the vicinity she can hear a tiger groan, hungry for its prey.

She spontaneously fires her gun in the air and beams like a beast. A Tiger for Tiger.

Chapter 5

In Cape Town Christmas is in the air: inflatable snowmen flutter in front of every shop, Christmas carols are sung at the corner of the main streets and even if the actual day is still far away, the Christmassy atmosphere makes people cheerful. Every man and woman seems to have a Santa Claus in their heart and every child sees a Santa Claus in the eyes of the vibrant grown-ups.

On the Waterfront tourists stroll looking at the beautiful, colourful, Old Dutch houses, children lick huge ice creams and parents cherish not having to worry about the cold because in this southern paradise Christmas is hot! Capetonians are less amazed at the beauty of a warm Christmas and avoid the touristy areas full of souvenir shops and ice cream parlours; they prefer to gather in quieter places that allow them to enjoy a glass of wine and some fresh fish or a nice cup of tea.

In a contemporary office building, the regional office of 'Action Against Poverty', a non-governmental organization involved with poverty reduction all over the world, a woman is typing on her computer. Her look is concentrated and her deep red nails tap the keyboard making it sound like a click clack symphony. If not for her passion to work for a cause, she would have made a good pianist. Music is her second nature. She looks like a girl so fresh, she would empty her cup every night to refill it again the next morning. Tenacity. On her desk there's a vase with a bunch of orchids and a red cup full of steaming coffee. Despite the warm weather the AC in the office is freezing and a cup of something warm is actually quite pleasant.

From the number of red items scattered around her room and on her body one can tell that she has a soft spot for this colour, but nothing about her is overwhelming. "Never too much" seems to be her motto, and she is sophisticated and modest at the same time. Her smile is warm and her eyes have a comforting sheen. Infact her eyes are a giveaway. She looks like an ordinary girl even if she is not touched up, but her attractive eyes never lets her pass unnoticed. Her stare can cut across all inhibitions making one want to go to her and greet.

Today she has given a special touch to her outfit as tonight she has a date: she is wearing red shoes and necklace to frame a pitch black dress, formal but fun, as she describes it. Her red bag is sitting on the chair in front of her desk and her short, wavy hair is cut in a modern but sober style.

As she types she talks on the phone, her mood is cheerful, she has taken a break from work and is chatting with her date and talking on the phone to her father "Is it 100% virgin olive oil? Father, trans fat, father, trans fat!" she smiles and her smile is turned into a laugh at her father's response.

Meanwhile her screen presents the conversation between Shy Gal, herself, and Hunky Dave, her date.

SHY GAL: Sounds good.

HUNKY DAVE: Pick u up at 7pm?

SHY GAL: Nope, let's meet at the restaurant itself.

HUNKY DAVE: Blind date... wat u wearing?

SHY GAL: Something RED... it's Christmas remember?

HUNKY DAVE: Santa's hat too?

SHY GAL: That's your garb. CU at 7.30pm, gotta go.

As she ends the conversation with "Hunky Dave" she tells her father she won't be able to watch the match with him tonight.

"Yes, it's a date, no nothing serious, in fact, it's another one of those blind dates... AGAIN! I know... Okay, I gotta go now, love you. I'll come by later tonight so we can watch the cricket match if you record it! Yeah well, provided you don't peek at it live and tell me the results half way through like you did last time! Ok, cool, I really have to go now, see you later!"

She hangs up and lets her eyes wander around the room. She works in a nice environment after all, there are problems and obnoxious people, like everywhere, but overall she's really happy with the vibe. She always wanted to help people, to have a positive impact on their lives, but she had no guts to be a doctor and no religious vocation, during university she came across the NGO sector and got a job in a small organization right after graduation. Then things moved forward and a year later she got a job here, a South African organization fighting against poverty around the world, where she could find her space. She's the gender in agriculture expert, she studies the condition of women all over the world and researches ways to improve them. So far she has mostly worked in Africa, but it has been enlightening to see what women do right next door to her. Many a time she has travelled less than a day from her posh Cape Town only to find herself in villages that had never seen the light of western civilization. She's happy with this job because it delicately offers her the opportunity to change her small slice of the world. Way back when she was far too small to nurse an ambition, she learnt something that would now change her life. One of her guardian nuns once whispered in her ears *"to change the world you must first change yourself"*. Back then she didn't know of its meaning or why somebody whispered in her ears of all the people, was it random or was it for a reason, she cannot recall. All she recalls are the profound words and she finds it most difficult to live by it.

Shyla looks at the small packet on her desk wrapped in red ribbon, she bought her father's Christmas present in advance this year and it lies there, a small but antique clock. Her father always spoke about time and often said that time is all you have as the real treasure, the rest is all a distraction. The card on it reads "Merry Christmas father, the man who taught me the importance of time!" Every time she looks at it she feels stupid: her job is all about talking, writing, being diplomatic and when it comes to Christmas cards all she can think of is that?

Damian, a colleague of Shyla walks by her desk, sees the smiley faces on her screen and jumps with excitement "Sooooo??? Meeting Mr Destiny tonight?"

Damian is a mulatto South African, the incarnation of a new generation of South Africans: when his parents met it was technically illegal, although widely accepted, for them to build a family due to the different colours of their skin, today he can be a feminine gay South African and find very few interested in people around him.

"Mhhh I don't know about that! Destiny is what you make out of life... of the life that is thrown at you… no man or woman can decide your destiny..." Shyla speaks in a confident tone.

"Whaaaaat? Please don't tell me you are one of those who don't believe in signs!!! Shyla signs are everywhere!!!" And he spreads his arms and turns around a couple of times in a jolly pirouette.

"Yeah, signs are everywhere, but whether to follow them or not is your choice... besides, destiny is not about chances, it's about choices... and right now, I choose coffee! Coming with me Mr Matrix?"

As she picks her coffee mug from her table to get a refill, some of the left over coffee spills on her desk, as she cleans it up with a paper handkerchief she sees a pop up on her computer screen. It's the commercial for Techno Marine Hummer chronographs and because her father is so fond of watches and clocks she takes a mental note, as soon as she comes back she'll have a look at their website. She already has a Christmas present for him but who says she can't get him two? After all this year has been a little hard on him with his health giving him trouble...

When she leaves the office Shyla is tired but glowing, her dark skin makes her red accessories stand out and the black dress highlights her very feminine curves.

Like all women she realized at six thirty in the evening that she's not happy with the way she looks "*How could I think that this would make me look good? I look like a whale in this dress! And these accessories? Nah...I gotta change!*" She thinks as she quickly texts Hunky Dave reminding him to meet at the restaurant instead of picking her up from the office.

She heads for home and as she walks the crowded yet tidy streets of her beautiful Cape Town, with lights that puncture the evening blue sky, she's happy. She imagines the pedestrians walking by with different musical instruments in their hands, playing music to reflect her vibrant mood. Having heard music in the best and the worst of times, Shyla has realised that music is what we carry in our hearts when we are ecstatic. Every cell in the body vibrates to create a symphony of sorts that elevates the mind to state of a soundless orgasm. This is also that occasion when she likes to suspend her beliefs to savour the opportunity of a faceless encounter. She always loves this passage of time, from two hours before meeting her date-guy to the actual moment. This is when woman's mind is at its creative best. Shyla at the helm of her womanhood enjoys these spurts of fancy that draws various imageries of her forthcoming date. She is well aware that the collage of this so called 'Mr Who' is so fascinating that if all there was such a guy existent, he would be classified as an alien from a universe parallel to her's. So far all the random men have turned out to be unsuitable for her but the excitement of the possibility of her 'Dream Man' is absolutely thrilling. She's an adrenaline junkie, always has been and most probably always will be.

A group of boys is playing in front of her building, a boy smiles at her and by smiling back she makes him blush. The boy is on top of the world, almost love at first sight for him. Shyla bends down and gives him a warm peck on his pink cheeks. Shyla is instantaneously transported back to her childhood albeit for a minute.

She remembers how she would fall in love with every boy on street dressed smartly just because it was Christmas and love was floating around as if Santa was a contagious Casanova. Christmas brings back the best memories of her life cause all her pain, grief, loneliness would disappear at the very thought of Santa Claus. Today she sees that wonder in the eyes of this little boy who is confused between Santa and Shyla, who between the two is going to be his date for this Christmas. Shyla turns behind to check out if the boy has moved out of his amazement. To her shock she finds him missing. He disappeared in a flash almost like a wormhole effect. Shyla flatters herself "was my kiss so magical that it can have a wormhole effect or did the boy time travel to planet earth just for a peck from me'. She knows that some things you never know. Serendipity.

In her mailbox she finds a leaflet, advertising soap, or face wash or whatnot. What strikes her though is the line that goes with it "Love is in the air, take a deep breath!" She takes a deep breath indeed. She can smell some fresh baked muffins from the neighbouring house. She knows that soon she would be enjoying a three-course meal with desserts being her favourite part of the appetising rendezvous. A generous dig into Tiramisu and that's her fleeting visit to paradise. The thought of relish puts her in a good mood and as soon as she gets into the house she turns the radio on, to a jazz station. She sways to her bedroom in perfect sync with the saxophone blaring out of the Bose speakers.

Shyla kicks her shoes on the two sides of the room and picks dresses from the cupboard, she looks at them in the mirror but ends up zeroing on the one she was already wearing.

Her house is small but very cosy: she has a huge photo of a tiger framed in the living room that tells a lot about her hidden character. The photograph has her mother's signature in ink. The handwriting is stylish and spells of clarity, written diagonally in red it reads as 'Rani…' On a shelf rests a photo of her graduation where she's hugging a white man, middle aged and dressed as a catholic priest. Her kitchen is tiny and her passion for coffee is clearly inversely proportional to her passion for cooking: on the counter Shyla has countless jars of coffee. Coffee powders, from different countries, of different flavours and intensities... whereas not one pot or pan can be spotted on the counter or anywhere else. Going by her elaborate collection of music, it's apparent that she is uncomfortable with too much of silence and cannot spend too much time in isolation. Music can be your loyal life partner she believes.

When she notices she's running fashionably late she leaves the house, heading for the restaurant. As she hops down the stairs she checks herself one last time in the mirror in the lobby "Shyla Thomas, destiny is a choice. Or maybe not" the thrill of the blind date is beginning to fade away, as she now realizes how many times she has had her hopes up and ended up being disappointed.

Sitting in the restaurant, sipping wine and listening to empty jibber jabber about veganism, Shyla thinks that this is just another of her "first dates" that never see the dawn of a second one.

Fortunately she has picked the place, the house music is soothing, this restaurant has really good wine and cheese, and so if nothing else, at least she can enjoy a good dinner.

"So... Vegan... like no eggs?"

"Yep! And also no cheese!" She suddenly feels judged and grows irritated against this goofy looking guy with his black shirt, his Donald Duck tie and his idiotic smile. What irritates her the most is that he is genuine! She can't even get mad at him because he is so kind! His smile cuts his face in half, that's how happy he is to be here with her tonight. She feels bad for wanting to get out of it but she honestly can't wait to be home, make herself a nice cup of coffee and get back to her book of her favourite genre- 'Espionage'.

"...Basically no dairy product..."

"Wait, hang on... How do you survive?"

"Oh, we eat a lot more things than you think! First all vegetables, then legumes, rice... all nicely washed down with lots of water! Pure, filtered water, at times even mineral water but spring water is a favourite!"

Shyla can't help making a disgusted face.

"Ooooook, right! Let's take a look at the menu, shall we…?"… 'Mister Water filter' she adds in her self-talk.

"Sure, I just wish this hippy would stop playing this noise!" she doesn't quite understand what he refers to and then sees a nice looking guy, long hair and a loose white shirt, tight denim jeans, who plays a flamenco, singing along his beautiful lament.

Ok, Shyla, relax. It's only a dinner; you don't have to see him again! So what if you will quit chatting online for the rest of your life!

As she thinks of ways to get out of this unruly nightmare, her eyes fall onto a beautiful necklace that a lady is wearing across the other table.

"Emeralds are forever… someday I shall own a gemstone ribbon like this one. But definitely not with this Donald Duck around" Shyla mutters to divert herself.

But before she can estimate the price of these emeralds, he leans forward as to tell her a secret, for a second she's faintly interested.

"We can't eat here!" he says enthusiastically. *What is he so agitated about, I bloody love this place!*

"I wonder why... I... I really like it..."

"I know but babe, look at the menu..." *Babe! Babe!!! This guy is evidently trying to push me off the edge, it's a joke... where is Damian? He must have organized it!*

"What is wrong with the menu?"

"Look... Fish, Meat, Eggs, Shellfish! This is a graveyard, not a menu! I wonder what the carbon footprint of this place is..." *He is genuine. He is genuine. He is genuine.* She keeps repeating to herself like a mantra.

"I like a simple life... I like to start my day with steaming black coffee and end it with a glass of red wine and everything that happens in between is incidental" Shyla tells the alien guy to shut himself up."

The waiter approaches, he refills Shyla's glass with a generous dose of cabernet. "*Much appreciated brother*" she thinks gratefully.

"May I take your order?"

"Nothing for me, thank you" the waiter looks mystified and Shyla, embarrassed, asks for one more minute "Yes, can you come back in a sec? Actually, do you have something that won't burst the ozone layer? Destroy the planet or blend the galaxy into a shapeless shake?"

The waiter looks even more bamboozled and walks away. Shyla is a little self-conscious as she has had a little too much to drink already and she wanted to be nice to the waiter but, considering how fast he ran away, she failed.

Just then her phone rings, she picks her bag hoping to fake an emergency and be able to run away. Escape to Mars forever.

"Sorry, it's my dad, I gotta take this" Dave gestures her to go ahead but not before advising "be careful of the cellphone waves, they can damage the brain". Shyla dashes off, as if an earthquake hits the place..

"Hey father... Oh, Sister Mary... what, where is my father?"

She looks clearly shocked after she hangs up. Holy Cow! Without even noticing that Dave is offering to drive her where she needs to go, she stands up and storms out. There is no place for a goodbye or time to pay her share of the bill. Shyla is visibly shaken to the core. This is an earthquake.

Chapter 6

Shyla drives up the winding road that takes her, turn after turn, closer to her father's residence. Every breath gets loaded with biting anxiety. It's raining heavily, an out of season shower, and her car strives up the hill to stay in its lane. As she speeds up she notices the lights of the town, it's barely nine. People, other people, are certainly having dinner or enjoying a stroll around the cheerful streets of Cape Town. They are casual.

For a second, a split second only, she remembers about Hunky Dave, did she leave him behind?

She arrives at the villa and parks the car ripping some of the nice green grass off the lane, she rushes out of the car and inside the building.

Sister Mary welcomes her, she is a middle aged woman, strong Boer features but a very gentle face, the face of a person who has learnt to love despite race, caste or wealth. She is a catholic nun and she is in charge of the wellbeing of Father Thomas, Shyla's father.

Father Thomas was the pupil of a very wealthy South African family, he had always been used to being served and, back then he was definitely a spoilt child. One day he was out with a group of friends, drinking and playing cards in a neighbourhood in the outskirts of the city. The world belonged to them, they had never been involved with racist of xenophobic raids as many did at the time, but they were well aware of the differences that tore the country apart at the time and were happy with the arrangement. In the split between blacks and whites they were white, they were rich and they were the ones who could get away with almost anything. Worst case scenario they would have gotten scolded and sent back home accompanied by a policeman.

Edward Thomas had never taken advantage of the situation but also never turned down the chance to benefit from it.

And so it was that one day, while playing cards and sipping whisky and soda he saw a boy collecting offers for the church who made the awful mistake of leaning onto his friend Larry's new car.

"Hey you *pisscop*!!! Move!!! That car is new and it costs more than your life!"

"I'm certain it does sir, let me just regain my strength, I have been walking all day in this heat..."

"I don't care what you have been doing, I'm not even sure you haven't been stealing you beggar!"

"I'm not a beggar, sir... I collect money on behalf of the Lord"

"Yeah right! The Lord being another *pisscop* like you around this corner?"

"No sir, the Lord being God the Almighty"

"Oh so now we are taking God's name in vain huh? Come here thief, let me teach you a lesson!" and Larry jumped over the table and stumbled on it due to his drunkenness. He got even angrier and ran after they boy who kept the box with the offerings as close as he could to his chest to make sure not to lose even one Rand.

The friends ran after Larry, unsure if they did it to stop him or, with the morbid lure of pointless violence, to watch him beat the boy.

The boy ran fast as his legs were young and he was light as a feather, besides he hadn't drank like the guys who ran and stumbled and laughed like idiots. Edward knew there was something absolutely wrong with it, but the force of the pack is always stronger than that of the individual, and he followed his friends without enjoying it particularly but also without pulling back.

The boy entered a church, the group followed.

Inside the church the light was dim and they had to stop to let their eyes grow used to the shade. When they did all they could see was a huge white priest, standing in front of them with a menacing face.

"This is the house of the Lord, I'm sure you have come here to pray, confess and beg for forgiveness for your sins"

At this point the only sensible thing to do was to apologize and leave, the priest looked like a very big rugby player and judging by his hands and his scarred face he was not shy when it came to teaching a lesson. But Larry was still high on his white power and on the scotch and made the fatal mistake to try and explain the issue to the priest, who listened carefully and then took Larry by his elbow and neck and lifted him to the entrance of the church as if he was a bunch of daisies. Larry was a big boy but the priest made him look like a kid, big and muscled as that he was. As soon as they had crossed the threshold of the church the priest gave Larry a solid punch on his face that made him fly down the steps and land on his bum.

Larry was speechless, like everybody else. The only one who had a great deal of talking to do was the priest, who said, "This country is falling apart because of people like you, you racist, useless fleas. There is a man, who those like you, have put him in prison, who one day will lead our great nation. His name is Nelson Mandela and if any of you had heard of him you wouldn't be here today.

In the eyes of God we are all the same. God is the one who gave us different colours not to make one stronger than the other but to allow us to learn from each other's differences. To grow together through a bunch of versatile attributes. You are evidently undeserving of forgiveness. Though I know He is so much wiser than me that he will eventually forgive you when you join his Kingdom.

Meanwhile please stay out of our Kingdom, this neighbourhood. The boy you chased here is a good catholic boy, he goes to school and wants to become a doctor and I will do all I can to help him. Every Sunday he goes out on the streets -risking to come across idiots like you- to collect money for the poor's of our church. He is more noble that you will ever be, and you treated him like a thief!"

"He leaned over my new car!" protested Larry as everyone else remained silent. The priest smiled.

"You know what the Bible say? "It's easier for a camel to pass through the hole in a needle than for a rich man to open the doors of Heaven" Do me a favour and get out of here, and make sure I don't see your faces around this neighbourhood again or you will be in big trouble. Even if I don't behave like you I'm very white, and if I go to the police I also have the priest bonus, priests tend to be reliable! Don't make me report you as church assaulters, because I swear to God I will!"

And by saying so he walked back into the church. His voice still echoed in the midst of the church bells that went off subsequently. Perfect timing! Does it ring a bell!

The guys walked back to their cars in silence, Larry was fuming, some of the other guys had grown angry at the betrayal of a fellow Afrikaner, but one of them, Edward, had been sincerely stricken by the priest's words. Like arrowheads the wisdom had lodged in his heart and wounded him forever.

The next day he had collected all his money, a few hundred Rands, and had set off for the church.

He didn't take the car on purpose, he wanted to take the bus, buy the ticket, see the colour of people go from pure white, through light brown, to black as he changed neighbourhood, hear different talks, smell different odours. Inhale life.

By the time he got to the church he was a little uncomfortable because in the streets everyone was looking at him, he was an outsider in his own town, and now, for the first time, he knew how the maids and gardeners and watchmen felt when they went to work in the posh neighbourhoods where only white people lived.

In the church he found father Sprong celebrating mass, the church was filled with people -it was a Sunday- and Edward was shocked to see how well the priest spoke Zulu. At the end of the function he also went to all the old ladies and men who had trouble standing up on their own addressing them in their language, Xhosa, Ndebele, Sotho, and helping them up and out of the church.

Edward sat there and at once felt uneasy, not because of his whiteness now, but rather because of his strict upbringing that cut him out of this life, real life.

He saw the boy from the previous day and wanted to go and apologize but the boy ran close to his family as soon as he saw him, what shocked Edward the most was that the boy's mother looked in the direction her son was pointing at but instead of giving Edward a look of reproach, or an apologetic grin (which black South Africans did at the time, as if they were to be punished for something they hadn't done, for the sole guilt of being black), the chubby lady looked at Edward and smiled with a sad and pitiful smile. Edward felt for the first time in his life in a position of weakness and what had scared him up until that moment, being in a room full of black people who could easily kill him if only they wanted to, made him now feel eager to learn more.

Father Sprong approached, his look wasn't full of forgiveness or pity or understanding: he thought that one of the boys had come back for more and he was ready to condescend him.

Seeing the menacing look on his face Edward, still holding the envelope with the money, felt the need to explain.

"Father, can we go to a quieter place?" The priest looked puzzled but took him to a room next door.

"Yesterday you said that the boy we chased, and I apologise for that, is collecting money for the poor's, and that he wants to go to university and become a doctor. These are all my savings, I want to help him"

"You think you can come here on a Sunday and buy forgiveness? Wrong century my friend..."

"No sir, ehm, Father... Look, I know my friend is an idiot. But this is South Africa, we were all born from the same group of friends, our parents are friends, our grandparents were friends, I can't turn my back on Larry because, as stupid as he might be, he is like a brother to me. What I can do is try to be different. It's a first step right?

I'm the only child of a wealthy family, I'm studying law but I've always been in love with literature, I dislike what I study because it forces me to perpetrate a system I don't agree with. But my father is a lawyer, my grandfather was a lawyer and so was my great grandfather. I feel I have no alternative and although I'm sorry my ancestors contributed to shape this country as it is today there's nothing I can do about it. I would like to learn from you..."

"Bro, I'm a priest, I have nothing to teach but religion..."

"Well maybe this is what I'm here to learn then!"

"It's a life of sacrifice, I feel, correct me if I'm wrong, that you are not quite used to the hardships of life..."

"You are not wrong Father, but I'm determined to change: all my wealth and possessions have not made me happy so far. I have mistaken greed for happiness, I saw you before, people love you, they seek refuge in you, and I want that. I want to be the shelter for needy people's hearts. I know I can't buy it, so I want to learn how to deserve it"

And so it was that Edward Thomas, against all odds and, most of all, against his family's will, entered a seminar in Bloemfontein and became a priest, he took over Father Sprong's parish when he became too old to run it and took care of his mentor until his very last day. Mpatso, the boy Edward and his friends chased that Saturday, did in fact become a doctor and cured Father Sprong until the end.

Over the years Edward found himself father of a girl born from a tragedy. His friend Mira, an Indian born photographer working in South Africa for NatGeo, an old friend from school, had gone to India for a photo shoot. She was after tigers in Chhattisgarh when she came across a young man who at first helped her but soon turned out to be a thug, a rebel who raped and abandoned her in the forest. She was found half dead by a nun and was sent back to South Africa, when Edward picked her up from the airport he knew that life had started to abandon her. She was determined to put all this behind her and not let it affect the rest of her life, but life often has more irony that we can conceive and a few weeks later Mira discovered that the man who raped her, a man who by now had lost all his identity, had left her with a part of him. She was pregnant. She told Thomas who, as a catholic priest, suggested she keep the baby. And so she did, transferring life to an unborn baby day after day and draining it out from herself. As her belly grew bigger Mira was constantly reminded that the evil man who had raped her was growing inside her and a deep, thick depression sucking the best of her, until, the night Shyla was born, she let go and died. Thomas had long started to feel the pressure of having made Mira keep the baby, he did see life slipping out of his friend's body and there was nothing he could do about it. Thomas had unknowingly buried that guilt deep inside. When Shyla was put in his arms as the only relative she had he decided to adopt her there and then. He knew he would have faced prejudice and possibly ostracism, but he owed this to Mira and he went on and did it.

And so it was Shyla who grew up calling him father and never really knowing all the details of her life. She wanted to know about her mother and her life but Edward was smart enough to divert her mind through noble talks. Whenever she felt lonely and restless about her roots, she would resort to music. Jazz, Latino, soft rock, retro, she could listen to anything that had profound lyrics, lyrics that could bring out the mysterious nature of life and its unanswered questions. And if music failed to sooth her nerves then a Hemmingway classic would definitely put her anxiety to rest- 'The old man and the sea' her all-time favourite.

Tonight, as she rushes escorted by Sister Mary through the dark corridor where she used to play as a child, her breath is short. Her mother died, father Thomas, her father, is the only person she has in the world. She still doesn't know what happened exactly, Sister Mary is saying something about God's plans "God has his plans, my child... Only He knows about them and we are not to enquire..."

"Plans? Enquire? What do you mean...?"

But as Sister Mary sniffs and holds her tears back they are in front of her father's door and doctor Mpatso, now with wrinkles and grey hair, is just coming out of it.

"Doctor Mpatso, what happened? I spoke to him a few hours ago, he was fine, and he was recording the cricket match so that we could watch it together... Please do something!"

"I'm sorry child, it's not in my hands anymore..."

"But he was taking such good care of himself after the second heart attack, I check on him too... we take long walks as you recommended, he eats healthy, I also go through his fridge every week to see if anyone is trying to spoil him, you know, he is very much loved by all the people down at the church..."

"I know Shyla, but there are some things that God faces us with and we can't do anything about them but accept them, perhaps it about a reason unknown to us"

"What... what do you mean?"

"Father Thomas doesn't have much time left to live, child..." Shyla's hands tremble and the watch she had bought him for Christmas falls from her hands and only now she wonders why she had carried it tonight. She enters the room, lit only by a feeble light by the side of the bed and kneels by her father's side.

He opens his eyes and from the intense blue it's easy to see how this frail man was once a vigorous South African, a handsome and strong man who took over father Sprong's parish and made no one regret his extremely loved predecessor. His face is radiating with the message that death is the only truth to life and death alongwith suffering gives life its correct meaning. "How can a man standing in front of death be so wise, in his very last moments of life" Shyla's thoughts race in her mind like a rocket. Even now, on his deathbed, Father Thomas emanates a sense of peace and wisdom that makes people around him feel at ease and in peace even when their hearts are troubled.

"Shyla, my child, I'm sorry I couldn't record the match..."

"No, I'm sorry... I left you alone for a stupid date... If I was here this wouldn't have happened!"

"Ahaha... No baby, this would have happened anyway, it's God's will and we are too tiny to judge His decisions.

We go through life to only learn how to die, if we live wisely, we die in wisdom and that is what we carry with us. Come closer now, I feel that life is beginning to slip away and there is something I need to tell you"

Shyla is devastated, her sobs are so loud that sister Mary is unsure whether it's her crying or Father Thomas choking, the doctor gestures her to remain outside. These are the last moments of a father with her child, she has no right to interrupt. If Shyla needs help or wants them in she will call them.

"Come on, come closer... Forgive me for hiding this secret from you all your life. It was all in good faith... But it is time now... Time you go and seek the truth"

Shyla is puzzled, her head is pounding, all the crying has made her eyes swell and she can hardly keep them open and now she hears about a truth... what truth?

"Although I have loved you since you were born more than my own life, you were not my daughter. When your mother went to India, for that photo shoot on tigers, the one I always told you about when you were young, remember? She was misled and raped by a rebellious Man who turned out to be the head of a Maoist terrorist group of Chhattisgarh in Central India. When she came back something inside her had died, her eyes were blank and there was no spark in them. But at the same time, something inside her was growing; you my child, and she lived for you, to allow you to come into this world, until the very last day. I was already a priest back then but I invited her to move here, my family was rich and caring for one more person was not going to be a problem. Remember grandpa and grandma? The day you were born they were the happiest people in the world. They had not taken my call to be a priest, very easily. I had no brothers and sisters and they wanted a big family, having you around was a sort of surrogate..."

He coughs and she mechanically hands him a glass of water, she doesn't know what to think, as a matter of fact she also doesn't know what she knows anymore.

The conversation goes on for a few minutes and by the time she leaves the room Shyla is a different person, her eyes are blank and she doesn't speak to anybody. She walks through the corridors where she remembers her grandparents teaching her how to walk and talk and write and read... but they were not her grandparents.

The doctor and the nun enter the priest's room and find on the bed only his earthly shell, his lifeless body. He has died telling his only and beloved daughter the truth, the one he knew. Now it's her job to take the journey backwards, twenty seven years after her mother got her here, inside her womb, to discover where her roots comes from. Who she is? Why she is? Why the why's?

Chapter 7

In the jungle of Kanker- Chhattisgarh, the night is cold, the eyes of the tigers, the human tigers that patrol the area, are watching one of their comrades ride a motorbike with a blindfolded man sitting in the back.

The blindfolded man has the thick red band the rider took off his arm over his eyes, he clearly can't see anything but seems pretty relaxed, he whistles the tune of a classic Bollywood love song, then tries to push the other guy to talk, asking questions about his favourite Bollywood film 'Sholay' and then his roots in Chhattisgarh. But the rider is only a messenger, Neil knows it only too well, he is not going to say a word he wasn't instructed to say.

The forest is drenched in the long and silver rays of the moon, a full moon that seems to cast a light over the entire world, bright as it is. Neil enjoys the fresh air, his driver doesn't know how he can keep his cool, *if it was me I would be shitting myself,* he thinks; but he is too inexperienced to know that Neil can't be afraid: he is a trader. He means business to everybody involved in the forest trade. And the Naxals are more of traders than anybody else in recent times. Traders always establish contact when they want something and have something to give. True, sometimes things turn sour, but it's in very rare cases and only because one of the two parties thinks he can outsmart the other. Trade is trade, when you try to be too smart you generally lose it all. Neil knows it, Debraj knows it.

This is why, when they arrive, the two of them talk to each other like they were trading in Cayman Islands. No ceremony because in business there's no need to be formal: it's a mere negotiation.

"How was the ride?"

"Smooth..." answers Neil massaging his back with one hand and his eyes with the other. A motorbike ride in the humid night of the Chhattisgarh jungle is not exactly relaxing, especially with all the bumps and holes that the rider seemed to know by heart and dive into on purpose, but the question was obviously rhetorical and only a short answer was expected. Besides, this doesn't exactly look like the Sheraton "Give us your opinion on how to improve our service!" it's a camp in the jungle where traders come in the middle of the night to do business with outlaws. Yeah, after the entire ride was smooth.

Debraj gives an order to a lieutenant "Organize some Daal Chaawal" and then turns apologetically to Neil "Sorry, that's all I can offer you tonight. Ganpath failed to deliver meat this morning..."

"Daal chaawal is perfect. Had lots of good meat in Pokhara, my system needs to realign..."

"Yeah, well, speaking of Pokhara..." and he gestures the backpack Neil still has on his back. He smiles and empties it on the ground, several small white packets emerge and a young gang member dives to catch them and tastes the dope. He nods towards Debraj, it's good.

Neil wasn't worried, he only deals with the best and for the best, he doesn't do cheap cuts.

Neil smiles at Debraj and quips, "That was in kind and here is the payment in cash". Neil hands him the bag full of money.

"Mhhh Baht... I prefer USD, you know that... They're easier to put onto the market..."

"I know... but this is what they had this time..." Neil is calm, it's not his fault, there's no need to be worried, money is money, it will take a little longer to turn Baht into USD but it's going to be fine.

"The stones are getting more and more precious by the day, I hope you understand that, well, fine, take some rest now, sleep here tonight and I'll get you dropped off on the main road in the morning. Your next consignment will be given to you soon"

Neil walks away and trips on his shoelaces. He kneels down taking the time, while he ties the laces mechanically and without looking at it, to get a clearer picture of the camp. He is curious to be in the middle of the militant camp to understand the working, but he has to be discreet. Any signs of peeking and he knows he would be left with no eyes for the rest of his life.

Earlier, after having taken the blindfold off his eyes, he couldn't see well, he was blinded by millions of stars and by the lights of the camp. Now he needs a minute to take a look around, and the shoelaces are the perfect excuse. Any piece of vital information could be handy in the long walk towards purpose.

Debraj looks at him, he is very confused about this guy: he admires his free spirit but although they have been working together for a while now and he has never been cheated by Neil, he can't really say he trusts him. He doesn't know how to explain it even to himself: there's something about Neil that is strange, he is different from all the people he has met since he joined the gang and yet does business regularly with them.

"Blindfolded again?" Neil asks as the mute driver hands him his red armband.

"Well my friend, one can never be too careful..."

"Oh come on, we have been working together for three years now and you still don't trust me?"

"Neil you were given the chance once, and I'm happy to extend the offer again, this doesn't ever happen... Join the gang, we work for a common goal..."

"Yeah... No... You know me, I'm the kind of guy..."

"Yes, who lives on his own terms and is happy with living and letting others live" says Debraj with the most paternalistic tone. They have this conversation every time they see each other and every time it ends with the same scene.

"Spot on. That's me! No grudges, no agenda. Just me, myself and I"

"But an able man like you... It would do you good to join our mission… A life without mission is a life totally worthless!"

Neil looks at Debraj, the cheerful tone has disappeared, swallowed by the deep voice that makes Debraj shiver. Neil's eyes have become black, of a deep black, as if the pupil has expanded the iris.

"What makes you think I don't have a mission?"

Debraj feels uneasy and Neil doesn't lower his look, he is staring into Debraj's eye and if he wasn't sure Neil has no reason whatsoever to hurt him or the movement, he would almost think this free flying trader could carve his heart out with a spoon right now.

A young gang member arrives and hands Debraj the radio set only saying "Purba" as he doesn't know if and how much he can talk in front of the stranger.

"I will see you in the morning Neil, take some rest" Debraj asks his men to escort Neil to an outhouse cottage. As a rule an outsider is not allowed to stay on their premises. There is a special guest villa located for traders and members of other parallel outfits. Debraj doesn't trust anybody except his gang members. Infact Debraj sleeps only a few hours and the rest of the time spends in managing his troop and security planning. Debraj has not only posted camouflaged guards at the periphery but also planted landmines at strategic entry points whose co-ordinates are only known to the gang members. The camp is well covered with dense trees and shrubbery that filters the sound from inside the camp premises. Debraj watches Neil disappear in the distance and then speaks in a steely tone to interrupt the static noise ejaculating from the receiver of the military grade radiophone

"Lal salaam, Purba. Yes, so I've heard. Make it seven thirty in the morning, sharp. I know I can count on you, over and out"

At dawn a police check point is set up on a road, routine, as they say.

A truck approaches slowly, it's driven by a woman and in the back it carries a number of tribal women in their colourful cotton saris going to the market to sell their handicraft. The police stops the truck and Purba, who is driving dressed in an unusually feminine pink sari, tells the policeman that they are going to the bazaar "We are all widows, we need some extra money and hope to sell some of these things, actually if you could be interested in a nice wooden bowl, or a frame... for photograph..."

"No, no, no… get out of my way woman, we got bigger fish to catch, we are men and civil servants, you think we waste time with these knick knacks?" the men laugh at unison and Purba smiles. They think she smiles at them, shy and apologetic for having been so stupid. The truth is that she has a colour changing Alexandrite hanging from her neck that is as big as a strawberry and if this idiot had looked a little better he would have probably made the hugest step of his entire career. But cops are cops and men are men, they see women and the first thing they think is that they have bigger fish to catch...

She restarts the car and the engine struggles so the truck hops and one of the women sitting in the back drops a wooden ornament. Habitual as she is to catch everything that falls, because in the forest you are buried in mud, if something falls it's generally lost, she bends down to take it and as she does so her sari is lifted to reveal black boots.

Now, cops are cops, and none of Purba's serpents has a great consideration for them, but even they think it's suspicious to see a tribal woman in her sari wearing thick, muddy boots.

Purba, who sees the face of the policeman in the rear-view mirror and hears him scream to the other two to stop the truck, has no choice, she gives a signal and three seconds later she straps her gun off her thigh and shoots the two policemen in front of her, someone else at the back has shot the two behind.

Four shots, four killed. If she wasn't in this awful situation right now she'd be proud of her team but right now she has four dead cops and she knows that the jungle has eyes and ears, before she sees Debraj, he will find out what happened. What irritates her the most is that she has no one to blame, she is the one who made the truck pass but someone else dropped the thing and blew their cover. So she had to take charge.

She keeps on driving, hoping to attract no more attention that she already has and to find on the way a good explanation for Debraj. The only thing that makes her feel slightly relieved is the gem, she has found. The gem will remain to be her security deposit for life. To be free of the thought of poverty for lifetime is a dream come true. Now she can pursue her passion of taking over the region. But one step at a time. Even the breeze in the forest carries the smell of treasure. Anybody gets a whiff and she will be killed like all the previous finders of this 'hope precious stone'-Alexandrite.

Not far from the accident the Turu Dalam is training: Kedar Singh conducts the drill, while he unloads years of frustration for not having progressed in the ranks of the Naxals on his trainees. His eyes are still red with rage and possibly some substance, like they were a few years ago. But despite the worn out and sloppy air he has he is an amazing shooter -possibly the only reason why he is still around- and right now he is teaching his men how to anchor a moving target. To simulate movement he uses birds. He releases caged birds caught by his men from the wilderness. The flock of wild birds struggle in search for a gate inside the huge can basket, the shape that reminds the militants of a circular globe. Are we ditto, but in a larger basket they ponder. As soon as the bird is in air, Kedar points it out to one of the men and makes them shoot them, when they don't succeed he screams and shouts and gets angry at them. Debraj looks at him and understands why he has never grown in the ranks of the organization: Kedar is the classic example of a man with a talent who expects everyone to have the same talent and is unable to accept that some don't and need training to acquire it. Kedar is a grotesque looking man with a neck that is smaller than his fist. His missing neck acts as a metaphor for his missing brains. His small round head almost sinks inside his broad shoulders. He is not able to teach, he has no patience and would like to be the glorious leader of a battalion of heroes. If only he was humble enough to learn from Purba, who spends time and a lot of patience with her trainees he wouldn't have so many people turning their backs on him. Debraj remembers learning about a Roman emperor, Caligola, who had the same characteristics as Kedar. He was so mad he had made his horse a senator of the grand Republic of Rome. It didn't end well. Kedar too is in limbo.

As he is looking at the scene Purba's truck arrives and the women, dressed in their colourful saris, download the ammunition. The men tease them for their outfit at first but run to help them as soon as Purba whistles with authority..

Neil walks out of his roof with a cup of tea, the night wasn't as unpleasant as he expected. But he was not lucky enough to get any information on the inner dealings of the Turu Dalam. Standing in front of the armed militants, he is astonished to see so many women around. Purba has arrived. He considers hiding, because she has the soft spot for him (conflict of interest) and is not shy about it, but then he decides against it.

He walks up to her and sees the massive amount of guns and ammunition she is downloading from the truck.

"That's a shit load of guns, lady"

"The name's Purba"

"I know, I know..."

"They're not just guns, Neil, they're our means to freedom"

"Freedom from what?"

"I see you haven't started thinking with your real brains yet"

"Whoa... lady with balls of steel... suits me like a gem"

She walks closer to him, so close he can feel the warmth of her skin and the cinnamon scent of her breath.

"I have been eyeing you for a while, I like the mystery that you always smell of" she rubs her chest against his "I perform like a tiger. Trust me, the fight will be worth it"

Neil "I am not so sure of that". Purba "You look like the guy who is in a perpetual conflict between angels and demons… well let them do their job while you enjoy a bit of a heaven inside my den".

Neil gets stiff "Well then we have a date... but when business is over... right now both of us still have unfinished business"

"I am waiting with bated breath" Purba growls. Neil feels the tightening of his muscles. Purba gives him a seductive look. Women like Purba have high rushes of adrenalin and if they find a suitable match that shares the same vibe, things can get out of control. But Purba knows she is at the headquarters so decides to capture the fellow tiger some other day. Had it been her den, Neil would have been in her private cabin by now, on his knees, speaks her confidence.

She loads her personal gun with more bullets, and as he watches her doing so a young boy, the silent rider who got him here the previous night approaches him with his thick red band.

Purba watches him taking off his sunglasses and tying a black band around his head, she says, "Be gentle to him" and laughs away.

"Look who is talking, the woman who holds a record of killing thirty three cops"

The young guy pats Neil shoulder and holds his hand telling him that it's really time for them to hit the road. As she watches him walk away, with the unsure steps of a blindfolded man she screams "Make it thirty seven after today"

He screams back "Ok, I surrender, we have a date... But please come unarmed, only I will be allowed to carry the weapon, the one I was born with!!!" Neil's laughter reverberates in the jungle like a roaring tiger under the bright morning sun navigating through the flourish of the Sal trees. This time it's the birds that sing. The forest echoes with different birds chirping a different note mostly one after the other. Nature plays Beethoven in a rustic avatar. Neil wonders "Isn't this what I call a life"

CHAPTER 8

It's a quite morning when, a few days after his funeral, Shyla decides to visit her father's, or rather Father Thomas', grave at the town cemetery. The weather is warm and the sun shines with compassion, behind the huge sunglasses she cries but she doesn't allow herself to show it and so she sniffs trying to be as quiet as possible, even though the cemetery is empty.

Father Thomas' tombstone presents his date of birth and death and displays his photograph. She has chosen one from when he was younger, and it was taken by her mum when they were at university. He smiles like an angel, Shyla is sure that her mum smiled too, behind the camera. It's strange how in this photo he doesn't look so much younger than when he died, one could very well think it was taken a week before.

As she prays Shyla remembers a day of her childhood, she must have been two or three, not older. The memory is blurred, as all the things we remember but are not too sure we have really lived. It's of the day she got her tattoo. Shyla doesn't show it often but on her forearm there's an Indian- Trishul with writing underneath it. Time has stretched it and deformed it a little but it's still visible. It was her mother's last wish: the moment she handed Shyla, a little bundle of no more than three kilos, to Father Thomas, she asked him to tattoo that symbol on her arm, to protect and guide her. She also asked him to conceal the story from her, for as long as he could, and only tell her when she'd be old enough to forgive and move on.

Father Thomas had waited and waited but when Shyla grew up to a girl with abundant joy in her heart, he had almost forgotten to tell Shyla about the scariest truth of her life. He was reluctant at first, after all he was a man of God, but soon convinced himself that if Mira's desire had to be fulfilled, he should grant her last wish on his death bed. Shyla doesn't remember what happened exactly because she was too young, but that tattoo was a rite of passage and she could sense, it was something that would have changed her life. And her father was there for her, with her. She remembers a perfume, a red curtain, a soft and warm wind, as if the very spirit of her mother had fallen upon her to protect her and to ease the pain. She recalls a gentle gush of energy surrounding her like a balloon.

Likewise Father Thomas had always been, euphoric to have been given the chance to have what most catholic priests would want but are not allowed to have: a family. When Shyla was born he gave her his name even though everyone, in the family and within the church, knew exactly who her mother was and in what circumstances Father Thomas had become also a father.

She wipes a tear from her cheek, now everything makes more sense. Or less, actually, but at least some things that always seemed strange to her about her life have cleared up. She had another father, a biological father, who is a stranger to her, who could be anywhere, dead or alive. And to makes matters worst, he is a rapist and a mean man. A chill runs down her spine when she recalls the name of her biological father that Thomas had mentioned to her. But all of this information sounds alien to Shyla. It makes no sense to her. She feels as if it was about her past birth and has nothing to do with her present avatar. But now that she knows about him, can she live without ever confronting her evil father on his heinous act that has perpetuated a bloodline. Will she be able to ever find him? And even if she does what will be the encounter like? Suddenly she feels her simple life thrown into a vortex. Her head spins like a dying star caught in the whirlpool of a blackhole.

Another part of her debates on the fact that a pious man without any blood ties raised her with utmost dedication: it's true that Father Thomas doesn't even share a gene with her, her greenish eyes are not his, her nose, so long and straight and so different to his... and yet he was there for the tattoo, he was there when she lost her first front tooth, and the second, he made her breakfast, he nursed her when she was sick, he even got chicken pox from her and they spent a week at home watching movies and eating ice cream. And now she gets to know that he is not her father? What changed? If he hadn't told her she'd still be his baby... she would be the girl who knew no complications. She would still be the girl who would get thrilled with the mere thought of a blind date. She would be the woman who would blush like an angel when a random schoolboy would give her a flying kiss from across the street. Has she lost her innocence!

The noises of the city roll around her head like waves in an empty glass. Her mind goes back to the day of the tattoo; it's probably still a vivid memory because she still bears scars of it on her body, the tattoo itself. Involuntarily she runs her fingers on her arm where a symbol of Trishul is inscribed. Tattooing a baby has disadvantages: above all, as the baby grows and so do his or her limbs, the tattoo changes shape, and today her Trishul is distorted, but it can still be seen. Underneath there are three words: Forgive Forget Further. The letters are tiny and unreadable but she knows that they are there now nailed in her consciousness. But why!

Shyla remembers a day of scorching heat, when her father took her to an Indian tattoo artist downtown, in what at the time was still called Indian town, upon Mira's instructions. She wasn't there, she had been dead for a while, but Shyla could sense her presence, she could nearly see her in the smoke of the incense behind the gauze curtains. The lights in the parlour were red, the smell of incense suffocating, her father sat outside, in a waiting room separated by the main room by only a thin curtain made of strands of beads. He had a rosary in his hand and kept rolling his fingers down, bead after bead, praying for his child and knowing only too well that the truth one day would come out, and from his own mouth.

Strangely enough she doesn't remember the pain, she does remember a gipsy looking Indian lady pulling her little arm forward and holding her so tight she couldn't breathe. She remembers the smell, intense, growing strong by the minute, she remembers the ceiling of the place: a sort of dark ceiling, black, blue? A sort of galaxy, or

Milky Way designed with a myriad of neon glow stickers. She was so captured by that universe above her head, the size of a room, easy to understand also by a child, that she didn't even notice what was going on. That day she fell in love with the Universe. Jupiter, Saturn, Moon and other distant stars became her close friends in an instant. She strongly felt they were watching her. Her loneliness is brightened by her mother's spirit that arrives from somewhere, near or far.

When she was brought out and her arm was a little swollen and red, yes, she did cry, and Father Thomas smiled with his broad smile and perfect teeth and blessed her. His spell was so powerful that the moment he recited a prayer she believed anything could happen, and that day the pain really went away. "When faith is backed by passion and endeavour, pain vanishes, miracles happen" promised Father Thomas to Shyla in her adolescent days.

A few hours later Shyla is seated in the meeting room of her office, absentmindedly listening to the conference call. The different offices around the world discuss what they call the "India Poverty Project". *India*, in her brain a bell rings and she lets it wander through the room. Her eyes stop on a picture that hangs from the wall with the organization's motto: there's a woman holding a starved child and a writing underneath: *Anya doesn't want a fish today only to starve tomorrow, she wants to learn how to fish. Action against poverty: help us change their lives. Forever.*

Shyla liked this line since she joined the NGO, the concept of a long term improvement rather than an emergency action which, in all likelihood could fall into a void, had always excited her, and working for an organization that seeks a solution that could last forever was, and still is, inebriating. The voices from different parts of the world collide over the airwaves.

"The situation in India is getting out of hand..."

"Call them Naxals or Maoist or whatever you want but we have a huge region where peasants have stopped growing crops or mining for fear of seeing it taken away from them... Infact they are brainwashed and recruited for militancy. The terror too can spread rampantly"

"Look, we are the South Africa office, why us? There are other offices that are not submerged by work like we are... London?"

"No, I'm sorry..."

"Jakarta?"

"Are you crazy man? We are geographically nearly as far as you and we cover the whole South East Asia region!"

"Ok, Delhi... its India, your people!"

"You are right..."

"Oh... thank the Lord!"

"Yes, you are right, but we have other problems right now. We have four education projects running and three health projects to launch. Besides we also cover Nepal and Bangladesh and we have no experience, not even a junior expert, working on governance. This time we can't help"

Shyla feels that she's in a playground filled with huge and greasy skinned babies with receding hairlines and expensive ties. But the matured officials today behave like children or even worst "He did it, it's his problem – this is my toy, why should I give it to him?"

She tries to interrupt with something clever that might draw their attention to where the problem really is, "Look, this situation is covering several states and the Indian government is severely underestimating it, action must be taken and we better do it fast".

There is a pause during which everyone acknowledges her.

Shyla is only twenty-six but she is smart, she got this job because she's good, not because she was the friend of a friend, and the head of the Cape Town office knows it and relies on her a lot.

"Shyla is right," he says "we must proceed with an *in loco* assessment of the damage and the risk for the next year as far as food and shelter is concerned, then we can sanction the funds and the team"

"Right!" says Charles, a fat old South African, Shyla knows his past is not exactly crystal clear, especially as far the racist riots were concerned, and he has always looked at her with gender discrimination. "But now we just need to write guidelines on how to do the assessment right? I mean we are not going to cross the world to teach our Asian colleagues how to do their job. Am I the only one who thinks it's crazy?"

Shyla interrupts him because Charles gets on her nerves even when he doesn't speak, as soon as he opens his mouth she snaps.

"Charles, the problem is not whose competence it is, this region survives on agriculture and mining, in a few months the rains will start and everything must be ready for a harvest by then, do you understand? We don't even have six months and we are already out of time for starch (rice and wheat, if you are wondering), we can put a patch on it with produce (fruit and vegetables, again, if you are not well acquainted with English) but we need to act fast. Besides, Charles, you might have not noticed but this NGO is called "Action Against Poverty" for a reason: to help poor people... The idea is to go there and see how much funding this emergency action will require and before you ask, no, the local government cannot provide information, it's like the problem we had with Malawi but ten times bigger. Plus the fight against Maoists, we have a tough situation here…Are we clear?"

Charles is irritated, getting lectured by a woman, he is had enough as it is, but from this cappuccino one… unacceptable!

"I do understand Shyla, what I don't understand is how you are going to overcome the problem? These things take time, countries go at war because of terrorism. Are you planning to go to India and plant tomatoes and beans yourself and show the locals that it's better to love each other than make war? Besides, why are you so eager to get your brains blown off?"

Shyla is at loss of words, she has to hold on to her hidden emotions and knows that if she answers now she will probably lose her job on account of being violent and impolite. Her boss comes in her rescue.

"Ok, let's calm down, shall we? I think you are both right. Delhi has asked our help and we will give it provided that they show their interest in the issue by giving us some resources. I'm not willing to go there and do their job for them, but the mission of our organization is to serve and help and we are going to do it no matter what! So, I will speak to Delhi today and see what they say, Shyla?"

"I'm fine with it and I offer to go if we need to send someone"

"Crazy girl…" hisses Charles between his teeth.

The director of the offices heads back to his room and orders Shyla to follow him. She is like a daughter to him, he remembers when a few years back she got the job and entered this same office, shy, with those big eyes looking around for something to say, feeling too young and scared for that big position. Over the years she grew and filed her claws to keep people like Charles in place, he is proud of her but also a little worried about her war-like attitude.

"You gotta watch out, kiddo, Charles can't wait to kick you out of the game... But seriously, do you really want to go? I know the death of your father has affected your life deeply and I wouldn't want you to make some foolish decision because now you are hurt and irrational..."

"Do I look like it, boss?" she answers with a smile.

"No you don't, but you might have not considered that, although Charles is a dimwit, he might be right. These people are terrorists and they won't think twice if it comes to blowing your brains off"

"Look Allan, I'm so grateful for all you taught me and all you have done for me, but I have grown now, I want more. I chose this job because I believe in it but also because I want a stimulating profession: this is what I've always wanted to do and if you trust me on this one, if you give me this last big chance it could really mean a lot for me, professionally I mean"

"Ok, you seem to have it all figured out... I'll make sure that Rosie books your flight and organizes your schedule..."

"Thanks" she says without a smile, a few years back she would have jumped and said things like "Oh Gosh!" and "I can't believe it", now she's just a professional whose idea is being valued enough to invest the organization's funds and resources on it.

"Oh, on a personal note... You watch out, any minor sign of risk you come back. And I don't say it because I worry about you but if anything happens to you I will be the one whose brains are blown off... by the headquarters, regional office, administration and so on... Am I making myself clear?"

"Crystal clear" she says with a smile, she knows that he is indeed doing his duty but he is also genuinely worried about her "You remind me of my father...Life is a purpose. . .attain it! He taught me that. And whenever I feel I'm fulfilling mine I know he's closer to me"

"Go on. Do it and make me proud, kiddo, when you come back I will have a promotion letter waiting for you!"

"Thanks boss!"

"Bon Voyage!"

This same night Shyla is doing one last tour of the flat to see if all the lights are off, if she forgot to turn off the gas, if the plants have enough water for a few days. There's a portrait of her mother with a professional camera hanging from her neck in the living room, she smiles at it and caresses it gently before her eyes fall on the post it next to it "KEYS"

Father Thomas wrote it once he had to come with her keys as she had locked herself out (again). This simple piece of yellow paper has an amazing value for her now and involuntarily she caresses it as well, as she has stroked her mother's picture.

The other hand is in her purse checking if she has the keys. She does. She picks up her small red suitcase and she's off. First stop: New Delhi

Chapter 9

Arriving in Delhi is a shock for Shyla: the airport seems ten times bigger than that of Cape Town or Johannesburg and a hundred times more crowded, the smells are what she thinks are most different. In airports around the world there's always a subtle smell of... nothing, here everything seems to bear its own, very distinctive smell.

She collects her suitcase at the conveyer belt and walks through the immigration, she's on duty and has no intention whatsoever to interrupt her listening of Debussy's *Claire de Lune* on her IPod to bargain if she can or can't bring facewash into the country, therefore she flips her passport nonchalantly and hoping not to be stopped and heads out where a smiling driver who is holding a placard with her name written on it.

Rosie called her last night -night? Afternoon? Bloody jet lag!- to let her know that she had managed to speak to the Delhi office, Shyla wonders who she might know to speak to someone at what? Three, four in the morning? And arrange for a driver to pick her up from the international terminal and will drop her off at the domestic one.

She is already firmly holding in her hand the boarding pass for Raipur.

The driver offers to take her bag and she lets him, she knows only too well that this is the last easy part of this trip: from the second she will leave the small plane used for domestic routes she's gonna be on her own, She might as well indulge a little now...

As she expected the arrival at Raipur is not as comfortable as the one at Delhi: for a moment she thought her suitcase was lost, then she saw someone picking it and had to run after them to get it back, apparently they wanted money, she threatened to call the police and they said they were "taxi drivers" who wanted to put it in the trunk to spare her the effort...

Now Shyla is at the bus station, she has bought herself a local simcard that fortunately works in her dual simcard android phone. She was horrified when the tea stall fellow-Raju asked for her passport but then she felt comforted when he took a photocopy and returned it with a lot of respect and also offered a packet of glucose biscuit free. Raju smiled "we are taught to treat visitors as angels from the skies" Shyla relished the biscuits thanks to the sparkling smile of an ordinary young lad who didn't have enough of clothes on him to keep him warm but knew his courtesy well. However he had zilch knowledge of the buses and their routes. Shyla is back to her lost self. She looks around for a signboard, a timetable, a... something, and anything that might indicate in a language that she can comprehend where all these busses go. Shyla has wondered for years, and certainly does so now, how all the people in countries where the literacy rate is so low can travel and understand where they are going, how much they have to pay for a ticket, how much change they should get.

Now all her doubts are palpable and the only answer she can find is that they ask, the sound of voices is so intense and so knit, voices into voices, voices over voices that the only reasonable explanation is that everyone is in her same situation: no one really knows where these busses with no sign on them go. The bus conductors stand by them and shout the destination, if you hear them you try and cut through the thick layer of people and reach them, if you don't, you ask if anyone has heard about a bus going to Jaipur, Delhi, Bombay, and Patna. Often you catch a bus and then get down in five minutes realising that there was a miscommunication or even worse, the bus conductor was confused.

Shyla is so concentrated on finding the bus that she doesn't see a man who notices her, he is wearing Rayban sunglasses and he is on his way to a bus too. Differently to her though he seems totally at ease: his white shirt is spotless, as if he just wore it fresh from the laundry, and his backpack falls graciously on his back as if it was filled with some fluff just to keep it in shape. But his eyes are screening Shyla from a comfortable distance.

Shyla on the other hand didn't expect this excruciating heat and feels that every inch of her body is drenched in sweat, she has the hangover-like feeling of the jet lag and her legs are weak, every step she takes she feels the need to crawl in an expensive hotel bed. However the soft rays of the sunlight keep her eyes glimmering and the perspiration on her forehead gives her an unusual glow.

She looks around to check if there's an expensive hotel around, she needs to lie down -horizontally- and sleep. Unfortunately the only thing her eyes allow her to see is a huge sign where a man in a singlet walks towards the square leaving behind a woman stranded on a motorbike, the slogan reads "Rayban eyewear – Forever yours".

Shyla is unimpressed, she honestly thinks Rayban eyewear could have done a lot better. *What is it a threat? If you buy our sunglasses you are stuck with the beefy guy who has abandoned his motorbike and girlfriend?* She thinks. But the one thing that strikes her is the resemblance with a scene from the great Gatsby: she remembers faintly how the lover, Daisy's antagonist and alter ego, lived with her husband in a house above the gas station, in a deserted place which had, as only attraction, the sign of an optician with a gigantic pair of glasses. Funny how two equally remote places have a pair of glasses as their only distinctive sign?

She shakes the thought out of her head and heads for a bus whose driver has just screamed a name that reminded her of the destination she must reach, she's relieved as she already has the ticket and everything should run smoothly.

Should. Smoothly. This is India.

"Look, I do have my ticket!"

"Yes I see ma'am" answers the bus conductor with a smile and shaking his head in the Indian fashion.

"So let me on the bus!"

"I can't ma'am, no seat"

"What do you mean no seat? Why on earth the guy over there sold me the ticket then?"

"I don't know, this bus, no seat, good earth"

"What am I supposed to do?"

"I don't know..."

"Should I wait for another bus?"

"I don't know..."

"Is there going to be another bus today?"

"I don't know..."

"What do you mean you don't know for God's sake, it's your job! How can you not know???"

"Sorry ma'am, I don't know!"

"Don't you say you are sorry because you have no idea how sorry I am?"

"Sorry ma'am, which country you are from? America?"

"Yes, I'm the President of the United States!"

"No, ma'am, United States: President Obama, Yes we can!"

Shyla has depleted of all her energy, she is so frustrated she could cry and she can't believe that only a couple of hours ago she was in an air conditioned airport where she had a fantastic cup of coffee and a French croissant and now she's trying to communicate with this idiot-Yes we can!

The man in sunglasses approaches her and tells her "New in town huh? This is India Miss Cleopatra, everything is possible, and my name is Neil by the way! He screams something from the bus window and two people step down and leave their places to Shyla and Neil, she's puzzled.

"What? What did you say?" In her head conspiracy theories erupt: *He's a secret services agent and wants to abduct me out of mistaken identity, there's a bomb on the bus and he's trying to get me killed, or he is aiming to loot me on the way,* but he interrupts her reverie with a hearty laugh.

"Nothing, I told them you were going to pay the price of the ticket plus hundred rupees to whoever left you their seats, I did the same for myself... Don't worry, it's safe, I'm safe! For these people hundred rupees is a lot of money, time has a lesser value here..." Neil pays the guys their fare plus the extra for both of them. He jumps onto the bus and disappears in the crowd. Shyla follows him, a little overwhelmed with the whole situation, she's fretfully tired and was looking forward to the bus ride to Kanker to sleep but as soon as she finds a minuscule spot she realizes that this is not going to be right place to enjoy a nap. Neil lands up sitting on a drum of kerosene that belongs to fellow passenger. Shyla wonders if there is anything like safety standards in the dictionary in this region. What if the bus meets with an accident? Before she can get any consolation she finds Neil sleeping like a baby atop the hazardous drum as it were a cradle. "Fools venture where angels fear to tread" the intellect reminds her.

Next to her sits a man who keeps turning around and smiling at her, she thinks he's old enough to be her father but also that probably he does not appear that old, he makes her uncomfortable though, she politely smiles back but his smell of old wool -in the afternoon heat- and vaguely of goat makes her regret with every smile...Why she left her cosy home in Cape Town.

In front of her a woman is nursing a child, her trip must have been long as she is evidently distraught, as soon as Shyla rubs her finger on the baby's face to stroke him the woman hands him to her as if he was a heavy package. Shyla thinks of her youth, she has travelled a lot and done quite adventurous things, but this is by far the craziest adventure she has ever been on.

She looks at the bus, it looks like one of those in the Guinness books of records "How many people can you stuff in a bus?" The bus also has something of a

Christmas crèche, the man with a bunch of chicken tight by their legs, the woman with the baby, another man with a perpetual smile showing his big silver tooth that he wears so proudly. Shyla thinks, before closing her eyes that each one of them has a book, a story, of their own, and she would like to be able to write them. "The stories that would come out of these ordinary people living such extraordinary lives would probably change the way the western world thinks about life as a whole. Oprah Winfrey could produce a never-ending series on these people titled 'wilder world" Shyla mutters to herself in jest. The bus zooms past diverse people, places and landscapes that could put the Wikipedia to shame.

She's so tired she can't keep her eyes open and bends her head backwards falling asleep in no time. After a day and a bit that she has spent awake she couldn't care less of her money, passport, house keys, she oblivious of everything around her except her sleep. In a second she is deep in Morpheus's arms.

Shyla's tormented sleep is ended abruptly by a sound. She hasn't managed to sleep more than five minutes at a stretch and she's unsure how much time has passed. She feels like she's rolling on the floor but thinks to her unconscious self that she must be getting slightly road sick. Then people shriek and she opens her eyes at once: in the little space between the heads of the passengers and the roof of the bus things, objects are flying, wild orchids, the bunch of chickens, the plastic cups for the tea...

There was a car crash, or simply the bus driver tried to save some passing cattle and the huge metal beast has spun out of the main road and into the fields, it's not going to be easy to put it back on track. In the commotion Shyla hits her head and blanks out, the last thing she can feel is a powerful hand that grabs her from under her arms and pulls her, she would fight back but has no strength.

Seconds later she wakes up in the field next to the bus, everything is a mess and the driver stares at the minibus like a tourist: curious but really careless. Fortunately the kerosene drum is lying safely, with its dangerous content intact- "how did that happen, this country surely lives on a miracle that the universe is trying to fathom" Shyla talks to herself aloud.

She notices the wreck: cups, clothes, flowers, bananas, water bottles and a dead chicken... She doesn't know India but she knows Africa and if these two realities are slightly similar, as soon as the bus is back in shape all these things will have regained their original place. Nothing is lost and nothing is wasted not even the dead chicken. She approaches the driver to enquire what's going to happen next, he seems uninterested to solve the problem.

"Ma'am, tomorrow morning!"

Shyla knows she's bouncing against a rubber wall so she looks around, trying to grasp something to talk about to the driver in order to draw him closer to her and see if she can get some better information or one of the first spots in the next ride.

"So, what's the deal with the Rayban boy? Why does he look like he's on a beach in Goa?"

"Ma'am, that is a frequent traveller, he knows things like this happen all the time" Shyla is a little thrown off by the stress the driver put on *all the time*.

"Besides, you might want to thank him, he's the one who pulled you out of the bus when you were passed out..."

The driver tries to start the engine idly and gives up almost immediately, he gets out and screams: "Ladies and Gentlemen no bus tonight, wait tomorrow"

Shyla knows that he has only spoke English for her, but everyone else seems to have understood and hunt for a place to squat for the night.

Frigging Delhi office! She thinks, and then why am I thinking that Charles was right all along? I have been in India for less than a day and already I've risked my life once, now I'm sleeping alfresco with all the risk of being raped, killed and robbed, if not by my travel companions then by some Maoist thug...

Shyla notices she has been thinking out loud and looks instinctively around to see if someone is looking at her. She sees Neil, who has crossed his arms and looks rather amused, he is shamelessly staring.

"I guess you find this rather amusing, don't you?"

"I don't know... Are you always this hyper? No, coz if you are I'd like to travel with you more often..." Shyla realizes that so far this man has been kind to her, he understands her language and in this less-than-optimal situation she needs someone to befriend. She will keep her eyes wide open and not trust him too much but she can't fight everybody...

"Yeah, no... I'm only this hyper when I crave coffee..."

"Well then you happen to be in the right place, I'm not even sure it wasn't your idea to make the bus break right here... Come with me"

"W-where?"

"To a human sacrifice! You want coffee? I'll give you coffee, but you gotta come with me, I'm not a waiter..." and he gestures her to follow him, she does.

They both indulge for a minute too long into each other's eyes. A feeling of excitement mixed with discomfort falls upon both of them, like the realization that this accidental meeting had been planned somewhere, by someone, a long long time ago.

The spark that crosses their irises suggests that their lives are about to be changed for ever, but right now they shake the thought out of their heads: they need coffee and none of them is prepared to look for, find or even stumble upon love. Love is so far away right now. And yet so close.

CHAPTER 10

Neil takes Shyla to a dhaaba, a local chai stall at the side of the road, the smell of spices and the warmth of the fire gives Shyla sense of cosiness and home.

I'm stranded on the side of the street with a stranger, possibly exposing myself to a huge risk and I feel fine... If I was wondering whether I'm crazy or not, well now I have the answer: I am.

Neil stares at her in awe. She is so lost in herself. Neil wonders: *She is a beautiful STORY UNTOLD. Just like me.* Neil hands her a cup of Nescafé and, still muddled, she looks in her purse for a bag of her sweetener; she notices how Neil adds fours spoons of sugar to his coffee.

"Oh sweet Jesus! Do you want to die? Do you know how long it will take you to burn those? Besides its bad for your health!" she bites her lower lip, for a moment she has forgotten where she is and who she's with and she said the same thing she would have told Damian at the cafeteria.

"Are you a fitness freak or something? You don't look like one!" Why is she so outraged; *does she think I'm fat?*

"Besides, you think too much, what are you? A journalist?"

"Something like that..."

"Something like what?" Neil is confused.

She looks around as she is short of words, she doesn't want to tell why she is here because in the safety package they have given her the first thing she read was that whoever has a position in a charity, NGO or international agency must be very careful of whom they speak to, especially if they are alone in the area, kidnappings and retaliations of every sort happen every day in India, she has to be careful. She had pondered about that... Exciting to have, for once, the chance to be somebody else, anybody, whoever you want! And then the thought became philosophical and she forgot to make herself a credible identity.

"Pho... Photographer... I'm a photographer, specialized in wildlife! From Cape Town" she adds with a grin. Then looks around and they are in the middle of nowhere, it doesn't exactly look like there's going to be much wildlife to see here... but she can always say, if this curious chap asks for more, that she's specialized in birds, or insects.

"Wild... wildlife, nice!"

Shyla looks at him with an enquiring look, it's pretty evident that now she wants to know what he does. Neil shrugs and smiles putting up his most innocent face.

"Ah, don't look at me, I'm unemployed and broke!"

"Pfff bullshit!!! Rayban sunglasses, Timberland boots, branded jeans; you can pull it off with unemployed but broke... Mhhh hard to believe!"

"Damn!!! Drop the wildlife and start a career as a reporter! You'd do wonders!"

For a second their eyes meet, they both have a look they don't generally have (fierce Shyla and shy Neil) and they seem to uncover the most secret side of themselves in front of a stranger, they both do it at the same time and for a second only they can really see into each other's souls. This scares the two of them and they both look away, aware that there's some tension pulling them together and, for different reasons, both aware that they should try as hard as they can to fight it.

Something is lingering in the air, it's a strange mix of love, tension and impending doom: something is about to happen, the air is electric, but neither Shyla nor Neil can be sure of what it is exactly. There's attraction between them but this is beyond that, it's more of a foreshadowing, and considering where they are and who could visit them during the night, it's better not to underestimate any of the stimulus they receive from the world around them. And yet it is so hard to think of a world outside of them. The romance of the night cages their spirit like exploding stars packed in a candy jar.

A group of women has gathered with a few of their belongings and, although aware of the risk they are all running by squatting by the side of the road, at the seam of the jungle, they sit down, sip tea and sings their souls out. Music has liberated their souls. Art protects them from fear. It's a beautiful chant and Shyla listens to it carefully, she can't understand any of it but it reminds her of the Zulu women singing around the fires, when she went on weekend trips with her father many years ago.

Shyla notices that the three guys with Metallica shirts, she had noticed them before, when she first got on the bus, walk behind the bus.

She had felt so old when, as soon as she saw them with their skinny jeans and black boots and rock band shirts. She had held her purse closer to her, as her grandmother used to do when a black person boarded the bus in Cape Town. She also amuses herself thinking that they probably went behind the bus to smoke weed or do something they couldn't do in front of everybody.

They truly surprise her when they come out of the dark corner with their guitars and join the women.

The scene before her eyes has a circle of women, of different ages but all dressed in colourful saris, one is holding a chicken, the other one with a baby goat on the leash -she was probably going to visit a relative with a present- one hugging a massive bag of rice, possibly her only source of income which she didn't want to abandon on the bus. They are all sitting in a circle and they sing, then the guys come, one by one, and sit between two old grannies, or next to a pretty but shy girl and her mother or again between an old lady and her baby granddaughter.

They sit down and strum their guitars, with their eyes closed as if they were on a stage, they tune their music on the chant and Shyla can tell that sometimes they go too fast or don't know where to stop, they follow a different genre, but music has glued together two worlds and the outcome is beautiful despite all the little mistakes they may be making. Being a sucker for music since a child, Shyla believes that music is divine because it brings together different beings on one common ground where they connect to each other like they were in the same space somewhere out there. *Music is a great leveller, a finger that points towards the light inside all of us.*

"What are they singing?" Shyla asks Neil who is sweetly looking at her. He travels a lot by train and bus and small incidents like this are not infrequent, therefore he has seen random groups of people singing together. He has turned blind by the frequency of folk and it's nice for him to rediscover the poetry of this act through somebody else's eyes. And when Shyla's eyes are poetry itself, the lyric reflecting in those eyes is pure magic.

Neil gets back to his chauvinist pretence "It's just an old ballad, it's in Chhattisgarhi and I can't quite understand all of it, from the little I understand this one is about love, how it heals all wounds and makes you a better person when it's true love..."

"It's beautiful..."

"Well, don't get too melancholic, it's just a song!" Neil gathers his wits.

"And what do you have against love, you brute?" she says smiling.

"Love is no cure… it sucks your adrenalin… Its escapism" Neil speaks from the cerebral side of his mind.

"Love is what makes you alive"

"Love kills…gets you off track"

Shyla looks at him with interest.

"Ok, Mr Buzzkill, let's talk about Chhattisgarh then!"

Just then they are interrupted by a boy who trots towards Shyla with a cloth filled with a few stone and metal figurines. He opens it before her eyes and says a few words in Chhattisgarhi, internationally understood words: he wants to sell his crafts!

Shyla hands him a hundred rupees note and buys an elephant and a tiger, Neil hands the boy some notes too.

"It's a savage, wild land, full of everything and with nothing in it. I think it's pretty magical... It's the land of tribes and minerals...precious stones and metals"

The night is falling over a steel plant, workers have either gone home or they are busy on their night shift. The night is warm and outside three men are talking. One of them in a safari suit- with the attitude of those who can pay and demand- talks to Debraj, over the phone. Two of Debraj's men are at a distance, checking the plant and most of all delivering the message, they are the ones who put this man in contact with Debraj, who, for security reasons can only do business over the radio or phone. The 'safari suit man' talks with the bravest voice he can put up but Debraj, from his chair in his den and behind the smoke of the brazier that is filling the room, can hear his voice tremble: this man is putting his life into the Maoist gang's hands, after all he has capitulated. He can try and sound as brave as he pleases but the truth is that he's scared to death. Debraj lets him brag, in the end he has the money and by now they have full hold of him, there's no point in stupid threats. From now on its only business, dirty, wealthy, gold covered shit business.

"Don't worry about the money. That will keep rolling in if all goes well. I just want commitment from you and your men here. No more tribal union leaders entering the plant. Not even the police. It's a two way street... you take care of my steel plant; I'll ensure your funds are replenished. I've already spoken to the MP"

Debraj hangs up the phone and looks at Kedar Singh, who sits in front of him with his usual red eyes. He has brought in two Chinese men dressed as musicians. The whole scene is quite curious: Debraj looks like an Indian, sad and disappointed Fidel Castro, Kedar Singh sits in front of him as a crazy mafia mob stuffed with God knows what drug -Debraj is not sure nor concerned if Kedar does drugs or in what quantity but the sure thing is that he would much rather have a junkie in his gang than a psychopath, and Kedar Singh looks like one-, the two Chinese men sit quietly handing him a chunk of roasted snake on a leaf.

They look nearly servile, in their worn out nomad singer clothes.

"Come on Debraj, he knows his hands are tight! If he screws up we'll blow his brains off, he knows it and the MP knows it too. Now guys, show us your talent!" exhorts them Kedar Singh, and the two Chinese men, who so far have been silent and Debraj wasn't even sure they understood, open their guitar cases, covered in stickers from all over the world and show the other duo their merchandise: two massive Chinese grenade launchers.

Debraj scrutinizes the two men, who still haven't said a word, and then the grenades, his head is elsewhere, he is rational and doesn't believe in foretelling, but he needs to be careful of outsiders cause a plan, a line of action, a daring undertaking, a resolute operation, is being lined up from this red terror camp buried under a sprawling façade of wilderness.

CHAPTER 11

In the deadly silence of night, the air gets chilly. Neil and Shyla sit next to one another for warmth... He likes being the man of the hour, calming her down and explaining, what happens in various groups that have squatted in different corners, he likes being in charge. She, on the other hand, has understood his liking for a Rambo role, and lets him play his part, she knows he knows more about this environment and she needs him. If he needs to feel in charge to help her she's not going to disappoint him.

He sips his chai as they sit in silence, she takes the empty plastic cup and throws it away, when he looks at her quizzically she only says, shrugging in her shoulders, "Well I've let you put a ton of sugar in your tea, you can't drink too many of them on the same day!"

Neil pretends to get upset but his eyes smile, and so do hers.

Shyla is tired, she looks around but all she can see is the white plastic chair with *paan* stains that she is sitting on, as Neil begins to unfold a sleeping bag he has fished out of his backpack she looks at her suitcase packed on the bus and lets out a sigh. She didn't necessarily mean to attract his attention but he turns around and asks her "Forgot the combination of your fancy suitcase, Miss All-good-things-in-life-are-dangerous-for-your-health?"

"No, I don't have anything to make a bed out of..." she responds, nearly to herself.

"Well I thought wildlife photographers were used to sleeping anywhere to catch the best time of the day... or the night..."

Shyla shivers, does he doubt something? But his was just a remark, in fact he continues as if nothing had happened "But don't worry, you can take my sleeping bag for tonight!"

"What? I mean, I don't mean to take your stuff... I should have thought about it really..."

"Not at all, I insist, we Indians might not have the best of everything but we certainly do have the best hospitality of all! I will be on the bench over there!"

Shyla thanks him and lies down, she is so tired she feels she's not even going to make it into the sleeping bag but once she is in, she falls asleep in a second. After what initially seems to her an eternity (but soon realizes were only a few minutes) she is woken up by an army of mosquitoes that aim for her as if she was a shooting target. She jumps up wagging her hands and slapping her arms and face in a vain attempt to chase the mosquitoes away.

Neil opens his eyes, woken up by the noise and the sight of Shyla jumping around trying to catch an invisible monster is quite amusing, so amusing he can't help himself and laughs his guts out.

Shyla looks at him, annoyed at first, she then realizes how hilarious the scene must have been and, because the few minutes of sleep make her feel like she has slept for hours, she goes to him with a smile and extends her hand.

"Shyla Thomas, I think I haven't been the best travel companion so far, I owe you an apology!"

"Not at all Shyla, I am used to women in their best behaviour, I'm Neil" she gives him and enquiring look.

"Neil what?"

"Isn't Neil enough?"

"Yeah, well, I guess... And so Neil with-no-surname, what is someone like you doing in this part of India?"

Neil looks around to grasp something that might give him an idea, he has tailored stories for all but had never had to make one up for a South African photographer. A pretty one too. And, quite unexpectedly, the clue comes from her: on the sleeping bag she has left the latest number of NatGeo, she took it out of her purse and was flipping through it before falling asleep.

"Wild... Wildlife fascinates me too..." he attempts, but he is a bad, bad liar and it takes Shyla a fraction of a second to tell he's making it up.

"Yeah sure, and I didn't tell you but I'm Cleopatra!" she says, going back to her sleeping bag.

Neil feels he owes her an explanation, a better one *why the hell women have to be always so curious? Damn it! And make us feel guilty if we don't tell them what they want to hear! Neil don't move, if you get up and go to her I'm never gonna talk to you again. And I'm me, so it's gonna be pretty hard. Neil don't go! Don't get up!* But before the message from his brain can stop his legs he's already up and walking to her.

"Ok, look, lets simply say, I am a treasure hunter and these forests have some unknown treasures hidden inside their bellies"

Shyla, afraid he's going to ask her something personal she doesn't want -and is not allowed- to reveal, cuts him short and ejaculates words out like a machine gun, she takes out the NatGeo magazine and shows him random pictures.

"You mean the wildlife... here check this out. What a tiger… Amazing huh? Do you know that there are more tigers held captive as pets than they are in the wild… sad but true. Listen, you seem to know your way around here. Can I tempt you to be my safari guide? I'd love to explore the jungle and get some candid shots... And really you look so at ease here, I really need someone like you!" She smiles at him with the sweetest eyes she can make and for a moment, as he stares into her almond eyes he seems convinced but then he regains control over himself and tries to dodge the question "Nice camera!"

But she doesn't give up that easily "So, what do you say?"

"It's not safe... the jungle"

"Oh come on... I'm from South Africa, wildlife fascination runs in my genes. What, you think I can't hustle a tiger?"

"There's more to the jungles here than just tigers, Ms Thomas"

"Like what?"

Neil takes her hand gently; she jumps, as she didn't expect it and stares at the two hands that, despite the scare, are still tight together.

He turns her wrist gently and peeks at her watch, as though he is not wearing one.

"Like it's bedtime... so no more questions, Miss Reporter"

He bows his head to gesture a goodnight and walks back to his bench, then covers his face with his cap. Shyla sees that and decides to use her scarf to cover her face too.

"Good night Neil the nature lover and treasure hunter with no surname!" she screams.

"Good night Miss Thomas. And off the record, it's Mahajan. But don't write it in your article on tigers please!"

She smiles as she is falling asleep. Neil starts snoring from his bench.

The night is troubled, for Shyla. In a sepia memory -or is it a dream? - A woman - herself? - is running through the jungle, a camera is hanging from her neck and she seems distressed. The forest is trembling, the trees are shaking and the sun plays hide and seek. Shyla sweats and feels fear, she doesn't know of what, she doesn't know if the woman is herself or someone else but the sense of impending doom hangs over her, blowing an icy wind behind her head.

The surrounding is calm and it's hard for Shyla's remotely conscious part to understand where this sense of fear might come from if the day is glorious and the woman seems to be taking photos of wildlife. It's strange, as the place of the dream looks nothing like South Africa and a lot more like this place, Chhattisgarh, where the bus stopped but also where Shyla has only spent a handful of hours in her life. Is it Deja vu!

At dawn Neil is woken up by a stray dog licking his face hoping to get some food from this odd man sleeping on the street by the bus. The dog has already feasted last night on the leftovers of the passengers of the bus and has come back for more, to enjoy as much food as he can before they hit the road again and he's left alone in this God forsaken place.

Neil gets up and instinctively looks at the sleeping bag. Empty. He is worried.

Shyla woke up early, before anyone else; the night *al fresco* is rough for someone used to sleeping with AC in a fancy Cape Town flat.

She breathed in the fresh air. The smells of earth and wood and water and grass colonised her nose, giving her a sort of nature drunkenness, she wanted more and strides away from the road, out of the clearing and into the jungle.

Like Alice in Wonderland, Shyla kept walking and walking, surprised at her every step by the amazing things she saw around her, things she, as any city girl, didn't even know existed. The hill Myna gave her company in spurts of pleasing sounds. The lush green Tendu leaves aroused her photographic instincts. And as she walked the path leaving no trace of her passage and letting the forest embrace her in a deadly net. Soon the birds stopped chirping to invite a climate of celestial silence.

After a good twenty-minute walk she hears a noise, she ducks and sees from the bushes a three-wheeler van passing by. On it there is Ganpath, a man in his forties who is the official grocery supplier of the Turu Dalam. The noise of his vehicle had covered sounds and Shyla, unsure of who they could be, keeps her hiding spot. Three men dressed in camouflage gear walk right next to her without noticing her and talk about the new batch of supplies, hoping, at least for today, to get a breakfast worth of this name. The men reach a nearby clearing and report to an older man.

How could she not have seen it? She was looking right in front of herself! - At this point they are too far away for Shyla to hear them but it's pretty clear that, given the tent and the uniforms, they are not hunters... Bam, she stepped across what she was looking for!

The Maoist terrorists are the reason why this region never gets aids delivered as they should: food, health products, even pumps and agriculture machines get "filtered" here. The sad truth is that they either never reach the needy as they are stolen at the storage plants or the corrupt politician of the day gives them to the terrorist groups straight away- if only she could report where they are...

She takes out her Smartphone and makes sure the exact position is recorded on the GPS and then reaches for her camera, hanging from her shoulder behind her, to take a couple of videos of the red gang members and of the makeshift training camp. From whatever they are yelling, she can comprehend three words 'Hail Turu Dalam'.

She knows only too well that she can't be this lucky on her first day but still, it might be useful to know who they are fighting against, provided that the Indian and Chhattisgarhi governments collaborate.

As she pulls her hand behind her back, trying not to make any noise she feels sudden warmth and at once the hand of a man covers her mouth.

She can hardly breathe, let alone scream.

The man drags her through the forest, she's afraid of losing her camera and her shoes, these are the only comfortable ones she has – strange how in difficult situations we all think of very simple things...-, she's also very afraid of this extremely strong man who drags her by her head with only one hand. She feels her neck getting loose and the lack of air makes her lose her senses.

As she closes her eyes, unable to fight back, she thinks that dying like this is so stupid...What a waste of a life... all this education and experience to get killed by lunatics. But it was all her own fault...she decided to land in this frying pan. Dead End.

Chapter 12

Shyla keeps her eyes closed to gain a few seconds to make out where she is and how many people are around her, there are no noises except a man breathing, his breath smells of chai and the light of the sun warms her eye lids, so they must be out of the jungle. She slowly opens her eyes and is invested by Neil's voice, he is freaked out and, even though Shyla can't make out the details of his face yet -she's facing the sun and her eyes have been closed for a while- she can tell from his trembling voice that he is scared.

"What did I tell you? Stay away from the jungle, for God's sake! Do you want to get us both killed? Is this the wildlife you are looking for? Coz trust me, these ones are as wild as it gets..."

Shyla whispers something but Neil can't hear her, he held her so tight he nearly accidentally strangled her and she struggles a little when she swallows and when she tries to talk. He doesn't seem to notice.

"Come on, the coast is clear, we are on the road, we have to walk back to the bus, it's about a kilometre and three hundred metres from here, we have to hurry if we don't want it to leave without us" and he marches after having helped her back on her feet.

Neil and Shyla are seated in a cab that scoots off from a bus station. Shyla can see the rickety bus filling up the next lot of a million passengers. Neil is as silent as a man in coma. He looks more terrified than Shyla herself. Shyla knows for sure that he can't be a red gang terrorist atleast and that is safe enough to begin with. The cab pulls over in front of the Government Circuit House, Neil gets off and helps Shyla out, he then takes the luggage and pays the fare. She checks if she has everything: camera, purse, and suitcase.

"Thank you, for today... for everything... This morning was a close shave, I'm sorry..."

"You must look after yourself, you are in a dangerous place now and if the next time I'm not around you might end up dead..."

"One day... just one day is all I need. This is your territory, you know it, you breathe it, and I need you. Show me around, I'll take some quick snaps of wildlife and that's it. I promise to reward you handsomely in cash or kind" Shyla sports a smile.

Neil feels more comfortable with the flirting "Haha, you never promise a man to reward him in kind!"

She gives him the evil eye and he smiles flirtatiously, they both walk into the circuit house and take their luggage.

"What is it with you and wildlife? Some old connection? Were you a tiger in your previous life?"

"Who's to say, anyways now there are just a couple of thousand tigers left in the entire world?"

"Look, we have had a rough couple of days, now we need a bed, well two beds, and a good night sleep. Tomorrow we will do some planning ok? Meanwhile... Have you ever been on a motorbike?"

"Well, I had a bike when I was small and motorbike, like bike bike... Mhhh"

"Well, whichever the case you haven't been on this one, and with me!"

The next morning, at dawn, Shyla is stuck to the back of Neil who is riding his bike and whistling a Bollywood classic tune; he feels her hands a little too tight and too sweaty around his waist but after all he doesn't mind it. The Robin is chirping, the river falls with a silvery sound from rock to rock and the green terrain is striking: in only a few hours there will be people follow their routine, going to the market, to school, to work, but right now everything looks as if it was pulled out of a fairy tale. They reach the Senmuda village. Senmuda is famous for the presence of Alexandrite and rough diamonds in nearby villages. Senmuda came to limelight internationally when in the eighties Alexandrite mines were discovered. Back then only Russia boasted of this colour changing precious stone and now India had huge deposits of Alexandrite named after the Russian Tsar Alexander.

Neil pulls over and stops the engine on the outskirts of the village; Shyla looks around and takes some photos of the surroundings, trying to figure out where they are and how far it is to the closest town.

"You stay right here, I will only be a minute! Shyla, look at me... Here!"

"I know, I know..."

Neil walks up to a man, an old man with a handkerchief tied around his neck. Shyla notices how his hands are wrinkled and his nails are broken around the edges: the hands of a working man, someone who lived fighting for his life and clawing his way through survival. His eyes are watery, slightly stained of white cataracts, his cheekbones and chin are pointy and the bones stick out, covered by a spiky beard.

"It's not a sand grain, I'm sure you'll recognize it if you see it..."

"We heard it was found months back but I haven't seen it myself, but..."

"But?" Neil doesn't lower his gaze, he is here for something and his ass is on the line: he is not going to leave without at least some relevant piece of information.

"No idea who has it, Neil. Trust me. As you said it's not a sand grain. Its 50 carats... and now it's gone"

"10%"

"50"

"30"

"Done. I'll do some more digging around, ask a few people in the mines.

"Dig fast Bhola... before it's gone!" and he pats the old man on the back. The old man nods as a roll of one hundred Rupees notes disappears in his pocket.

Neil crosses the rivulet and goes back to the motorbike where Shyla was trying to catch bits and pieces of the conversation he had with the local. She only understood "50 carats" and now she is almost sure he is after something big.

"So? Clues on the hidden treasure? Are we going treasure hunting?"

"This whole state is sitting on a gazillion carats of gemstones. These locals here travel around, set up camp and excavate. If they find something, they end up selling the gems for a few hundred rupees"

"Are you serious? Let me guess, you're one of their buyers right? You look like a man of many professions!"

"One of them is forest guide and I charge extra to take around women who are extraordinarily beautiful... so your bill is sky high already... I'd be worried if I were you..."

"Yeah... I feel I don't trust you anymore" and she laughs.

Neil produces a stem of tiger orchids and hands it to her flirtatiously. Shyla enquires, "Where do you get orchids from in this dense forests". Neil shoots back "Google it... Chhattisgarh grows more than thirty types of orchids and more than five hundred species of flowering plants" Shyla "wow and what about tigers". Neil feigns ignorance and continues his whistling; this time it's Neil Diamond. She smiles, she can't deny she's attracted to him but at the same time she feels confused by the fact that only a month ago she had a different life. A month ago she was chatting with Hunky Dave, looking for a dress for a date, talking on the phone with her father... Her father... One month ago she had a father, a family, a life ... She had... And now, she can't even think about it... She's in India, doesn't even know where exactly and with a man she hardly knows, who pulls out a tiger orchid from nowhere, who might be involved in God knows what kind of business.

He gets back on the bike and is humming "Girl you'll be a woman soon..." Shyla is at the back and she smiles while she breathes in his strong and manly perfume.

Neil takes Shyla to a corner of the jungle where they are likely to find tigers. He warns her that tiger spotting is a matter of great luck but today he can smell a tiger from a distance. The two of them are staring into the bushes with absolute silence. Soon Neil's charm works with the wildlife. A couple of hours of staring at still life, they spot a movement of yellow fur with thick black stripes. The lone tiger, majestically walks through the deep green bushes. The tiger's eyes pierce the greenery and look at the two people taking pictures. Shyla tries to be as quiet as possible and the snapshot of the Tiger is one of the best photos she has ever taken. The animal yawns showing two rows of perfect, deathly sharp teeth, Shyla thinks that everything about this animal is majestic. She is profoundly grateful to Neil for having brought her here. Neil reminds Shyla of her school days when she was the one who would boldly walk upto a guy and ask him to take her for a bicycle ride. The boys barely in their teens would mostly shy away out of fear of being teased. But there was this one boy who not only took her for a long ride but who also bought her ice cream and poured cola on her dress. That was one hell of a day for Shyla, out on the streets with this American boy who cared a damn about the world. He smelt of freedom, of a liberated soul. She was taken aback by his audacity but she tasted liberty in his carefree attitude. All Shyla remembers of him is the peck he gave her on her pink lips when he dropped her home. Since then she has been kissed several times but nothing matches to the kiss of the young boy riding on passion. She stares at Neil blankly.

Her reverie is interrupted by the sound of an engine, the memory of the previous day still lingers with fear and at once she looks at Neil to see what his reaction is. Their eyes meet. He is scared.

A jeep appears from out of the bushes, four men sit in it and rush for the tiger. The agile animal darts and the jeep chases it without even noticing the two people. Shyla can only hear the sounds of the jungle opening before the tiger and behind the jeep, like a wound. Neil can guess the distance between the predator and the prey shortening, ironically the two roles are inverted now.

The engine stops and a few shots are fired, the lament of the tiger peaks high in the sky, Shyla covers her ears as if the piercing sound of death could break them. She wants to run but before she can even figure which direction to take another jeep cuts the jungle leaving behind a clearing: fallen trees, leaves, broken bushes. This vintage jeep is boarded with a few tribal leaders. For a moment the sky can be seen, blue and brutal with the rays of the sun concentrating in one strip rather than filtering through the branches.

More shots, screams, voices, shootings.

“Salwa Judum” whispers Neil to himself and at once, without him realizing it or even wanting it, his mind goes back to the Tiger. So there are two opposite gangs fighting for a solitary tiger. A game in the wild. “Run” he screams to Shyla, whose fear has paralyzed her.

He grabs her by the sleeve and forces her to run, they run with no direction, anywhere opposite the shots but they don’t really know where to.

As they go their feet slip, Neil, running in front of Shyla, falls into a ditch and loses his pocket diary and one of the dices he constantly plays with. His left leg hurts, he must have hit it somewhere. He takes a deep breath, as he can’t see Shyla and the shots have stopped. One of the two gangs has won and now they'll have time to look for any witnesses.

Neil has heard countless times how the gangs raid the forests for anyone who might have witnessed a shooting or a trade or a killing. If they find them there's gonna be no way out.

Why the hell did I offer to take her around? She left and saved her ass without even thinking about me... he doesn't have time to finish his thought as a strong hand grabs him by the shoulder and pulls him up. His bones, flesh and skin hurt because the hand is so strong, it obviously can't be her.

Before he can say anything a country made pistol is pulled under his chin and a raspy voice asks, "Who the fish are you?"

"Save the lotus flower" It's a password, Neil prays for a second that this squared faced idiot knows it. In fact the brute loosens the grip on Neil's throat.

"Why here? Who sent for you?"

"Check with Debraj Dai... I work with him. I was passing by so..."

"Get out of here before I blow your brains off"

"Easy brother... easy"

As soon as the guy leaves, Neil looks around for Shyla, she's nowhere to be seen and just before he can get angry at his idiocy for having trusted a stranger, and a woman, he hears her voice.

"Am I going to get any help to get out of this ditch?" it's her voice, strangely calm.

Neil pulls out his phone, which has an inbuilt torch, he still had in his pocket and sees her open his diary and holding his dice. He helps her out, she doesn't look as shocked as he expected her to be, and right now it's not a good time to enquire what she has read in the diary. But she definitely knows something he was trying to hide, otherwise she wouldn't be this calm. Or is she just shocked?

Chapter 13

Back on the motorbike the atmosphere is a little tense again: Shyla came to realize what just happened -her travel companion might well be a broke, jobless Indian, but sure enough a few minutes ago he had a gun piercing through his chin and with a sentence that made no sense, evidently a code, he got himself out of the pangs of dangerous men. Neil is equally worried: he still hasn't figured out who Shyla really is: he has researched her but her name doesn't seem to appear anywhere, on the world wide web she doesn't exist and although she claims to be a photographer and so far she hasn't done anything to make him doubt her, he still thinks there's more to her than a camera hanging from her neck and a passion for wild animals.

The uncomfortable silence is broken by the arrival of a village by the name of Kondagaon. Shyla is amazed at the variety of handicrafts that are exhibited outside the pastoral village houses. Men, women and children are all absorbed in the fine arts of metal figurines. Neil shares with Shyla the fact that these handicrafts have a global demand and they get exported to various countries around the globe. The irony being that these tribal get peanuts for months of hardwork. He stops the bike and buys a bronze statue- that of a tiger made by the Dhokra artist of this region. Shyla is flabbergasted by the precision of the artefact. She gives Neil a peck on his cheek 'a big thank you'. Neil caught off-guard, blushes like a baby. Amongst his several encounters with women this kiss was the most spontaneous and innocent he ponders. Enroute he stops by at a local bar that serves the Bastar Beer obtained from Sulphi- the extracts of palm trees. Shyla loves the freshness of the rice beer. It's natural and yet gives a mild kick. She needs this more than anything after the narrow escape. A slight miss-timing and she would have been buried with centipedes in the soil. Sometimes the distance between life and death is hair-thin yet it cannot override the shackles of Karma. She is alive.

Neil accelerates his motorbike out of sheer exuberance. The red dust goes flying around like a twister. And so with the dust Neil tries to unburden his guilt over meaningless relationships of the past. For a change a realisation dawns in his perked up senses. "Maybe Shyla is right, Love brings meaning to life" perhaps the first lesson on love was deduced by him today.

"Please slow down" Shyla reminds a lost Neil, her voice is not excessively worried but it triggers in Neil the need all men have to reassure women and prove to be completely in control.

"No worries, I know these roads like the back of my hand!"

But as he says so the front wheel of the motorbike slips on a carpet of wet leaves and Neil loses control over the bike. Its weight does the rest: the motorbike falls to the ground grating its body against the asphalt and spitting out millions of sparks. Shyla screams but Neil manages to grab her and therefore the motorbike is on its own, they fall on the other side and roll down a small hill.

By the time they open their eyes again and can stand up- Shyla, who is still terrified and keeps her fists pressed against her eyes, a longer time- they find themselves in an amphitheatre. They look at each other's clothes, red with dry mud. What matches with their attire is the redness of the arena of arts. Shyla is mesmerized at the beauty of this temple of the arts, made by men, in the heart of a jungle. What would their performing arts be like, what were the stories that they would portray…Shyla contemplates? Over the years the people have abandoned it and nature swallowed it back: as they look at it she notices trees growing inside it, plants sprouting where people have been sitting, hundreds of years ago, nature exploding before her very eyes and taking back its space. At the same time she's fully aware that, for the first time, she's really alone with Neil, this curious stranger she's utterly fascinated by. Shyla can feel the thin hair of her arms rising against the sleeves of the cotton shirt, goose bumps tickling her arms. He looks unimpressed and uninterested in her. To her.

The truth is that he has also just realized that they are alone in the jungle, and the mix of adventure and her perfume is getting to his head at a dangerously fast pace. Her face blends in with the greens like a moon in the galaxy of stars. The way she smiles, with her lip balm shining in the dim light and uncovering her perfect white teeth, the small wrinkles around her eyes, he's attracted to her with a strength he has never felt before. It's like being a magnet trying to resist a perfectly crafted piece of iron.

"This is so beautiful..."

"Yeah, it's one of the most ancient amphitheatres in...." but it's getting dark, black clouds are gathering in the distance and through the hot and humid weather a cold wind is blowing, cutting the heat with a sharp blade. Shyla is caught up in this context, hypnotized by everything she can see and feel, and of course she's not listening to him.

"This is the moment I've been waiting for all my life..."

Neil looks at her, unable to understand what she can possibly find in something so boringly obvious. But he has seen this place several times during his wanderings, for Shyla it is the very first time in her life.

He brushes off some insects that have stuck to his clothes during the fall and are now crawling up his arm.

"Oh no, please Miss Shakespeare spare me your love fever..."

"What's so wrong about love? It is only with love that you touch the sky, which you can fly into the universe, that you can feel stars. How deeply you love others shows how deeply you love yourself"

Neil looks at her and pulls out of his side pocket a small flask, before drinking from it he raises it to his face and clears his throat "To love or not to love, this is the question!" he recites with a deep voice like that of Sir Lawrence Oliver in his famous impersonation of Hamlet. Neil tries a baritone "love is like a shot of rum, it gives you a kick instantly, and then it gives you a hangover for almost the rest of your life"

Shyla is amused as he keeps reciting and drinking. He passes her the flask several times, she refuses to taste the sour tasting rum and thinks that it's not right, but on second thoughts she's in the heart of Chhattisgarh, this may as well do!

"Love is a like a tiger waiting to hunt you down and someday kill you, they say people fall in love, I want to rise… rise to live for the moment. I love this very moment and this moment that will burst open and spread its spirited wings beyond the horizons of time and space."

Suddenly he gets closer to Shyla, wraps her around him in a very theatrical way and pulls her body so close to his she can hardly breathe.

"One regret, my dear world that I am determined not to have on my death bed... that I didn't kiss you enough!" Shyla gets a little iffy. Neil sounds like a confused man stuck in a maze searching for an exit that will renew his faith in love. And Shyla doesn't need to be a victim of Neil's sentimental duality. Shyla manages to get free from his passionate grip and runs to a pond from which she splashes some water to his face, laughing and trying to get him back to his senses. Neil is high on life and tipsy on rum, Shyla notices. He is stupid, he is over confident, he is confused but he is cute, Shyla blushes with her mellow thoughts. Neil runs to her like a child.

He lifts her in his strapping arms. He loses his balance and they both fall into the water body and burst out laughing until they have tears in their eyes. They are lost in a glee like two kids playing in the pool and then he helps her out of the water. The night is falling, on this corner of the jungle, and the sound of water reminds the two of them the tranquil picture of a school fountain. The cold air is making them nervous. Neil without much ado gulps a mouthful of rum from his hip flask. Shyla gives in to the chill and matches up with his swig of rum on the rocks. Shyla a wine drinker tastes rum for the first time but then it's all about the survival of the fittest. On the other hand they both know they are in danger, the tigers hunt after sunset, and the thrill of peril runs through their spines giving them shocks of adrenaline. Is it love? Is it lust? Is it fear of fear? None of them knows, and none of them would tell the other, but their hearts beat faster, their eyes are glued together. Shyla, generally a cheeky yet virtuous girl is overcome with instincts that escape the route of her brain, going straight to her stomach. Frank Sinatra's- "Strangers in the night" the song replays albeit in her mind. Is this for real? Neil extends a hand to her and she knows only too well that his hand cannot be touched unless she wants to give up every control over herself. She has been touched by men earlier but she knew them well. Also she was in a more controlled locality. But then the man in front of her presently is more enticing than anyone else that she has been in physical contact with. Like a beautiful rainbow torn between the sun and the rain, she feels vibrant from head to toe but her logical mind is controlling her decisions. However the zeal of the attractive man wooing her in the most surreal surrounding that she could have imagined seems straight out of a romantic novel. As her lips get moist by her own saliva, she feels itchy in her thighs. Is it the oestrogen that is tickling her nerves! Is this the real me?

Neil, on the other hand, is silently hoping to have a blow or two of a colder breeze that could allow him to inch closer to her, he's hoping for a moon big enough to confound her, for the sound of the river to cradle her. Making the most of unusual situations, that's what he does best. And the risk factor, the stray tigers that populate the jungle, but the nights of central India, purely romantic in their secrecy, this time help him. *The most beautiful poetry is never recited, its just heard. Two shadows get still as the eyes make love to each other. The most beautiful words are the ones that are never spoken, they are simply felt. The deep forest glows with chemistry, the starlit sky blushes into pheromones. The most beautiful dance is never performed it's simply experienced. Two destined souls celebrate the silence of the universe.* The droplets of water roll down their dusky dark skins and shine in the dark like small diamonds being thrown against the light of the moon.

Water is being splashed also in another corner of this inhospitable forest: Debraj is shaving and the big fragment of mirror that reflects his image drips with the soapy water he used. His sideburns still hold some of the white foam but he cleans it away with a towel.

In this damn forest even a manly pleasure like shaving becomes a hassle, the water is dirty and never the right temperature, the soap stinks... Debraj remembers his first time: his father took him to the barber shop on the road, in front of their house, and although it was a poor setting, in essence not much better than this one, the whole ritual was very special. His father was not a man of science or words, a hard worker who believed in communism as the only way for all men to be equal. Men. Women were a different story.

Debraj was never taught to understand or respect women, and up until now the only ones he has treated as equals are the comrades like Purba. Infact he is silently attracted to her, like a painter to his muse. Purba is his protégé and a sense of reward for Debraj. That makes Purba the only woman Debraj has some consideration for, although a lot can be credited to the fact that part of a man's brain lies in the muscle between his knees.

His father wasn't a good example in this respect and from what he could see in his own house Debraj had grown with the idea that women were more or less useful and mobile objects who could have several uses, including that of reproducing. His father was a brutal man and Debraj grew up thinking that he, like his father, like all men, was supposed to take whatever he wanted from a woman, no one had ever taught him how to love. Love was simply not an option. Love was ambushed by hatred or even worst- self-loathing.

From what he saw in his house he learnt that whenever a man is stressed or angry or has just been mistreated by someone more powerful (which was usually the case) he can go home and lie on his wife, or the maid, or any woman and release his anger and frustration inside her.

This was what made his father calmer. And his mother more ashamed and depressed.

But for young Debraj this was normal, his house wasn't any different to those of his friends, and when he himself felt the desire to indulge in the same, he often found women who endured the pain. These women were usually from very low strata and they did it for money or were forced into it by scheming from a man who would someday lead a red terror outfit. Some were paralysed with fear; some needed some fierce stroking, so to say, before passing out. But everything always went more or less as expected.

Despite his modest background Debraj was very bright and managed to go to university and, after a few years, also become a professor. He soon realized that what happened in the poorer household wasn't very different to what happened in the richer ones: all men were the same, his father was right. All of them took what they wanted, the only restriction for choice being their caste or their status. And this is why he never felt he was doing something wrong when he took a woman for an emotional release, it was just natural, everyone did it. What they studied at work, about women being thinkers and politicians in ancient Greece and Rome was a parallel thing: they were women of a past time and of a different world, women in this world, of this time were different, made to work and please men. Or at least so he thought until that day.

Now, trying to see his entire face in the triangular fragment of mirror, hanging from a nail in the wall, he takes off his red scarf, the one he never takes off, to reveal a very long and spiky scar.

The scar.

Of all wounds and scars that decorate his body this one is the only one that still hurts. It reminds him of the day he found a woman to release his anger into and she cried and screamed until she found of the ground a piece of glass and cut right through his throat.

As he felt his blood spilling out, warm and fluid on his manly chest, caught into his black hair, he saw her face, distraught by pain and fear but with that flame in her eyes. It was as if the blood spilling out of him, draining life from his neck could turn into a new life for her. The power of revenge. Instant. She had the look of a tigress that would disengage its prey by cutting into the neck. It was about thirty years ago but every time Debraj runs his fingers on the scar he still feels the pain and the warm and viscous blood spilling out of it.

At the same time Neil and Shyla enter a city on Neil's rugged motorbike.

"This bike is ancient..."

"Well princess, it took us here, didn't it?"

"Mhhhh..."

"Look, I need to go into that building, its job, I'm gonna be a while, can you promise me you won't get into trouble and you'll be safe? I'm watching you..."

"Of course Mr I-Me-Myself-up!"

As Neil is about to cross the street Shyla screams after him "Would it be a problem if I borrowed this piece of history for a couple of hours?"

"Oh, so now you like it huh? Be my guest, but even though I know it doesn't match your personality try and be gentle, my lady likes to be treated with kindness!" and he throws Shyla the keys which she catches in mid-air.

Shyla rides away smiling and Neil stands on the corner of the building, catching even the last glimpse of her as she leans on his World War II motorbike and drives it with smooth movements. Neil has always thought that a woman who can ride a motorbike, especially an old and rusty one, has a particular charm. She is hot and dynamic. It's like being able to show respect, tenderness, affection and strength all at once.

When Neil is sure to be out of Shyla's sight he keeps walking and, instead of entering the building as he had told her, he turns into a narrow lane and, as soon as he sees the dark SUV with tainted windows, he gets in it even if, apparently, no one had invited him to do so.

In the car, with the engine on, Anand Sharma is waiting for him.

Anand is a big man; his body could easily be shown in commercials advertising sportswear because every muscle in it is flexible and fit. Even his face, despite being rather regular, is a striking face, cut in half by a thick but very nicely trimmed handlebar moustache.

He is not rich, he comes from a modest family from Nagpur, and all the men in his family for three generations have served the nation in the armed forces. Once he became a policeman he spent a few years in Nagpur but, knowing that he was one of the few who was willing to give his life for his country, he decided to move to somewhere where his wish to serve could really be used at best. He was transferred to Chhattisgarh, allegedly to fight terrorism, he soon found out that many of his colleagues were as rotten as the guys on the other side, but instead of giving up to frustration Anand decided that this would be his mission. He found an opportunity in chaos. And he worked every day of his life since to protect his country and try, when possible, to get rid of the bad apples. Neil doesn't dislike Anand, but they are fairly different people, and their differences draw them apart. Anand is a family guy, he has an adopted son and still no wife but Neil can tell that he believes in love and would do anything to fall in love with the right girl, get married and have children. But Neil doesn't judge him for these traditional wishes, on the contrary he values a man who knows what he wants and is not ashamed of it. Neil could never do or desire what Anand wants, he's a free spirit, and this difference doesn't allow them to be close friends, but the respect for one another is enough for them to have an open and durable relationship, based on trust. And a common enemy.

In the car that smells of new upholstery and leather wax the two men shake hands.

"I'm happy you could make it" says Anand in his slow, raspy and deep voice.

"I'm not the kind of person who lets people down..." answers Neil with a grin. He sees himself in the car, with his dusty clothes, which he has worn on the nearly deadly bus ride and on the long bike ride through the jungle... and the incident...

Anand and Neil park the car in a quiet spot just outside the town.

"Did they say what they would do with the guns?"

"No, I didn't stick around long enough... it's not exactly a tea party..."

Neil takes the cash Anand is handing him and puts it in his pocket.

"They are up to something, we must find out what it is..."

"Yeah, but as I said it's risky... It's not like going to a holiday resort?" Neil retorts.

"Look, I appreciate you taking those risks, believe me I do. I don't understand why you abandoned your cop training. You would have made a fine cop"

"Yeah, well things don't always happen the way we want them to. But then this will also lead me somewhere... someday all the dots will get connected" Neil smells of being self-assured.

Anand nods in agreement and checks his watch.

"Sounds like the cool dude with a secret mission. Come on, I'll drop you off where you parked your bike"

"It's hard to tell where the bike is, I left it in the hands of a very charming lady... What can I say? I'm that kind of dude, after all..."

Chapter 14

Shyla crosses a number of paddy fields and gets directions from people who speak a language that is Greek and Latin to Shyla. Somehow she reaches a rustic landscape. She is at a crossroads that seem to lead to nowhere. The road is uneven and air holds the colour of dust. The only saving grace is spicy smell of wild flowers. It reminds her of her first blind date when she had experimented with a new spicy perfume that left the guy sneezing out of allergy throughout the evening. He literally went blind with tears rolling down and a running nose.

She parks the motorbike near a mud hut, she has left the centre of the town and has tried to ride backwards to where they were before, where Neil asked about a fifty carat stone. She needs to understand more and this seems like a good lead: if the ground is filled with gems no wonder the red terrorists want to keep it. And at the same time some corrupt Government officials have all interest to stand back and say it's too dangerous to take any action. Meanwhile people die of starvation, this story is only too well known...

She switches off her I Pod just in time after listening to Louis Armstrong's 'What a wonderful world'. With irony written all over her face she parks the heavy motorbike and enters the hut where a group of women sit and weave.

She has managed to change and take a sort of shower -ah, her Cape Town shower! - And she feels more comfortable now, in her brown trousers and white shirt, with the camera hanging from her neck. This is what she should look like, as a photographer, and this gear is less likely to blow her cover than the dress she was wearing before and which she had to throw away due to its smell and also because it was literally torn into pieces. She has found a bottle of nail varnish remover, as she was wandering through town, and although they made her pay full price for what really was a half-bottle, she's happy to have been able to remove those creepy red residues of nail varnish that were biting into her nails like spiky teeth.

Inside the hut she needs a few seconds to get used to the light: the room is poorly lit and coming from outside her eyes only register a small source of light on the side and a black mass. But the mass, although fairly still, is moving untidily and in different directions: Shyla's guess is that it's people sitting and doing something with their arms and hands. There is no particular smell so it's not food processing, or at least no food produce she knows is involved. She moves closer.

Now the picture is clearer: it's a circle of women sitting on the floor and weaving. Some are spinning, some are weaving, and a few are trimming. It's only women, all ages, all shades of brown; they are all there to work together. There's silence, or rather a soft lament, a song, emerging from the silence, but Shyla can't quite make out who is singing. *Some songs don't have a voice. Some wounds don't have scars.*

She needs to fructify her official assignment. She accepted the task of surveying the truth and now she is in the middle of the game, so she thinks. She clicks pictures, as she's supposed to do if she were a journalist, and smiles at these women who have such sad eyes. She wants to liven the moods, the energy of the room is dull and no words can describe the grief that floats in the air. There is a tragic world and then there are these miniscule volcanoes buried inside this tragic world waiting to erupt someday. Shyla can guess the extent of misfortune just by looking into their deep irises and at the wrinkled skin around them. All of them have aged much earlier than they are meant to. Shyla mulls "a life with a fast forward button in the hand and no food on the plate, how can a curse be so uncompassionate, what have they done to deserve this"

One in particular attracts her attention: she is old but her hands work with the precision of a young and skilled person, she's hunched onto her work but notices that Shyla is taking a picture of her by the flash that goes off in her face. She slowly lifts her head and squeezes her eyes to try and make out Shyla's shape against the light of the door.

Shyla misunderstands this and lifts the camera, embarrassed, she's afraid this might get her kicked out. But it doesn't. As soon as the lady recognizes a young woman behind the flash that for a second lit her work like it had never been lit before, she gestures her to come closer. Shyla goes and as the lady moves to the side making space for her Shyla understands she wants her to sit next to her. A story is evidently about to come up. She sits.

"Bidesi ho?" says the woman, with a smile.

"Ji ha" answers Shyla.

She shoots pictures of the lady: of her work, of her hands, of her torn sari and a key she has tied to it with a knot. Shyla had never thought about it but saris don't have pockets... the idea of tying keys to it is genius!

The woman looks around and then smiles at Shyla asking her to come closer, she rummages through an old jute bag; it still smells of rice and of the writings that adorned it. Shyla can still see the bright colours but can't distinguish the letters anymore.

The wrinkled hand emerges with a small wooden box, the care she handles it with makes Shyla think that it's something so very precious and she can't quite think what it could be. For a moment Shyla remembers those two words: fifty carats and her heart beat speeds up, she holds her breath. Mentally she pictures the scene: her, Shyla Thomas, being photographed as she gives the stone back to the Government of India after having taken it away from thugs, she would certainly have a preferential channel to the information she has come here to gather. Personal information, unrelated to poverty. She's about to discover something as interesting but she doesn't know it yet.

Shyla is woken from her reverie by the woman who is now pulling her shirt to show her the content of the box. She has opened it in front of her very eyes and Shyla was too lost in her projections to notice the rather simple and hugely disappointing content of the box.

A family photograph.

There's the woman with an old man, her husband, two men that definitely look like her, her sons, at each man's side there's a woman, their wives and finally there are three children, who evidently didn't want to stand still for the picture and their eyes show all the impatience they are trying to withhold.

Shyla looks at the face of the woman, then at the picture: her eyes haven't changed one bit but the rest has fallen apart. Shyla even thinks that the woman in front of her is so old that this picture must have been taken fifty years ago.

"Your family?"

The woman nods in agreement, proud to show off her clan to her.

"I would love to meet them! Is it possible?"

The woman's eyes go teary and she looks away. Shyla figures that the woman would like to say something but she only speaks Chhattisgarhi and Shyla herself only speaks very poor Hindi. Another woman comes into the conversation, younger and whose English is astonishingly good considering her age and where they are. She is a social worker from a neighbouring state.

"They killed her entire family. Even the children. That photograph is all she has of their memories and she cherishes it with her life"

Shyla is sad, confused and puzzled, how can this woman still be alive, besides... who would ever do something like that? The children? The oldest one can't be older than six or seven!

"She smiles... though she has nothing to smile about... but that's her choice, to get brutalised maynot be a choice, but to smile like an angel inspite of all this, is the essence of human divinity"

"We have no option. They claim to be fighting for our happiness... instead they have taken away our near and dear ones... but we won't let them take away our hope"

Shyla doesn't need to ask who "they" are, and the woman doesn't need to tell. "They" are a continuous presence in their lives, they don't need to be mentioned because their presence lingers around anyway.

"I never thought the Red Terrorists or the Maoists, if you prefer, were killing innocents... I thought they were only fighting against the Government"

The lady smiles sadly and shakes her head, her tone is soft as she tells Shyla something natural for her and unbelievable for the South African bred Indian in front of her. "The Maoists didn't kill her family"

"Then who did?" asks Shyla, confused.

"Salwa-Judum... a part of this outfit had a few devils dressed as angels. Salwa-judum otherwise was a civilian militia appointed by the government to protect the local community from Naxalites. However it was disbanded by the Supreme Court in 2011 declaring the outfit illegal and unconstitutional. It's thanks to Mahesh Babu that we have shelter and this weaving job"

"Alright, where can I find Mahesh Babu?"

Minutes later the motorbike is roaring in front of a small office, Shyla had to ask for directions a couple of times but everyone seemed to know this Mahesh... *He's more famous than a TV star*, thinks Shyla.

She enters the small office, it smells of paper, chai and curry but the atmosphere is cosy, the man looks like a good person who struggles with a broken system that is so much bigger than him. He clears the table from all the papers and bits and pieces and offers her a cup of tea.

It's pretty clear that he is not used to receive international guests in his office, so to speak, and he looks a little embarrassed and out of place. He looks for a nice cup but the best he can find is a china cup with a small chip on the side, he moves fast and desperately looks for something fancy to offer Shyla. She has introduced herself as a journalist and he feels she's by far the most influential person to have ever crossed this threshold.

She smiles and puts him at ease by complimenting him on the marvellous scent of his chai. She sips it graciously and asks him questions; he is charmed by how much she cares about this issue, which no one -or no one with power- has ever cared about so far.

"They are right..."

"But according to the government the Salwa Judum is supposed to be helping the people by fighting against red terror"

"As you rightly said..."supposed" to be... the truth is different... tragic rather. The Salwa Judum has violated many human rights. Likewise the people here are torn between whom to support. If they side with the Maoists, the Salwa Judum tortures them, even kills them, branding them as Naxalites. If they side with the Salwa Judum, the Red Gang, or Turu Dalam in this district, stops protecting them, branding them as traitors"

"Oh my God... this is terrible"

Mahesh gets up from his seat. He gently takes the empty glass from Shyla.

"Let me show you what is really terrible..."

And he takes the keys of the office motorbike; the one he uses during office hours (he otherwise uses his own bike for personal business, people like and respect that because it's different to what everyone does) and asks Shyla to follow him.

The motorbike is parked outside, it's rather old, even older than Neil's, and rusty but Shyla doesn't want to offend this kind and self-conscious man, she jumps on, ready to ride.

She puts her camera on her back and as Mahesh starts the bike, which coughs away a black smoke before idling, she smiles. In the last few days she has been thinking very often where she was four, five, seven days ago. It always strikes her how ten days ago her life was perfect, she did have problems, but like everyone else, her biggest problem was having forgotten to buy tomatoes or soap. In the last seventy two hours she has risked her life twice, she's on the other side of the world and right now she's on a motorbike with a total stranger who, for all she knows, might be taking her to the jungle and handle her out to the Maoists.

But she's serene, the fact that no one is worrying about her anymore is kind of exciting: all her life she has always evaluated how dangerous things were and then decided against them. The few times she did something a little over the edge she felt guilty and afraid something would happen and her father's heart would be broken. Now she can ride a rusty motorbike with a complete stranger in a terrorists ridden district in the heart of India and no one worries, no one cares. *What can happen when you find a cause, when you stand larger than fear itself, fear scampers away like a squirrel!*

Of course she would prefer to be still giving things up and not make her father worry, but he's not around anymore... It's hard to picture going back home and not watching the last cricket match with him or knowing that he won't call before a date, worried that the date might be a freak.

It's hard, but she's on her own now and she must face it. Life is yet not as bad as it can get for several others on the same planet. *When you are left alone to explore, to discover yourself, it's not by accident, it's by design.*

Chapter 15

Mahesh drives carefully, his motorbike is old and noisy and Shyla can't avoid thinking how different he is to Neil. Of course Neil has that brutal charm of mysterious people we hardly understand and therefore imagine that they hold something special about them. The mystery maybe real or it maybe fake but surely it does make an interesting journey. Mahesh, on the other hand, is rather upfront and if he doesn't come up with an unpleasant surprise like handling her to a terrorist gang, which she doubts but is still unsure of, quite dull. He is soft spoken and calm.

As she's thinking about this, the motorbike claws its way on a country road, the scenery is green and extremely fresh, *this corner of the world looks like my guide here*, she thinks. And it's true, Mahesh does look like the place he took her to. What Shyla does not know is that Mahesh is taking her to a refugee camp, he only said "Come with me" and of course she thought he would show her something related to the red terror (her covert interest) but the pleasant ride took her mind off to a calmer land of whispering greens.

They take one last turn and then find themselves on a small hill, Shyla expects the scenery to be as lush and as scenic as it has been so far but in the small valley below all she sees are shacks and huts, people, looking tiny like ants in the distance, who walk everywhere, bringing buckets of water and taking food from a centre, washing clothes and running after children.

A refugee camp.

The colours have changed too: from green to yellow through a myriad of shades of grey and red, everything in the valley is dry and arid, the people gathering in the refugee camp have walked over the green grass drying it up and have dug wells to suck water from the ground, turning the rich earth into sand. As they approach on the coughing motorbike Shyla can distinguish details a lot better and she notices the wrinkled faces and the empty eyes, of people who have seen and suffered more than they could bear, she sees the malnourished children and the hunched old people, the women and the men, carrying all they possess and staring blankly ahead, hoping to reach the camp before it's too late. If hell descends and mellows down, it has to be this.

Mahesh and Shyla pass a never-ending line of people and he doesn't need to tell her anything as much as she doesn't need to ask, and in this overwhelming silence they reach the camp. For the first time Shyla realises that silence can be as creepy as this. Mahesh flashes his badge to the guard who nods at him but he stops Shyla and stares at her from head to toes.

"Don't worry Umar, she's with me, she's a friend..."

The guard lets her in and Shyla breathes, now that destiny took her this far it would be a shame to go back and not see what she came here for. *Some roads have a blinding bend but it's still not the end of the road.*

She catches up with Mahesh and follows him into a mud hut like the one she has entered only a couple of hours ago and where she met the social reformer lady who took her to Mahesh.

"Anjali... it's me Mahesh from Nari Niketan. I have someone I'd like you to meet" calls Mahesh in a soft voice, the hut has no door, only a curtain, therefore calling is the only way Mahesh has to knock and announce his presence.

Shyla wonders who Anjali might be and how she could help her but she doesn't wonder for long, as she sees something moving on the floor. A girl. She looks really young and she's lying on the floor, covered by a black shawl so Shyla is not quite sure how tall she could be. Mahesh enters the room and goes to Anjali. He strokes her face and help her to stand up. His body covers hers and Shyla can only see that the girl is having trouble moving, as he moves aside Shyla observes that the girl is pregnant.

At first Shyla is a little shocked, Anjali looks really young, far too young to be pregnant, her face is thin and her features have been beautiful although now she's mostly worn out by the pregnancy and the life in the camp. Shyla shoots a smile at Anjali but the girl seems to be waiting for an introduction. It's evident to Shyla that she has been heavily hurt and is now afraid of everyone. Shyla ponders how long it took Mahesh, especially as a man, to earn her trust, as, around him, she seems to be at ease.

"Anjali, this is Shyla Thomas. Your new friend. She wanted to say hello to you"

Anjali walks up to her guest without saying a word and takes her hand. Shyla's nerves are on the edge of breaking, she's tired, afraid and altogether not a person who likes touching or being touched and the touch of Anjali's ice cold hand makes her take a step back. It's absolutely involuntary and, if thinking rationally, she would have preferred to be friendly rather than so abrupt but Anjali looks at her with her head leaning on one side and tries again.

I break into her house where she lives alone and pregnant and I'm the one who's afraid? What am I thinking ???

But Anjali looks unimpressed and not afraid at all, she takes Shyla's hand, she does allow it this time, and places it on her belly as if it was the most natural thing to do in the world.

"See how he kicks! ...Didn't let me sleep all night"

Shyla can indeed feel the baby kicking inside the girl's stomach, none of her friends have had babies yet and she has never touched a pregnant woman's tummy. It's strangely tense and hard, *she must be almost due to give birth*, Shyla thinks.

As she keeps her hand on this hard container of a live baby who kicks she's overwhelmed with the miracle of life. It has never happened before: she is the girl who always wears something red and goes on blind dates she can bitch about with her gay friend Damian... She's not the one who has ever wanted children or got emotional about them. But this one here, this is so strong, it's life springing out of a person despite the war, the fear, the hunger... For the first time she realises *–Miracles don't happen in churches, they take place in the spirit of humans who connect with divine.*

A siren blares outside and Mahesh walks to Anjali and puts a hand on her shoulder.

"Lunch time, Anjali. Go, make sure you eat properly okay and drink sufficient milk?"

Anjali nods and takes Shyla's hands, kisses them and runs outside as if Mahesh was an uncle who told his niece to go out and play. She runs like a little girl, even though the weight of her belly must be overwhelming on that bony body... Shyla ponders at the wonders of nature 'A child carrying another child'!

"She was brought here eight months ago when her family died, caught in the crossfire between the Turu Dalam, and the Salwa Judum" Mahesh Babu breaks her flow of thoughts.

"Let me guess... the Turu Dalam bastards did this to her" Shyla swears through her own wounds.

Mahesh nods, helplessly "I've been bringing her some medicine to cope with her depression. She tried to commit suicide... they gang-raped her and she got pregnant. She will never be able to put all this behind her, a baby will always remind her of where he or she came from"

Shyla doesn't know what to say, this story reminds her of a painful one, the story that Father Thomas told her on his death bed, her own story. She is the baby of a rape victim, and, one day this boy or girl inside Anjali will be a man or woman who, just like herself, will want to know and seek revenge. *It's a bizarre coincidence. It's a sign. It's a beam of light that shows her where to look. An enormous tragedy can destroy you, define you or fortify you.*

She has made her choice. Now she has found somebody who shares the same choice.

"Do the police and the Government know about this? And if they do how come they are not doing anything about it?"

"An FIR has been registered but... the legal system sucks in this country... And besides, Anjali is one of a thousand cases, she's no different to all the other girls who have been victimised like her..."

Shyla smiles sadly, hearing Mahesh with his strong Indian accent say that 'something sucks' is ironic and tragic at the same time. This simple word that she uses dozens of times a day has a totally different meaning here, his tone proves to her that he is highly disillusioned and frustrated. She can tell that he could cry about each of these people. He is gifted with undying compassion. A gift that everybody is born with but seldom recognise. She finds his drive and motivation to work here, even if it's like emptying the sea with a teaspoon, absolutely admirable.

Mahesh takes her back to the motorbike and the ride back is silent and at the same time filled with thoughts, words not spoken and unasked and unanswered questions.

As Shyla takes her bike in front of Mahesh's office where she had left it, she feels a strange sense of emptiness, as if she had something more, something else to feel or say but emotions and words wouldn't come out. This has been a strong experience, stronger than any other she has ever had. And she doesn't have an easy job, but somehow in her job the poor, the desperate, always had a natural cause or an enemy to be so. Here it's a war between two clans of thugs that traps people in between, and the worst part is that all three actors, the Naxalites, the Government and the people, should all be on the same side, *they are all Indians for God's sake...*

She says a dry goodbye to her travel companion who smiles, a sad and frustrated smile, and stands on the door until she's gone. He will then go back to his little dusty office and will keep doing his job, saving lives, day after day, a silent and unknown hero. No one will ever hear about him, about people like him, they will never have a book written about them, never get interviewed, never receive praises by Government officials.

The perks of working and living in a no man's land! At best the Government officials will be broadcasted as a hero of some party or the other side's hero during an electoral campaign.

And they, the social workers, the few honest ones, smile sadly like Mahesh does and walk back into their offices, where between a sip of chai and a million cigarettes to release the stress of having to save lives, including their own, they keep doing their job. He depends on the old Bollywood classic songs on the radio for company in the daytime and at night one phone call to their family living in a distant town is good enough to let life pass by at a snail pace. No celebrations, no travel, no moments larger than life. And one day they grey and turn old. *But still they have found a purpose in life: to be content and useful. A very potent combination of virtues that could someday change the world. Someday.*

Shyla thinks about this as she rides back to the hotel, if that is what she can call it. She drives nervously as she knows that the only person she knows, Neil, will be there but she will have no chance to speak to him about her hidden agenda. Vengeance. She doesn't even know what side he's on and the last thing she wants to do is to feed such juicy information, about Mahesh, about the camp, to the wrong side. No, she will take a shower and keep this to herself, but it's going to be hard. This is not just some story, this is as personal as it can get. *She will have to contain this pain today till it becomes her strength tomorrow.*

In front of the grocery store though, a couple of red eyes are looking as Shyla as she parks the motorbike and turns the screechy engine off. She doesn't notice it, of course, caught as she is in her thoughts. But Ganpath has been watching her, she left more than four hours ago and drove into the forest, and now she's back with that look in her eyes... suspicious... he'll keep an eye on her.

CHAPTER 16

Back at the Government Circuit house Neil is going through his contacts and trying to track Shyla, who was supposed to be away for a couple of hours and ended up disappearing. He holds a bottle of red wine in his hand and smiles at the irony of organizing a rather romantic night with her in a place like this. *Red wine in the midst of red terror sounds like poetry in blood. Never seen a lotus blossom in muck. It's never about the outside, it's always the inside that paints your real world. If you can find love in the midst of bedlam, you know the Truth*-Neil stands reassured.

He finally finds Shyla's number- "Yeah, hi... hope you're treating my baby fine... she likes to be handled with care... hey... are you okay? Shyla... Sh... Shit!"

He hears the line being cut and tries calling her again, in the long, echoing pauses he asks her for a landmark so that he can go and pick her up.

As he hurries to find another bike he thinks that this woman has a natural instinct for trouble, and that he is not going to keep saving her life everytime she gets into some deep shit, he has his own goals, this is a distraction and… But as he thinks all these things his heart pounds in his chest so hard he can hardly breathe. It's unusual for Neil to be so worried- "why can't women be simpler, and why am I getting so hyper, is it her or is it me!"

Shyla is on the riverbank, throwing stones into the water and looking at the circles exploding from the point where the pebbles touch the water. The circles become bigger and bigger and then vanish. The reflections, which are originally crystal clear, keep getting distorted with every piercing stone.

Neil arrives in a rush, he sees Shyla and, in spite of himself throws a look at his bike, i*t's fine, so she didn't have an accident... so what the hell is wrong with her?* He walks next to her and can sense her anger but he doesn't know where it comes from and there's little he can do about it if she doesn't speak to him.

He puts the bottle on the ground, next to it a stem of tiger orchids and then sits next to her, patting her back gently.

"What's up with the attitude, Shyla? You got me anxious and I hate that..."

"I'm good"

"Bullshit! This place is not safe" He realizes he has shouted and the last thing he wants right now is to scare her, he softens up his voice "especially for a beautiful girl like you... Even I'd be tempted..."

"You think you are some macho huh? But you know what? You are just like everyone else, an outer observer, silent and careless!"

"What the hell are you...?"

"Nothing! Just piss off okay... and take your bike. I'm fine..."

Neil knows that there is something wrong and that this place is unsafe enough as it is, there's no need to make it any less safe by sticking around after dark. He hugs her, Neil has lived long enough, and been through enough crap, to know that when people are angry on their own there's something buried deep down that has been suddenly brought up and which they need to sort out. *When something is unmasked it's likely to stay that way and the only way to solve the problem is to actually face one's skeletons in the closet. To kiss them, to make love to them till they turn into fairies and disappear into thin air.* But this, even though rational and intuitive, is hard and painful when turned into reality. Shyla needs to sort her shit out but she can't do it alone. Her cup is too messy and it's spilling all over. She can't think clearly.

She has gotten up and left, she hurried toward the bushes, away from the clearing, but has slowed down, *as if she wanted to be followed*, thinks Neil. And so he does follow her, wraps his arms around her and hugs her tight, but she fights back, the idea of having to rely on someone, Neil of all people, makes her angry and powerless at the same time. She wants help but she doesn't want to talk, she wants to be hugged but doesn't want the other person to expect sex from her, she likes Neil but she would rather be in a fancy restaurant on the Waterfront in Cape Town than here in the forest. Overall she's just very confused, and exhausted. She fights back his hug, but Neil knows better than that, he hugs her even more, whispers soft words into her ear and finally she gives up. Her body is shaken by a shiver, she's either about to cry or throw up because too much tension has built inside her frail body.

Neil wonders what could have happened today to make her feel so blue, he can't exactly think of anything: this is a troubled area indeed but the only thing she could have really been shocked by are the refugee camps and it's unlikely that she found one on her own, let alone enter it without a special permission...Unless...

Neil, used to camping in the forest, quickly collects some wood and pours, broken hearted, some dark rum on it to light a fire, he takes his old zippo from his pocket and lights a majestic fire. It will not keep the Naxalites away, that's for sure, but at least it will prevent animals from approaching. The bike works fine but by the time the emotional crisis would get over it might get too dark to hit the road with a lady: roads are patrolled by the terrorists, especially at night, who stop cars and motorbikes and take whatever they consider useful. Being in the forest it's not much safer but they can hope no one comes this side tonight, whereas on the street they'd have the certainty to be looted.

Shyla holds on to the bottle of wine, a good half has already gone and she's a little tipsy but also considerably less irritated. Neil looks at her, she's so beautiful and yet behind this petite girl there is so much to be discovered, it's as if she had a massive black shadow stuck behind her. He understands that she is stuck between two separate streams of conflicting thoughts. And currently the streams are behaving like oceans with a high tide. When a woman is caught in the cyclone of love and hatred, the perfect storm, it can get very catastrophic.

She approaches and hands him the bottle, all they have for the night is the clothes they are wearing and this bottle, no food, no glasses, no sleeping bag.

"You got a family, Neil?"

"What?"

"You got some dark secrets. I can sense it. I don't know... a wife? Children? No... It's something dark, hard to explain... There's something dark and dangerous about you... Can't quite put my finger on what exactly..."

Neil is a little concerned but conceals it well behind a hearty laugh.

"You're nuts" He can count on the fact that Shyla is on her way to getting drunk and she probably won't remember this conversation tomorrow.

"Nope... I'm drunk... you know something else?"

"What?"

"I'm drunk and I'm liking it. And you know something else?"

"What?"

"I'm drunk, I'm liking it and I like you... you're a good guy... oh, and you know something else Neil?"

Neil takes the bottle gently from her and smiles softly at her stream of words.

"What Shyla?"

"I'm drunk, I'm liking it... I like you... and... And..." *Alright here we are! Sad drunkenness, what a lucky man I am! I get to spend the night in the forest with a gorgeous lady and not only she gets drunk but also has the blues...*

"And Neil, and... I'm a daughter of a rape victim..."

Neil did not quite see this coming and for a moment he is left speechless. Drunken people tend to alter reality, but it's generally what they see around them, not a memory, or not such a painful one anyway, this is evidently something that was buried deep down and came up today.

"Father Thomas took care of me all my life, like my own daddy. Mum died giving birth to me... She was a photographer, specialised in wildlife. Then one day, in these very jungles she was raped. She fled to Capetown before she would be cheap breaking news. Father Thomas helped build for her a new life. But she died shortly after I was born, when she discovered she was pregnant with the child of a rapist, it destroyed her dreams, her desire to live. Her last wish before dying was to inscribe this tattoo on my arm as a memento..."

Shyla uncovers her arm, Neil reads it, Forget, Forgive... but before he can read the last word she rolls her sleeve down and continues telling her own, painful story. "My mother told father Thomas that it will protect me and one day it will all come together… Only recently I have discovered who I am and where I come from, who could be my real father. I decided to come here even though the story and most of all the meaning of the tattoo still makes no sense to me. Am I searching for my rapist father, the reason why my mother died? Don't know, but I am alone...now, and they are all up there" Shyla looks up and with her tiny hand points at the stars, which from this darkness look huge and the brightest she has ever seen. Neil doesn't know what to say after such a painful and heartfelt confession, but he feels it's only fair for him to come clean and be honest with her.

"I'm an orphan too, Shyla. Mum and dad died in a train crash. My brother and I were in the same train but I guess it wasn't our time to go. But life has its cruel moments... my brother died a few years ago. He was my only family after our parents passed away. Since then, because I had no obligations, no ties, no family, no one to be there for, I decided to live life like a free bird. *When you have nothing left to lose you have nothing to fear*"

They are sitting close to one another, feeling each other's pain and, for the first time, fully understanding each other. They are naked from the inside. He moves closer to her, stroking her face, kisses her neck gently and then moves towards her mouth with his full, soft lips.

She is stroking him, nothing he has done so far seemed to have made her feel uncomfortable and before they know it he is making love to her, for the first time in years taking all the time he needs to make her feel loved and feel her love in return. He presses hard on her, locks her palms, and she holds him on top of her to release herself from inner strain. Her nails scratch his back like they were removing stains from her soul while he fondles her chest for comfort that he needs the most. Their feet rub against each other to give each other a sense of security. For both of them, for very different reasons, it has been hard to feel at ease with another person: for Neil, sex was always a quick thing that more often than not had nothing to do with love. Shyla always looked for love and always found herself either with people who had no intention of loving anybody or with those who could only prove to love by suffocating her with empty attentions and a parasite-like love.

For the first time, right now, the two of them enjoy sex not just as the act of sex but also as a means of communication. Their bodies entwine with each other with equal passion. Neil tries to be gentle but to his surprise Shyla gets fiery. She gets onto him and presses her thighs against his. Neil turns into a Tiger who has met his match. He turns her upside down and climbs onto her with his hands pressed against her chest. She bites him in the neck. He tries to kiss her on the lips but she turns her head away.

Suddenly though, Shyla, her eyes closed, sees a woman smiling at a man, she has a camera strapped around her neck and a strange resemblance to herself, she smiles but only Shyla, outer viewer of the scene and with no visual on the man's face, can sense a strange foreshadowing, as if something tragic was about to happen. The man comes closer to the woman with wicked intentions sketched all over his partly pockmarked face.

Shyla also sees herself, as if her soul had flown away from her body, she sees her own body twitching under Neil's strong and experienced arms. It's not a pleasant feeling and she suddenly gets up screaming.

Neil, completely turned on, taken aback, pushes her down gently, whispering in her ear "Don't worry baby, it's all right, I will be as gentle as possible when I am inside you." Shyla pushes Neil aside and yells "get out of my sight". Neil is bewildered. She begs Neil to leave her alone for the night. He slides away under a tree like a rabbit and dozes off without uttering a word. Shyla falls asleep with fatigue. Her body turns cold and numb.

The night passes without any surprises either from wild animal or from the Turu Dalam and in the morning light Shyla is woken up by the buzz of the phone. Hers and Neil's are close to one another and, as she expects a call or a message from her boss, she picks up the phone and absentmindedly reads the message before realizing it's not her phone.

Her suspicion is stirred by the cryptic message she has just read, the damage is done, and she may as well read it again.

"Bogey no. 2A. 1.45 PM TODAY. DELIVERY. AS PER PLAN"

She remembers the talk of last night, the lovemaking and trusting him by almost surrendering herself, but this is something big, she feels it, and there's no way on earth she's going to let him wander out at 1.45 today... Neil continues to sleep like a log in the comfort of his huge bedroom- the wilderness.

Chapter 17

Next morning, Neil drops Shyla off at the Government Circuit house but there's a bit of awkwardness between the two. When they woke up this morning they quickly packed their few things and put the fire off with some water from the river and left. Neil got on the bike, passed Shyla his helmet and rode off, they didn't speak, but even if they did the wind would have blown away their voices.

By the time they get to the house it's nearly noon and Shyla is both awkward and tickled about what happened the night before - yet sleepy for the night passed al fresco.

Neil seems very concentrated, he had the expression of a man with a mission and drove like a devil, but now, seeing her face and getting the helmet from her small hands, he seems to be softening up.

The weird feeling of not knowing what might happen next persists but Shyla also feels a lot more serene now that she sees his eyes sparking with light: he is a man, a real one, and he won't run away.

"Want to come in for some coffee?" she stammers.

Neil grabs her wrist as he has started doing in the last few days, since they became a little more intimate, to check the time on her wrist watch "Nope... gotta go. I'll see you tonight... Have planned something special for you. You, me and starry skies and destiny..."

Shyla smiles alone on the stairs of the building as he rides away on his old motorbike that now carry her scars as well. She smiles and thinks to herself how fast life can change sometimes, she would have never thought of a man like Neil as a boyfriend... boyfriend? Well yes, boyfriend, companion, whatever... He is quite the opposite actually of all she has been looking for in a man so far: she wanted someone soft spoken and sweet like her dad, someone who could take her out to nice dinners and quote poetry, not quite an outlaw of the Indian jungle...

She laughs thinking of what Damian might say about this and all of a sudden she's brought back to the whole purpose of being here... work, material for reference, data, field study, evaluation reports... Is she doing what she's expected to do? So far it's been like living in a dream and things have "just happened to her" without her having to make them happen. On the other hand she knows only too well that her time here is limited and if she doesn't want to lose her job -which she doesn't- she better come up with something fast.

The good thing is that because information on the area was so narrow they didn't quite tie her to specific things she should report on, more like the lifestyle of the Chhattisgarhi people, the involvement of the government, the logistical problems of the tribal, the economic conditions, the actual presence of a terrorist group... the extent of damage caused by insurgent gangs...All these things she has seen first-hand so now the only problem is to write them down in a report that might quench the thirst for tragedy that only development workers seem to have. For additional facts and figures she has got some contacts like Mahesh Babu but she needs some more officials on board.

As he drove away from her Neil too was pensive. He has dropped her off for the day and now he is alone back to his lonely self. Life brings two beings together in a defining moment and then you don't want to keep that person away from your eyes even for a while. But Neil was never insecure or crazy for companionship. Today, On the contrary, he is thinking that for the first time in years he has found a person who is exactly like him, a girl, with wounds to heal and with nightmares to wake her up in the middle of the night. He wonders then, being together will destroy them or actually help them sort out their own problems. He muses about her, she stirs in him an urge for protection, he feels that she's like a chick just out of its eggshell; she needs to be looked after and loved. And only he can understand how much love she can give in return. *A match made in heaven or hell,* he laughs in jest as he enters the Jagdalpur railway station.

Inside the railway station Neil becomes a different, cold blooded, expressionless person: he knows what he's looking for and he moves through the people as if they were a jelly, he slides past without them noticing him. This is his job, what he's good at and what makes him who he is.

The platform is not very crowded at this hour of the day. A few vendors sell fruits and tea with an expression of boredom and mundane. The only excitement is a toddler who is running around on the platform with a water pistol and tripping over baggage. His mother is chasing him with her *duppatta* falling all over the place. Neil is devoid of any emotion or empathy for the masses around him. He is on autopilot.

As the clock on the train platform displays three numbers -1.45- he hurries to the carriage Two-A, motionless on the railway track. The goods train is waiting for the signal to proceed. On the side of the track a passenger train arrives. The chaos gets diverted towards the passenger train. Neil opens the door of the goods carriage and gets in and in a second the noise, the voices, the colours, the beggars and the soft yellow mist of the station turns into amber. His eyes take a while before getting used to the darkness but he's calm, he has done this a million times and, to be fair, Turu Dalam has many issues but when they do business they are very trustworthy.

In fact as he sits alone in the carriage, after having left the sliding door open by a couple of centimetres to let some light in. Through the slit, he sees three men dressed as peasants finishing off their tea at once and paying the boy who sold it to them. The boy doesn't seem to notice anything and is pretty happy when they tell him that he can keep the Rupee of change, but Neil smiles at their naiveté: if they wanted to be taken as three separate individuals, not as part of a group, they had to pay separately. Who on earth pays for three teas when two of them were drank by people he didn't know and didn't even exchange a word with?

They get in the carriage, one at the time, over a period of about three minutes and the oldest one, with a cavernous voice due to smoking like a chimney, addresses him with the usual kindness displayed by the gang.

"Debraj will send for you once you get back from Pokhara with the cash"

"Well, good afternoon to you" the man doesn't exactly seem to be either understanding or appreciating Neil's joke.

"Ok, I will be in touch when I come back from Pokhara" says Neil putting the package in his pocket. The youngest gang member is watching the platform, no one is around except for a lazy policeman, too busy to look at village folk passing by to actually go and look for Naxalites. They hear a whistle blowing and at once the train plies, gaining speed as it leaves the station.

"Get off at the next stop at the next signal. The auto waiting outside will drop you back into town"

"Where are you people heading to?"

"Where is the stuff you are transporting? I hope it's safe"

"You may be Debraj's friend, but you are not mine. Mind you own business"

"Man, I am on your side. I have got a tip that you are being watched and this is my business because if they catch you I sink with you, I'm just protecting my business, as you can see"

"Don't worry, the stuff is well hidden, nothing to worry about..." cuts short the man, visibly annoyed with Neil's tone.

All of a sudden they all hear a whistle, it's different this time, not the jolly whistle blowing of the train master but the dry whistle of steel cutting through air. They all know what it means but because of the close compartment and of the dim light they don't know where it comes from.

It doesn't take long before they find out as with a dumb noise of flesh being pierced the young gang member who stood watch by the door falls to his knees. The door is shut open and a policeman walk in shooting, the man with the cavernous voice kills him and the man falls back, but behind him two more are climbing up and shooting like there's no tomorrow. The smell of gunpowder burns Neil's nostrils, he came unarmed and therefore the only thing he can do is to duck and pray that no bullet hits him. Turu Dalam shoots, the police shoots, the noise is hard to stand and Neil finally breaks out through a breach in the door, as he is hanging out of the train the only thing he can think of is that he must have a pretty powerful Karma of past life for having dodged so many bullets.

By the time he reaches the other compartment, full of jute bags filled with food grains, his fingers and knuckles hurt from having hung too tight from the rails, a bruise on his palm from rusty iron gets irritable. He would like to stop for a moment and catch his breath but a bullet comes whistling so close to his right ear that he's momentarily turned deaf.

In his numbness he sees the jute bags torn by the rain of bullets and small packages of Marijuana falling off of them. *This is where they hide it, that's why despite the humanitarian aids for the famine stricken areas there's never enough food*, quickly thinks Neil, making a mental note on where to look the next time. He also smiles to himself, this is by far the most life threatening situation he's been in since a long time and all he can think of is the hiding spots of the Turu Dalam... Hiding spots... his mind races to the previous night. She touched him like a beast. This woman really is changing him! Hope to see her tonight! Shyla the tigress! He smirks.

He sees a bullet fly close to him, he turns around and sees a cop standing on the carriage behind his with a smile on his face, and he's aiming at him and won't miss this time. But in the seconds he takes to aim at Neil something hits the Khaki clad cop in the back and his victorious smile turns into a grin and seconds later, before he even falls down, a stream of blood springs from his mouth. When he falls a gang member appears behind him, against the sun Neil can't quite make out who, and waves a thank you salute to him with his arm in the air. Neil keeps running, he hears shooting and turns around, the gang member is falling onto the jute bags as also the policeman he killed before him and as Neil had done before them all. The bags and their seeds inside get soaked in blood as the corpses pile up and Neil has the feeling, from the noises he still hears inside the carriage, that these are not going to be the only two corpses today. The dead-body count might put the cluster of jute bags to shame.

In fact he keeps sprinting and jumps to reach the next carriage when a hand drags him down making him dodge a bullet that would have otherwise pierced his chest, right through his heart.

The fear and the shock leave him speechless and motionless for a second: he can't see what's around him, he fell on his side and therefore all he sees is the floor of the compartment, a piece of paper, a beer can -funny how object belonging to a relatively quiet time stay behind those who have used them and witness completely different scenes: this beer was probably drank by a father on his way home, wondering if his wife had made him something special, and now... here it is, in the middle of a shootout-. Do animate things also have a destiny? Neil is drunk on thoughts about Shyla.

Neil can feel a presence behind him but can't quite distinguish who it can be? Maybe the youth watching the entrance of the carriage? No, that one was shot before his very eyes... Then who? This one is small, too small to be a soldier or a cop... A cargo passenger maybe? But what passenger would save a runaway jumping from a cargo carriage with corpses on it.

Before he knows the small figure gets up with rare agility and pulls him up.

He is so surprised to see what he sees that he doesn't even recognize the person in front of him, saying something he can't hear because of temporary deafness.

"Thank me later... guess you're not the only superhero around"

"Shy... SHYLA? What the hell are you doing here?"

Before she can explain a gang member comes into the carriage and seizes her, lifting her up and pointing a gun right under her chin. Neil panics but a cop walks in too, pointing a gun at the man. Now Neil is worried twice as much, there's no negotiation here, the matter is out of his hands, and he and Shyla are both hostages, but loyalty to which party is the confusion. When you see death pointing at you from either side, you wonder what's a bigger joke, life or death.

Shyla is too shocked to blink.

"You let her go you bastard" says the cop in the most movie-like voice he can pull out.

"I'll blow her brains off, I swear..." answers the other, used to making threats but also, Neil fears, to keeping promises.

"I'm not your enemy. I'm one of you I swear. I can prove it" And she whispers a code into the gang member's ear, the same safe word she had heard Neil pronounce a few days earlier - Save the lotus flower.

The man is rather shocked to see this woman, evidently not one of them, who doesn't speak Chhattisgarhi and whose Hindi is also clearly not a mother tongue, take the situation in hand. Maybe she is a foreign counterpart that Debraj interacts with he assures himself. While he looks at her in confusion, he lets his guard down, fatal mistake to make when Neil is around, as he seizes the gun and shoots him. For Neil it's the first, there aren't too many instances when he has even held the gun. Most of the time, holding the gun with the right stance does the trick. But here, he knows that if the timing is not correct, it will make him history and a rotting specimen for the biology lab.

The policeman takes care of the other gang members who are entering the carriage now. How many are they? It seems like they stuffed the train covertly just in case things turned sour, thinks Neil.

He and Shyla duck down to protect themselves from the bullets shooting all around them, he keeps his arm on her head and strangely enough she feels safe here, with the mayhem above their heads and Neil next to her. Romance on a train with bullets ringing. Not exactly music to her hears, she recalls watching 'Die Hard' with bullets screaming out of the Dolby system on her first date. But this is more of a reality show. The train finally crosses a river, the bridge is quite high but it's the only chance they have to try and make it alive, if they stay here either the gang or the cops will kill them... or worst- stray bullets.

Neil opens the metal door in a dash. He grabs Shyla by the arm. In a split second he reassures her. To eternity and back. They jump almost in a motion blur. They cut through the static air with their souls suspended between heaven and earth. The fall takes forever and Neil actually wonders if they are already dead, when they finally touch the water, Shyla regains her senses. She virtually passed out for a few seconds. Not her idea of a bungee jump without a harness and rope. The water is cold and both are messed up in their minds. The sound of random bullets continues to ring in their deaf ears as they painfully try to swim to the riverbank. The train and its feast of bullets enter a tunnel and the noise of the engine covers that of death. The elusive sound of bodies falling off the train echoes in the silent skies.

Chapter 18

Neil and Shyla reach the riverbank panting. The swim wasn't too long but the current was strong and they never managed to even touch each other to see if they were safe. Now they are both sitting and without major injuries they take their breath and try to look at one another, sharply, with the relief of seeing a loved one safe and with the rage due to finding out a betrayal.

Shyla knows that she shouldn't have been there, Neil will surely find out that she has either read his text or followed him, whichever the case he's not going to be happy. But on the other hand she's more angry at him, enraged, she repeated the password she had heard him say and it worked, the insurgents bought it, which means he's one of them. So what will he do now? Kill her? Finish the witness? She's also confused by the fact that all of a sudden both the guards and the thieves were at him and she's not too sure how to read that duality. She has always been a big fan of Harry Potter books but Dan Brown is not on her favoured list of authors. Neil is a chameleon. But how poisonous can he get!

Sitting next to her, short of breath, is Neil, soaked in water and with his boots and jeans covered in mud from trying to walk up the river. She knew the password, how did she know it? Did she spy on him? Was she following him? How was she even on the train? Who is she? He has been watching a lot of pirated Hollywood movies but this one has real emotions and her eyes don't lie? But is she a highly trained spy?

As always when someone is desperate for a clue and there seems to be nothing to hang on to, Neil feeds his brain with his own fears.

I knew it was a bad time to trust someone, this one... a spy reporter... I wonder why she's after me though... Fish! Why did I sleep with her, why did I trust her? I'm bound to be alone and abandoned by those whom I love. I should go back to Pokhara right away and date Xian, she's too young, ok, but this way I'm sure she'll always love me.

Suddenly, in the rush of anger and fear that still runs through his bloodstream, he checks his pocket for the only thing that, until two days ago, mattered. Out of a small package a few small sized alexandrite gemstones appear and shine in the afternoon sun.

"Do you wanna explain yourself? What was all that about?"

"Why don't you go first? Who are you, exactly what the hell where you doing on that bloody train? ...Who do you think you are, huh? Snooping around like this?"

"I wasn't snooping..."

"Bullshit! BULL SHIT! I heard you in there!"

"So what? I followed you, and what I said... well it's just a code!" Shyla is obviously underestimating Neil's anger, which is quite evidently about to reach its peak.

"Just a code? Why don't you just take your friggin NRI arse back to Cape Town and do your little tiger hunting there! Stop interfering in matters that don't concern you!"

"Yeah right, so that jerks like you can screw up this country some more... right? Those are alexandrite... you're smuggling them, aren't you?"

Shyla's anger raises by the minute, although she has only started shouting to defend herself, she's now truly believing her words, discovering a patriotism she didn't know she had. Perhaps her mother's genes are lighting up her bravado bulbs.

Neil begins to walk away, trying to keep his cool and not say things he might regret or that could not be undone: he knows only too well how words can't be swallowed back once they linger in the air. Shyla has been drowned into a vortex where anger can only generate more anger and keeps shouting louder her accusations. She knows this has been her weakness from the days of wonder. Once she is overtaken by rage, no one can stop her. And the serene Father Thomas is no longer around.

"You're working for those gangs... you're one of them! God, I knew I couldn't trust you, I knew it, you diabolique traitor" Suddenly, Neil pulls a gun out. It was the gun he got earlier from the Turu Dalam gang member, he knows he has shot but he's not sure whether he has killed him or not. Was it him or the cop who also shot simultaneously? He points the gun at Shyla who, for the first time in minutes, freezes.

"You know nothing! I'm warning you... whoever you are, whatever spy or cock organisation you work for... get the hell out of my way and mind your own god damn business!"

Shyla paces up to him, with the eyes lost in space. By pointing a gun at her he has made everything easier, how could she ever be so stupid to think she loved a man so evil?

The scene, from an outsider standpoint, it's frightening: two people high on adrenaline keep mistaking each other's actions and words and look into the empty space daring one another. One of them has a gun and is pointing it at the woman. Who, strangely enough, races towards him and lifts her chin, she walks so fast that the gun, extension of Neil's stretched arm, pokes Shyla in the neck. Neil doesn't bring his arm down and she doesn't take a step back. The tension is in the air and it's so thick it can almost be felt on one's skin. The ill vibes and noise perhaps disturbed the migratory birds trailing on the riverbank. The friendly flock of sandpipers fly away in disgust. Deafening silence.

"I dare you... go on... let's see if you've got what it really takes... Neil frigging gangster... Kill me if you think it's gonna change something!"

Neil shoots a couple of bullets into the shrubbery and then looks into her eyes for a moment, bites his lip and curses under his breath. He takes his gun and puts it back in his pocket.

"Piss off... just go away... you know your way around if you meet them..."

Shyla walks away, only now she understands that there is something deeper in Neil: she had an insight of it the other night, but she was drunk and then the whole episode of sex and drama happened and there was no time to talk about it.

She regrets having said those things, now that her adrenaline is going down and she's more clear headed she wonders what the damage is but she's still too proud to go and talk to him first.

In another corner of that same jungle Debraj is receiving the news. Most of his men were afraid to go and tell him and they sent ahead a younger boy who explains in plain and clear words what happened, without much emotional involvement. There are no survivors.

Debraj kicks a bucket that was close to his foot, right now he is so angry he could go and shoot the cops at the police station with bare hands.

"Bastards!!! They will pay for it, you have my word, and they'll pay now"

Outside Kedar is spit roasting a wild cat with his grin that always looks like a sinister smile. Debraj sees him and is momentarily irritated by the stupid grin.

Shyla and Neil split, she has gone back to the only place that, although different to everything she knows, makes her feel at home: the Salwa Judum refugee camp. She stops to play with a kid and is reminded of herself, though a million years ago it feels now. She was in front of her school, the girl's convent school in the suburbs of Cape Town, all the mothers were coming to pick up their children and she was standing there, two thin braids at the sides of her head and a big black hole in the place of one of her front teeth. She was waiting patiently and stepping on the tips of her toes to check if daddy was still far away. That day her father had taken her to the Cathedral and told her to pray so that her tooth could grow back stronger than before: this would be a tooth she'd keep all her life, until she was old. Shyla remembers how hard she had prayed that time, with her eyes squeezed closed and her hands into one another, pressing the palms against each other to be more effective in her request. She was the first one in the class who had lost a tooth and other children were making fun of her, she had to get a tooth back, any tooth!

Shyla is brought back by her reverie by one of the children of the camp, who throws an inflatable ball at her and hits her in the face. He looks starved. His undernourished mother scolds him but Shyla gestures to her that it's a matter of no consequence, she kneels down and smiles at the boy, he smiles back and she throws him the ball. She gives him a flying kiss. He catches it like Robinhood.

She thinks to herself- a page of Harry Porter that she remembers. She wished she could have a magic wand that could create a wormhole and she could disappear in it, escorting with her, all the deprived kids and the heavily pregnant Anjali. Travel to a land, a planet, a universe where the kids are given back their innocence, they are treated with love and respect, where God is reminded of the truth that he too must have been a kid, in some day of his existence and it is he who has created this wonderful world full of blissful children. Then why discriminate with these distressed children with pure souls. Why play a ruthless game with their fate? Why Children? Why?

In another part of town, in fact in town, Neil is clearing his room and packing his stuff to go to Pokhara. His head is stuck in a whirlpool of feelings and there are so many things he is thinking of he feels his eyes are going to bulge out. He feels like he is standing in a rapid river with thousand undercurrents pulling him apart. Shyla.

He can't stop thinking about her, though he's angry. But also more worried than he has ever been, that something bad could happen to her. If only his brother was here now... Anil always knew what to say. Right now he would have probably said "What are you talking about Neil? She betrayed you, forget her and move on..." This is what Neil would want his elder brother to say.

What he would really say if he was here is "She saved your life you idiot, and you gave no explanations, how is she supposed to have you all figured out if the only thing you did with dedication was hitting on her?"

He's still thinking of this when he arrives at the border between India and Nepal, says hello to the guys at the Border security force and drives off after having given them a little present to speed the process up and don't indulge in a thorough checking. They have seen Neil a million times, they know him, or they think they do, and he has never caused any trouble neither in India nor in Nepal, so his presents are always welcome but the truth is they wouldn't stop him anyway. Neil's charm works like a diamond.

Neil knows it but still prefers to be sure to oil the mechanism, if anything happens he'd much rather be in the position to say that the two police officers knew and got paid to shut up rather than say that he acted alone. Atleast he will have a bargaining chip for his lawyers.

In the circuit house Shyla is lying on the bed and absentmindedly watching the news on TV, today's action was huge, it's was like a movie, she knows they can't pretend it hasn't happened, someone must report about it.

She has knocked on Neil's door earlier, but has received no answer. The cleaning lady said something in Chhattisgarhi that she didn't understand but from her gesticulation it was pretty clear that he has left for some faraway destination.

Shyla is disappointed and slightly worried: first because she had gotten used to the company and to not being here alone, which, after what she has seen in the last couple of days, is terrifying. The other part of her is angry, at Neil and at herself, because by leaving he has basically admitted his fault. Was he worried they'd come to look for him here? "They" who? The police or the rebels?

She's probably more confused than angry. Lost in her train of thought, misses the first few words of the interview.

On the TV screen Anand's face looks small but all the creases on his forehead are pretty visible: this job, if done with conscience and determination, wears people out, they just age prematurely seeing all their friends dying one by one and witnessing insurgents overpowering them.

"And the narcotics packed with food grains?" shouts from the crowd a young reporter.

"We are trying to find its origins. The 'Red Radicals' trade in them to finance their operations. Thus we are trying to curb all their illegal trades but these operations are delicate and take a long time"

"Yes, some might say it's a little late in the day..." ventures another young reporter.

"It's never too late to stop terror, we kill their business, we finish them" answers Anand taking his glasses off and cleaning the lenses against his shirt.

"It's not long before we get to the bottom of this red terror. We have some important leads and of course the CM's support" there is a faint laughter in the crowd: some people have just been let down so many times by their leaders that they can't afford to trust them anymore.

Shyla listens carefully, she's interested in what Anand is saying but also in what everyone around him seems to think and whisper. She takes her wallet out of her purse and extracts the picture of a middle-aged woman, her eyes are sweet and ancient, as if she had lived many lives. Shyla stares into them while the sound of the TV numbs her thought and accompanies her into a deep sleep.

Anand's voice echoes also in Debraj's den, as it seems to echo in the whole of Central India tonight. Debraj listens to the interview but his eyes are filled with flames of rage and his hand is so tight around the glass of scotch he's holding that his knuckles have turned white.

"These fools think that they are helping their country... somebody tell them they are all going to die unsung heroes while politicians are filling their pockets and overseas bank accounts and feeding the country to the dogs! Invoke the CM's support Anand, you fool! The CM is the first one who would walk over your dead body when money is flashed before his eyes..."

Other gang members nod in agreement; Kedar Singh has his usual psychopath expression and is digging grenades out of a bag mixed with potatoes, smelling them in ecstasy as if they were ripe fruits. He licks a grenade like it was a mango.

"Speed, we need speed... That's the reason I brought you here, in Debu"

"I know why I am here Kedar"

"Mr Professor this is war... See what I do next"

"Focus Kedar. Don't forget we are fighting this war because we have a cause"

"Yes Professor... Destroy and survive. You plan the Mega Event, meanwhile I'll create some fireworks. Before any big show there is always some fireworks... right guys?"

Chapter 19

A young tigress fondles a tiger at the crack of dawn. She is brimming with lust. The male tiger is sleepy after a long night's caper that he went alone, for a change of prey. The tigress strokes the tiger in the ears. The saliva trickles down the tiger's neck. The Tiger gets turned on and jumps on the tigress and makes passionate love to it. Vapours fly as fur rubs against rich fur. The sound of an oncoming train doesn't interfere with their wild moods. Neil watches them from his motorbike. He is trespassing the jungles enroute to Nepal. He sees the vintage steam train coming close to these tigers lost in their carnal madness. As a sigh of relief Neil notices that the tigers are on the neighbouring track and the train passes without brushing the two wild cats engaged in ecstasy galore. Once the train has passed leaving behind a trail of smoke, Neil finds himself on the railway track making love to the tigress. There is no male tiger. The feeling of mating with a tigress is the most awesome experience that Neil could ever have in his wildest dreams. He feels the thick coat of fur on his skin. The spicy smell of its perspiration is ethereal. Next he sees Shyla's eyes instead of the tigress's eyes staring into him with intense lure. He leaps on Shyla the tigress and pins her down with the lust filled energy that has inflated his body. Shyla takes over and they begin to take turns over each other in frenzy. The iron railway tracks vibrate more vigorously than the tremble of an overriding train. Stones on the track get flung into the space with the quaking vibrations.

Neil's reverie is broken when he rolls over to the floor after dropping from his bed. Thud. His wet- dream crashes into fragments of recognition. The smell of his shoe wakes him up fully. He looks outside the window of the forest lodge that he has halted for a night's sleep. He is breathless. His sturdy motorbike stares at him with the lure of a jaguar, ready to cruise on rough yet familiar terrains. Neil is powered by the inch. He kick-starts his mean machine with a gush of vigour. Racing through the sun kissed Sunderbans' has been vanity for both the rider and the ride.

The morning sun illuminates the porch of the government guesthouse at Bastar, where Shyla gets up and starts working on her report. As she types on her small laptop she thinks of everything that has happened in the last... what week? As things happen she keeps being struck at how fast life can change: not even twenty-four hours ago she was dodging bullets on a train and now she's sitting in this nice garden sipping coffee and trying to recover from the bad hangover only bad wines can give. Since a child she always feared loneliness, even if it's daytime. This isolated guesthouse surrounded by shrubbery and silence, with the caretaker always missing in action, gives her creeps. She nervously types her report on her laptop just to get some company out of words. Words to her hold great significance. Words soak her, caress her, dress her and at times undress her.

She hears a jeep coming, her guest, she tries to clean up the room as much as she can, she hides everything under the blanket and evens it with her arms, it does look a bit fluffy but at least she doesn't have clothes and shoes scattered all over the place.

Shyla hears the engine stop, a man's voice asking for her room and his steps approaching, by the time he knocks at the door she's already behind it, ready to open it with a big smile.

Anand's face seems to have been pulled out of the TV screen: he's wearing the same shirt as yesterday and his wrinkles seem to have deepened around his eyes and at the corners of his mouth. He is definitely tired, the police station yesterday must have been mayhem, dead cops, people coming and going, counting the wounded, but he hadn't left, he spent the night there. And this convinces Shyla that he is one of the good ones, one of those who give their lives for a cause, which they are unlikely to see the end of. Instinctively she's drawn to him, of course emotionally she's somewhere else, but this guy really seems one of those people you want to know in life: a trustworthy, solid, open, good guy. A good man. And as boring as that might sound a woman sometimes needs a man in her life who doesn't disappear, so what if he is privy to secret codeword to rebel gangs...

"Shyla Thomas- Thank you so much for making time for me"

"Anand Sharma- It's my pleasure. Bad timing though. I don't always get the opportunity to meet someone from a renowned magazine who is keen on finding out about the terrible events in Chhattisgarh and wants to help by taking the story to the rest of the world"

His smile seems genuine and open and Shyla can't wait to interview him as she feels he is a goldmine of information.

She invites him to sit down in the little garden just outside her room and take a cup of coffee.

"Plain black... good for hangovers... suits me... will be good for you too…all that turbulence on duty"

Anand is a little taken aback by her definite Indian look and her not so Indian behaviour, he has always lived here and is unsure what she is doing here, he looks around trying to find a clue.

He feels a little uncomfortable and sits at the very end of the chair, looking at her he got a very good first impression, of course she's beautiful but there's also something very special about her. She's a woman who has endured, who went through a lot and is seeking for concord. They might have similar paths, and Anand surprises himself hoping that these troubled paths could meet. He hasn't said a word about it and yet when she looks at him with her almond shaped enquiring eyes he feels his face on fire. Sweet.

"Hmmm... Nice camera, have you been taking lots of pictures?"

Shyla nods, she gets up and fetches the camera to show him some of her pictures. By looking at them she realizes how many things she has seen that are not related to one another at all. But they all have a story. A mixed bag of arrows. Finally she finds the picture of the tiger she had taken that day with Neil, when they nearly got killed...

"My son loves tigers," says Anand to try and warm up the atmosphere.

"Really? Well there you go... I'm not the only crazy one then! I love the way they look, the way they move, and the way they seem so fluffy and all of a sudden turn into deadly predators"

Shyla is not quite sure how to introduce the subject of her interest. She has called Anand saying what she wanted to talk but now, even though the mood is a little more relaxed, there's clearly an elephant in the room. She picks up the newspaper and lets the first page do the job for her.

"Your men did a fantastic job, you must be proud of them..."

"Oh yes, this is our routine. We are always in the line of fire"

Anand has kept the camera in his hand and is flipping through photos as they speak. He lands on a photograph of the Turu Dalam- the red gang on a hunt and stops for a few seconds.

"You're a bit of a risk taker yourself, as I see..." he says with a smile.

"Yeah, curiosity always gets the best of me"

Anand opens a photo of Neil and smiles.

"Neil Mahajan... always the poser!"

Shyla is clearly shocked to hear a police officer say something so personal, and not so judgmental to be fair, about a Rebel.

She feels a little uncomfortable, as if she chose to interview the wrong person and as if she realized now how she has invited into her own space, her room, another one of them. Brothers in cahoots.

"You... you know him?"

"Yes, nice chap..."

"Nice? Are you serious? He's the guy you should be interrogating about yesterday... he seems to know a lot about the red gang rebels, the Turu Dalam..." says Shyla without thinking what the consequences of her statement may be if Anand really is one of them.

"Ms Thomas, look, I'm a police officer, I'm used to reading into people and gathering information about them before I go and meet them in their guest house. I know who you are but I'm more than happy to play by your rules, you belong to a higher institution I have no power over and besides I think that me and you work on the same side, despite what you might have heard about Indian cops.

Mr Mahajan, Neil as you might know him, is one of my most trustworthy men. He's an informer, although not strictly an officer, but if he chooses to take up this career I'd fully endorse him because he is a silent warrior in this war"

"Neil? Warrior?"

"Yes... Neil's a good guy"

"I don't think I could trust him anymore"

"Anymore?"

"Long story..."

Anand perceives that something must have happened between the two but at the same time feels like he needs to tell Shyla something more to restore Neil's image, whatever he might have done was only driven by circumstances, he's sure.

"I'm a cop. I follow my instincts about people. I ran a file check on him. A long time ago Neil was training for the Police Force when his brother, also a cop, died in a bomb blast planted by the Maoists. Later it was discovered that the minister whom his brother was escorting was a very corrupt official who had tried to play around with Turu Dalam and, as you might have noticed, Turu Dalam doesn't like getting screwed.

I remember arriving on the site of the explosion and the bridge the cars were blown to pieces, a car was in the river and corpses scattered everywhere. They didn't spare anybody, those who didn't die in the blast were ruthlessly killed. When I found Anil's body it was half blown up..."

Shyla is horrified "Oh my God! Does he know that you know all this? He seems too private to share any of this with anyone...besides this information that I have witnessed is no sports bar conversation"

"No. I didn't want to poke a dagger into his past wounds. I know he does some of his own stuff to live comfortably, like smuggling illegal stuff, but I choose to overlook all that because of the classified information that he provides, which no other guy would be able to gather in such a short time. His side business allows him to get in touch with people we would never suspect and this gives us a huge advantage. Besides, our resources are limited, my informers can't live on what I can give them, they all have some sort of side business... shopkeeper, nurse, they all do something else, Neil is the only one who went out for the big money, but can you blame him, he is wicked smart? In the end he only has to care for himself and I'd give up all other informants if I was asked to only keep one, I would have him a million times"

"What about the gemstone smuggling... I saw him dealing with the Maoists. On the train, I saw him"

"Neil is trying to enter their inner circle Shyla, he'll do whatever is necessary. He has to be in nosiness with these rebels. Only then will they trust him. And it was Neil who informed me about the Red gang trade delivery and the appointment at the Jagdalpur train station"

"When you say "whatever is necessary" you mean putting his own life in danger, right?"

Anand smiles sadly, this country needs martyrs, lots of them. Anand is one too in his own way. Suddenly Shyla is worried about Neil, she regrets saying what she said down at the river and she wishes she could go back in time and undo what she did. She doesn't know where he is now and for all she, or Anand, know he could be in the hands of the Maoists tied to a chair for interrogation. What if they suspect him now? What if they are extorting the truth from him right now?

Shyla shudders with her imagination as Anand turns passionate with his words.

"Meanwhile we have corrupt politicians involved in drug and weapon trade... also the illegal smuggling of diamonds and precious gems. The irony of the people of this land... We have Mahatma Gandhi printed on each and every banknote and yet leaders use banknotes with one of our brightest national heroes on them to corruptly buy their way into power... to bribe and to profit from illegal trades, I find this rather disgusting"

But Shyla isn't listening to Anand, right now all she can think of is Neil and why he didn't explain all this to her. He forced her to go away in order to protect her, in spite of his own life.

"I wonder... why Neil never clarified... what is his hidden motive?"

Anand is about to answer when his phone rings, he picks up with that indefinite smile of his, hard to detect and at once his smile becomes grim and soon an expression of panic covers his face.

Bad news, Shyla can tell even if he hasn't said anything yet.

She is afraid for Neil, all she can think of him right now, what happen to him!

Before Anand has hung up the phone Shyla is already dressed and has her purse in her hand.

Chapter 20

From the top of the hill Kedar watches the wreck with his usual grin, this time is more of an impish smile. His wicked face is camouflaged in the wild shrubbery. What he sees is the closest thing he can relate to Hell, that very Hell, once a nun that he had kidnapped had told him about, where people burn alive and cursed souls languish forever.

Beneath the cliff he's standing on, a helicopter has crashed, it hasn't just crashed by fate or by mistake, he, Kedar crashed it by bombarding it with grenades that have exploded in the air making it so hot and unstable that the pilot lost control and fell to the ground like a ripe pear. The sound was different, a lot more appealing to Kedar's sadistic ears: it was the sound of a prey that falls into the claws of the predator, the sound of metal being brutalized and melt onto the ground, the sound of lives vanishing, abandoning their burning bodies. The sound of death, truly music to his ears. He can hear the noise of a band, an orchestra of demons playing their slimy instruments while they hover around to consume the last breath of dying spirits. Kedar applauds with his ugly scarred hands like the master of the ceremony. He indulges in a gentle dance of the devil that he is nursing inside him from many births. He knows at some level that the evil inside him is a humungous monster; a malicious collection of predisposition from several lifetimes, redemption is as distant as the edge of the universe. Or maybe as close.

The first cars arrive, helpless before the tragedy, Kedar loves this moment more than that of death itself: he can picture in the eyes of those who have arrived the fear, he can nearly smell the revolting stench of burned flesh mixed with gas. Right now they fear him, they don't know who he is but they look around to see where he's hiding, like scared animals that can sense the presence of the tiger but can't see it. They don't know it yet but the tiger is him, rather the hyena- Kedar Singh, the embodiment of all their fears.

When Anand and Shyla arrive the scene is hideous: more people have gathered, some are helping and some are just watching -Shyla has always detested those who gather to just stand and watch tragedies happen before their very eyes- there are people running, the smell of burnt flesh is ubiquitous and disgusting. All the people here look like millions of ants, apparently running in different directions but all with a plan, and Shyla notices it through her camera, which keeps clicking and imprisoning fragments of those lives into its lens. These photos will stir the right emotions and the funds will flow in time to stop terror and their maniac masterminds. For once people present on this fateful ground forget about the biting cold. Anand looks around to find some of his men, to understand who exactly died and if by any chance there are survivors. As always neither the mind nor the hand behind all this were found.

News vans arrive, after everyone else, like vultures, to feast on the remains of the tragedy. Desperate Reporters break into a nervous cacophony while they shiver in the cold winds- "How many deaths? What happened? Find some witnesses so they can speak on TV, no that one is too old, find someone young... find a dead body… it would be nice to also film someone injured, maybe someone who can't speak... Find me someone in a state of shock please!!!" This is all Shyla hears, and she hates them for being so cruel and showing so little respect before what really is a tragedy. But they are just doing their job sans sympathy. The curtains to this tragedy have opened up, the show had begun!

In the cosy safety of a hall, not too far from the accident but far enough to be safe, the CM is giving a press conference. He didn't feel like doing it so soon but he was forced to when events escalated and so many journalists turned up on the spot... the thing couldn't be kept a secret any longer. Anyways he is on an apparent mission to combat these rebels.

"I express my deepest condolence to the families of these brave men. The victims' families will be compensated monetarily for this tragic attack. And I will personally begin my visits to promote goodwill... My first one will be at Kanker Public School on Republic Day"

His words sound empty and echo into themselves, goodwill, tragic attack, condolences, these words have been repeated over and over by all those who came before him and by him and will likely be repeated by those who will come after. The people have heard promises and seen them shattered like their hopes and their dreams. Who cares if this one too makes false promises? Promises are like Tendu leaves, to the citizens here, they sprout green in spring and then they wither and fall off. They have been cheated on so many times that it hardly matters anymore: journalist have to invent yet another lie that may sound remotely believable and people will buy the newspaper again tomorrow more to comment it at the *chaiwalla* stand than to actually learn what happened. No one knows what happened and yet everybody knows.

A reporter stands up and shouts over other voices, "Sir, with all due respect, aren't you concerned about your safety?"

The CM'S security commander interrupts the interview to reassure the audience that all security measures are being taken, at the school visit only children, their teachers and designated media will be present. There will be a lot of prior checking, executed by special task force.

From his den Debraj is watching the press conference broadcasted on TV. He spits on the ground with vengeance embellished deep inside the retina of his deadly eyes. He has a neutral expression on his face, somewhere deep down he is celebrating his victory of today, but he is in anticipation of a bigger blow to civilised society. Kedar is his usual mad, but someday Debraj will have to deal with his insanity, Debraj knows, but today he was grand. And yet another part of Debraj has grown tired of all this, more and more often he wonders what life would be like if one day he took a plane, one of those he sees over his head every day in the jungle, and left for good. And escape to Goa...Nepal or China. He has saved enough to have a rather good life there, or maybe faraway from India altogether... But he is tied to this jungle and all his fantasies always fall on the same spot: he grew up in the neighbouring state, his parents died here, his entire life is here, if he went anywhere else he wouldn't be Debraj, the terror of Chhattisgarh, he wouldn't be anyone, and he's not sure he can come with being just another Indian, in line at the super market and watching cricket with patrons at a pub while the wives are out shopping. Too much water has gone under a bridge. Debraj is like a dead robot, mastermind, meticulous with no heart. But then every human has a soft spot buried deep within till they themselves discover it. The awaking of the unconscious.

Anand has taken half a day off to spend some time with his son, Raghav is growing so fast, right before his eyes, and he's very seldom there for him. He is a good boy, he knows his dada is fighting a good battle but for how long is he going to be ok with it? When will the bonds weaken due to his father's busy duty calls? Today they play scrabble in the porch, whenever they get a whole day together -a real luxury- Anand tries to play but also indulge in less active games so that they can get time to talk. There are so many things he would like to tell his son... So many things and so little time.

Anand smiles in his own sad way when he sees that his son has completed a word and that word is "bomb", he must have heard it so many times in the last two days, in fact in last few years, that he doesn't even associate the word itself with destruction anymore. It's just another word, an inanimate object on the scrabble board. Just like any fruit. Apple, mango, bomb!

When Shyla walks in Anand looks pleasantly surprised.

"Shyla! Welcome... What a surprise!"

Raghav runs to see who this Shyla is and smiles as soon as she sees her, she's wearing jeans, a white singlet and a yellow shirt open on it, and she looks like one of those actresses in action movies, nothing like the women of Kanker. He immediately likes her and welcomes her with a broad smile extending his hand like his dada taught him.

"Hello young man, you must be Raghav! How are you?"

"Very well thank you. Dada told me you like tigers" It was pretty obvious that he had been bursting to ask her this question from the second he heard the gate creaking.

Shyla glances at Anand and smiles, she most definitely didn't expect to be the talk of the family after a whole day spent together with Anand, she actually thought he might find her annoying.

"What else did your daddy tell you about me?"

Anand breaks into the conversation "Raghav, scouts honour, remember?"

Raghav smiles and nods and his gaze falls on the thin and long package that Shyla is holding. He hadn't seen in before but now that he has he's dying with curiosity. Shyla notices it and hands the package to him.

"Yeah, I got this for you, but you must promise me you will teach me how to fly it!"

Raghav opens the package and a beautiful, brightly coloured kite emerges with its wide wings and long thread. Raghav can't contain his excitement, he knows that it's the day he's supposed to spend with his dada but he can't wait to show this beauty to all other children.

"Wow, everyone is going to envy me now!!!"

"Alright guys, chai time!!!" calls Anand.

The usually serious police officer shows a side of himself Shyla would have never expected to see: he's making sandwiches to go with chai, wearing a very normal pair of jeans, a blue shirt, barefoot. Shyla would prefer not to stare but his soft, warm, comforting normality charms her in spite of herself. Could Anand be a family man? He already is. Neil? He has disappeared; he's that kind of man. Always on the go! Future? There seems to be no future.

Anand slips some intense looks at Shyla, while she isn't looking back: he sees her playing with Raghav, laughing, and apparently forgetting what kind of trouble she's in. If given a choice, someone like her, is who he'd like to marry. Isn't that what love is? Looking at someone and hoping to grow old together, chatting about common interests, listening to music, watching TV at night and waiting for the grandchildren to come visit?

Shyla used to have high expectations from love: romance, passion, and mystery. But since her father died and she discovered that the first twenty-eight years of her life were a perfectly crafted fiction, she has reconsidered her outlook. She wishes to come home to a man who can be trusted, one who is unlikely to disappear or cheat. A man who she respects cause he has a purpose to live for? Is love a burning thing? She doesn't know, she thought she did: she thought she knew everything back in South Africa, until everything changed. Shyla is confused, attracted to two very different men, in a foreign country that she's only starting to understand, generally confused about what to do next.

The trio moves into the kitchen where Anand grinds fresh ginger, Shyla takes the milk from the fridge and they both look through the door, at the living room, where Raghav is assembling the kite with religious precision.

"He's amazing! I don't see much of you in him... Does he take after his mum? Where is she, by the way?"

"Who?"

"Your wife?"

Anand takes time to answer the question, as if he was deciding whether to tell the whole story or the short version; he knows Shyla well enough by now to know that if he goes with the short version she's not going to be satisfied and enquire further, but he gives it a try anyway, maybe today she's not in detective mode!

"Uh... I'm not married"

Anand looks at Shyla and can tell that she would like to ask more questions but doesn't dare to.

"He looks just like Madhav..."

"Madhav?"

"His real father, he was one of my most faithful informers, he wasn't as reckless as Neil but he was good, he was a very ordinary man, besides, he had a family. Therefore no will to be as daring as our friend... He died, shot by the Turu Dalam. I have always suspected Kedar Singh, a madman, but I have no proof it was him. It's always the same story with these people, they are a legacy and defend each other, even when we get one of them alive he'd much rather be executed than rat on his friends... And so Madhav died, he had probably discovered about the plan to bomb the bridge where Neil's brother died, we will never know. He called me from a pay phone but the only thing I could hear by the time the call was passed on to me were the three shots that pierced his head. His tormented wife died shortly after and left behind Raghav, three year old orphan of this insane war. I felt like I owed it to Madhav to take care of his son.

Raghav knows the whole story, I wanted him to grow up being proud of his dad, I had taken from him so much already that I didn't feel it right to steal even his past"

Shyla looks at Raghav from the kitchen window, he has assembled the kite and is attempting to fly it, and she smiles and now understands why Anand's smile is always so sad.

"A victim of rebellion is our future... Will he ever forgive the country that allowed red terror to remain fertile?"

Anand registers the depth of Shyla's question, he would like to answer that yes, it's true, India is not deploying enough forces to deal with this plague, but people like him work their asses off to build a safer country. But then he stops his train of thought abruptly: it's true, there are a few crusaders like him, but isn't she right in a sense? He hates the red terror as a concept and thinks that murderers should go to jail, but he also understands -and tries to teach Raghav- that it's the people of this region that are responsible first. They are often uneducated and faced with acute poverty and problems, they think can only get overcome by supporting a despotic power like Turu Dalam.

Anand pities the youths of Turu Dalam, they think they believe in the principles but really they are just cannon fodder at the mercy of one or two visionaries that promise a lot and think the only way forward is violence. Sadly these so called terror Masterminds are themselves mislead by external outfits and other smuggling syndicates.

He is teaching his son not to hate anybody, to make peace with everyone but will he succeed? In this world where innocent people are robbed, raped and blown up, will Raghav be so balanced to distinguish between good and bad or will he take one side and follow it blindly. "Blood for blood" yell some of his own policemen, but blood only calls for more blood and the war never ends.

Will he be strong enough to teach his son what so hard to believe in, even for himself?

Shyla sees that Anand is lost in his thoughts and from the curve of his eyes, pointing down as the eyes of people who have grown accustomed to crying, she knows that he is not thinking about the shopping list or what car to buy. The only way she can have him on her side is by turning his despair into fire, she knows him well enough by now to know that he is not a violent man, he's one of those cops who still shoots in the air before aiming at a person, and he is exactly what she's looking for.

She needs his calmness, his reflective brain, his logic, to get where she wants to get and that is why she calls him out of his reverie with an abrupt question.

"Who is Debraj Roy?"

Hearing that name is like an electric shock for Anand. He keeps calm but smiles, looks at her and seeing the fire burning in her eyes proves to him that from now on they can trust each other thoroughly, they are in the same team, a team made of two: they are the only ones who have the most powerful reason to find Debraj and seek for justice once and for all.

CHAPTER 21

Anand takes Shyla to the office he has set up for himself at home: with a child there are only so many hours you can spend at the office. He has managed to get one of the mums of Raghav's school mates to pick him up and take him to her house, it's a safe place, she's the wife of another policeman, a clean one, and she knows what their life is like. After work he goes and collects him, sometimes he has already had dinner but sometimes, once home, Anand still has to cook, check the homework and tell a story. He never wanted to hire a maid because, given his position, he wasn't comfortable with having somebody he didn't know snooping around the house while he wasn't there, so they have a lady coming in on Saturday and Sundays for laundry and some cleaning up but they do most of the work themselves, which of course doesn't make Anand's life any easier.

When the lights in Raghav's room are off he can finally start working again.

Shyla enters this small room with a whole wall covered in newspaper clippings, photographs, notes, the smell of paper and coffee is very strong, this is evidently the place where Anand spends most of his time when he's home. There is also a small couch, it looks old and in bad shape, but Shyla guesses that it has been Anand's bed for many a night.

While he switches on his laptop Anand explains to Shyla the tale of Debraj, the kingpin behind the terror in this region of Chhattisgarh.

"Debraj Roy is the brain behind red terror in this region...Once a renowned college professor. He got abducted by the alleged head of Turu Dalam back then-Kedar Singh. It is believed that Kedar brainwashed him with a lot of false bravado. But from what I know Kedar is a madman, an obsessive visionary and a psychopath, his cruelty has no boundaries and quite frankly I don't see how a man as educated as Debraj could get trapped in this demon's game plan. Debraj must have been in his confused youth phase then and so he got overpowered and trapped. Sometimes even victims of violent upbringing lose their scruples overnight and make bad choices. But Kedar has others above him, international insurgent wherewithal. I'm certain of this because Turu Dalam's resources, from what we know from ballistic investigations we carry out after attacks, are very advanced: nothing the two of them, Kedar and Debraj, could get without external help. There sophistication of weaponry and tactical support is routed through bigger vested interests. These external sources will never be identified because the network is often complicated and misleading. The Turu Dalam have income coming from smuggling and robbing but definitely not enough to finance such a huge operation over such a long period of time. I do feel money and arms keep pouring in from other neighbouring countries, I have no proof of that but I'm almost certain. My intelligence sources are scanty and unsophisticated but I am sure about the roots that can be traced to some international insurgent outfits"

Anand plays a couple of videos on his laptop, videos he got through the intelligence office, showing the training of Turu Dalam gang members and their "day job": extorting money from mine owners and land owners to keep trade unions out of the mines. There are some exclusive short clips on smuggling of precious stones and rough diamonds, sound bits of carriers who deliver these packets of loot within the region.

In the last video clip, there's a three-wheeler van filled with young men from the village, their faces are expressionless and blank, as if they were being taken to die. Shyla gives Anand an enquiring look.

"Human shields. The gang members go to remote villages and persuade young men to show their allegiance to the movement. Instead they use these boys as human shields at their base, which is surrounded by landmines. The villagers are aware of their misuse but there's nothing they can do about it: if they don't go they get shot in their village outright, if they go they at least have the hope not to be blown away..."

"This is barbaric!" Shyla has no other words for it, she's horrified.

"And despite all these informers and information you still don't know where exactly their hideout is?"

Anand shows her more pictures of the actual place and some maps but shake his head.

"It's somewhere in the very dense part of the jungle... almost impossible to get to. Not to mention the tribal support. Even before we can get anywhere close, chances are we will get ambushed by militants who are stationed at various strategic points. The militants are sons of this very soil and therefore can map every tree, every water body in these amazons of India. So far all information we have is based on photos Neil has sent us when he was there and before you ask, yes, on his private business. But his private business was the only way he had to go and meet Debraj right inside his den, without him we would still be shooting in the dark"

"Does Neil know how to get to them?"

"I doubt it. He always told me that when they take him there he's blindfolded and I have no reason to doubt it, it makes a lot of sense: he is just someone they do business with, not one of them, why should they trust him? Shyla, something tells me you're digging too deep into this. I know why you do it, but as a friend I suggest you not to go too deep down this road. It's way too dangerous"

Shyla smiles and would like to say something but at the same time she doesn't want to lie to him. So far Anand has been the most sincere person she has met: he hasn't hidden any truths from her and has been upfront about everything, she wants to reassure him but the only way to do it is by lying to him, which she can't do.

Fortunately Raghav comes to rescue her as he storms into the room with his new kite shouting that it works so well and that they should come out and see it themselves. Anand smiles and follows him. Shyla lingers in the room where Raghav, while running in, has bumped into a pile of files that are now scattered onto the floor. One of them reads in black capital letters "Neil Mahajan".

In Pokhara Neil enters the usual pub, the one he always goes to and which until the last time looked so familiar. Today as he walks in he is welcomed by a somewhat metallic voice singing a rock song in English with a Nepalese accent. Is it Wanderwal by Oasis? It could be... the accent is so strong it took him a while before realizing the song actually in English.

He takes a look around, what before meeting Shyla looked cosy and at the same time adventurous -an obscure bar in Pokhara with live music at any time of the day and night, where a Chinese twenty year old waits for him and where obscure businessmen sit at the tables waiting to strike a deal on something that is more likely to be illegal than not- now just looks sad. The adventure is gone leaving room to an emptiness filled with metallic music.

Neil looks around him and sees the colours faded and things for what they really are: the singer is just a woman waiting to be picked by one of the men at the tables, the so called businessmen are only the henchmen of someone more powerful who can't be bothered to come to this no man's land.

He sits at his usual table, looking around and noticing for the first time a bunch of red roses dried up in a beer glass, reminds him of tourists that he himself must have picked up in his wild drunk days, probably.

Xian approaches with her usual cheerfulness, she's twenty, and she's not bound to acknowledge decadence around her for another ten years at least. To her this place is a playground, she knows everyone, she's safe as everyone knows she's untouchable due to her father's influence and therefore she plays like a child. She has prostitutes on the barstools instead of dolls on the bar shelf, and patrons instead of school friends coming for cheap scotch, she has got tourists who are smashed and want more fun, but who cares? She's the owner of her doll's house, she makes the rules and she breaks them!

"Old Monk on the rocks... just the way you like it"

Neil downs his drink and passes the glass back to Xian without even looking at her.

"Same... no wait... double"

"What's her name?"

Neil lifts his eyes and stares at Xian, he is surprised but just for a second, he then pretends to ignore her but the damage is done, she knows. She's disappointed; somehow she always hoped she could be the one who would drag him sad and lonely, lost in the pain of love, to a bar to talk to an expressionless bartender. Today the bartender is her, which means she can't be the cause of his broken heart. But Xian is young and yet smart, no heartbreak lasts forever: if he's here it means he's not with her, there's room yet for pretty Xian if she plays her cards well.

"That look on your face... you don't fool me lover boy, do you know how many people like you I see here every day? Dozens! Come on spill, what's her name? Did she break your heart?"

While saying so she slides the glass with a generous refill back to him, he takes it and downs it again.

"Told you before. I ain't got no time for a woman. Women are only good to screw up a man's life... Except for you little one, you are a saviour..."

"Cut the crap, Neil, I know you. She's screwed you real bad, hasn't she? Well, she must be something..."

Neil is unmoved. He feels Shyla's touch in the confines of his memory. She is soft yet steely. She is gentle yet fierce. She is the not the girl of his dreams yet she is.

A Chinese waiter comes and whispers something into Xian's ear she nods and pats him on the shoulder.

"He's here. In the basement"

Neil is a little tipsy now but he pulls himself up and tries to regain his balance before he goes down. This is an important meeting, he shouldn't have drunk but he needed to clear Shyla out of his head. Wipe the memory out and wash it down with a generous amount of rum, the vintage one Xian keeps only for him. It goes without saying that he hasn't, the rum has only heightened the fact that he has created such a huge wall between him and Shyla that chances of seeing her again are impossible. There has been too much of an exchange of anger and hatred. Bad timing. Bad choices.

Of course he doesn't know about Anand meeting Shyla, about him telling her who he really is, all he knows is that he left her on the riverbank and that most likely she has gone back to her business, whatever her business is, wherever it is. Cape Town? Delhi? New York? Who is to say?

A doubt cuts his breath for a second: has she made it out of the jungle? He has read all the newspaper in the last two days, if anything happened they should have written something, but again, she looks Indian, no one would know she is a foreigner, and people die in the jungle all the time. But Anand knew about her, he doesn't know her personally but Neil has asked him to run a background check on her, he hasn't received an answer yet but if anything had happened to her he would have told him... Right?

As he walks down the stairs Neil curses his stubbornness and his inability to say things as they are, his urge to run away everytime someone tries to know him better, to attempt to love him. He's afraid to love and to be loved because all the people whom he loved have died. He has come to the conclusion that if he really loves her he must let her go, not just let, but push her away, because if she stays anywhere near him she's bound to die, like everyone else. He is doomed.

Before entering the room he takes a deep breath and tries to go back to the old arrogant Neil everyone knows here. A man of his existence wears different masks, which he needs to change at the drop of a hat. Neil with a thousand faces is what he believes. He pinches his ears, a trick he uses to get sober in a flash.

"Let's go Neil... it's Showtime... yet again... for love and glory..."

CHAPTER 22

Neil enters the basement where Gao Yee, a Chinese guy, evidently already high on drugs and who likes to play the dude-gangster, is waiting for him.

Gao Yee greets him and checks him out to see where he's hiding the product, that's how they call it "product" as if it were some sort of product that you find anywhere.

The guy is unusually tall for a Chinese and has long hair that he keeps tight behind his back; he is wearing a white singlet that highlights his small but strong muscles covered in tattoos. Neil sees a huge dragon crawling down his right shoulder and some Chinese writing on the other arm.

The guys moves jerkily, constantly touching his nose and his arms, as if he was the only one who could see insects climbing up his forearms.

The dude is drugged to the bones, I better get the business done soon and get out of here. Not a good day to listen to a Chinese tripping...

Neil hands him the package and Gao Yee opens it greedily, his eyes spark when he sees the cluster of the gems, pieces of alexandrite cumulatively as big as a fist, something very few lucky people have seen before. A lot of work has gone to accumulate these.

After having handed out the package Neil lingers, he wants to stay long enough to convince the guy that it's good stuff, if he leaves early it might look that Neil is cheating, only God knows if junkies are paranoid.

Neil's gaze falls on the table where Gao Yee has made himself comfortable with a few lines of cocaine, or whatever he shoots up his nose, a few joints and a pipe of opium. Gao Yee lifts his eyes from the stones and sees Neil looking at the table.

"Oh, I'm sorry, so rude of me, help yourself..."

"No, thanks... I need to head back to my dear country"

The tension is palpable, even if Neil doesn't know why the rivalry between the two – in the end they are both only here for business- takes many shapes, including that of patriotism.

"Yeah...right. Don't worry... The Chinese will destroy it before you know it... they have some interesting plans going on there..."

"Yeah, yeah... I feel I have heard this story many times before... We'll see what they are able to do, as far as I know all attempts have led to fiascos..."

Gao Yee stumbles closer to Neil and points his finger at him, his attempt is quite clearly to be menacing but the fact that he's totally lost in his trip doesn't help his purpose.

"I ain't joking, brother. The big invasion is coming part by part... you won't know what hit you until it's over"

Neil wonders if Gao knows something he doesn't, but he keeps a foot in every shoe in India, he knows that if something was to happen so soon Anand would have told him. Anand shared his intelligence and gave him warnings on prior occasions. No, Anand doesn't know. This looks like the external Maoists' at work... But they fight for a greater cause; destroying India would only mean a huge deployment of resources and a great risk for a very slim chance of success. Or maybe it's for illegal trade. But again, this is only his conjecture, it may very well be either case, but this junkie is too unreliable to make an official report on what he says.

"I feel it's your cheap Chinese heroin that's talking, try this: Indian stuff, it may clear your mind" and hands him a small white packet.

Gao Yee looks at him intensely, he may have gone too far with this one, Gao's eyes are flaming and because Neil doesn't know if he's unarmed -Xian generally checks, but this is China vs. India, he doesn't know where she stands- and Neil feels he has to bring the tension down. He throws a red gem at him, Gao fetches it and looks at it against the light bulb, then parts his lips in that awful grin of his.

"Ok Let me tell you a little secret, Mister India..."

Gao bends down to sniff a line on the little table then, as he tries to stand up again he loses balance and falls on the beanbag. He opens his eyes and looks at Neil, who stares back at him with an inquiring look.

"So?"

"So check this out..." he throws his phone at Neil who presses play on the video that Gao has selected for him.

The video portrays two Chinese men planning a bombing of an Indian politician; the quality of the video is poor, as one of those videos shot by terrorists in the Middle East or in South America. Neil is not at ease as he can't understand if this is a real thing or something that this idiot of Gao Yee has put together himself. In his mind Neil keeps going back to Anand, should he get in touch and let him know or would it be a false alarm?

The conversation between the two Chinese guys has English subtitles, strangely enough; perhaps for trade of international secrets, Neil listens to an extract of it.

"C4 plastic, grenade launcher, automatic guns, the works. Delivered without a glitch. Inform the office?"

"Sure the show is on"

"Never let you down before, have I? Who are you blowing up this time?"

The older guy shows a picture which is not shown in the video "Oh... he is some minister"

"Who is assigned to the job?"

"The most dangerous guy in that region, effective rate-ninety percent"

The video is over and Neil is left without an answer, he looks at Gao with and inquiring look.

"Who?"

"Can't tell you, brother. Wait and see"

The Chinese waiter enters the room with a plate of momos and leaves them on the table in front of Gao, he looks at them and then screams something in Chinese that frightens the poor guy who scampers away like a rat faced with a cat.

Neil can't quite make out who this Gao Yee is, he must be someone's son if he is so powerful despite his young age and the abuse of drugs but he knows too little about Chinese gangs to figure out who he might be.

Gao loads the opium pipe and rolling a joint, it's pretty clear that their conversation is over, Neil turns around to walk away but, unexpectedly considering how much drugs Gao has inside him, he jumps up from his beanbag and grabs Neil by the shoulder. Neil looks at him intensely.

"One of your terror gangs in India has already received the stuff... highly explosive stuff... the clock is ticking... ahahahaah... tick tock... tick tock..."

"Which gang?"

But Gao is already too lost in his trip to hear him or even acknowledge his presence.

Neil walks away with a strong sense of foreshadowing, what is going to happen? How reliable were those people? Why the subtitles in English?

He is confused and his mind goes back to Anand, should he let him know, what if it's true?

Then all of a sudden, like an arrow striking through his brain the thought of Shyla comes back to him. Where is she now?

Neil sets his tent by the lake, the sound of water has always been soothing to him, and tonight more than ever he needs to be pampered, if not by someone at least by something.

He sits on a bench, looks at the full moon that has never seemed bigger. People come here to camp, from all over the world, without knowing what happens a few kilometres from here. He wonders if what Gao said is true and what the tourists would think if a bomb exploded right near their happy tents with lots of comforts and inflatable mattresses.

Without thinking his hand slips into his pocket and digs out the *Pachisi* dice that follows him everywhere. He rolls them in his hand; it's a soothing gesture that he has done all his life, something that makes him feel better whenever he is down.

He remembers when he was just a boy, his parents had died and his brother took care of him, they would play *Pachisi* to decide who was to do what in the house: dishwashing? *Pachisi!* Cooking? *Pachisi!* And the worst of it all... Laundry? *Pachisi!* His brother was a lot better than him, maybe he knew a trick or two, and always won so he was left him with the housework.

Neil has an especially fond memory of his brother who, just back from police service and still wrapped up in his uniform, came home and called him outside to play *Pachisi.*

The dice were all worn out by now but to Neil they were like an amulet. Strangely enough they were among the few things that hadn't burned in that dreadful fire that killed his big brother.

Neil remembers it only too well, that day of six years ago... He was at the police academy begging his brother to get his annual leave at the same time as his so they could spend time together, by then Anil had a higher rank and had been assigned to escort politicians around the region. His days of leave were more and more scarce but he still tried all he could to spend as much time as possible with his little brother.

Neil remembers the last word Anil said and his bright laugh, he remembers the blast and then the phone going mute, he knew, he was sure, that if his brother had expected something like that to happen he would have not laughed that way.

For the first few hours this was of great comfort, the phone must have just fallen somewhere and the connection had been cut. But then a call arrived; he was called in the Superintendent's office, who also delivered the news with the most plain and dull voice Neil remembered having ever heard.

"I'm sorry young man" that was all he had said.

Anil, his brother, his whole family had just been blown up and the only thing this old turtle was able to say was "I'm sorry young man". For Neil this was more than a good reason to leave and seek justice on his own.

The army, the police, took for granted that some of their officers were going to die, but this is India, there are a lot of people, a lot of them who are charmed or pushed by their families into the armed forces, who cares if some Anil Mahajan and his men die in a blast?

Neil became a sort of renegade, travelling the states around in search of a good business until the day he accidentally stepped onto the Turu Dalam. He remembers his days when he would visit the Deobhog region in Chhattisgarh to purchase gemstones from the locals at dirt-cheap rates. One evening he made friends with a couple of Rebels over drinks and then perpetually landed up doing business with them. With the patience of the spider he knitted his web, did business and shared their life as much as he could to juice all their secrets and sell them to the only person who really was committed to closing this bloody, never ending, match: Anand.

The day he met Anand for the first time in a social gathering, there was conflict to begin with but when Neil saw the honesty and passion in Anand, it instantly reminded him of his elder brother. Neil felt immediately drawn to him cause Anand had the same values as his brother. Neil gave him the secrets and as he got back on his motorbike, which had once been Anil's, he said, "Information will keep coming, just ask me what you want to know and I will fish it out. My only condition is that you don't step into my business. Are we clear?"

"Clear"

And so they sealed the deal and started a long friendship, if this is what you can call it. They had never been at each other's house -in fact Neil didn't even have one- but this was no common friendship, they were both survivors and dreamers in their own way, their friendship was based on principles more than on shared experiences.

A metallic sound brings him back to reality, his phone, he has just received a text message. ZEBRA TENT 6. He approaches a cluster of tents covered in black and white stripes that somehow remind the pattern on zebras, he finds number six and enters. Inside a man is lying on a bed twitching under a woman who is seducing him by dancing right above him with lingerie that leaves nothing to imagination. The light is red and everything -the tent, the furniture, the bed, even the skin of the two people- has a red shade.

Neil considers having gotten into the wrong tent but no, this is the one. Suddenly the man stands up and turns towards him but he is so heavily drugged he doesn't see him and falls back onto the bed. But Neil has recognized him, it's Gao Yee. And the woman is Xian, it's hard to tell because he has always seen her dressed but there's no doubt, it's her.

He leaves the tent and waits outside, after a couple of minutes he hears a numb sound, like something falling heavily onto the floor. He still has that gun... He could intervene, but Xian comes out of the tent as if nothing happened, she's wearing a long coat that covers her tall black boots and the see through lingerie. She hands him a piece of paper without saying anything. Neil opens it "Turu Dalam, chief: Debraj Roy". Neil stares at her in disbelief, she smiles back at him.

"Neil, when do I get my share of the barter...one night with you is all I am asking for..."

Neil smiles and looks at this girl who looks like any college girl but who also has a dense life behind her, even if Neil doesn't know what kind exactly.

"Xian, you are the sexiest bartender in the world... let's keep it at that for now and I would love to make love to you till eternity but strangely enough my heart doesn't agree with me… one of the few times when a man actually listens to his heart and not the crocodile between his legs" Neil hugs her tight. Xian is touched for the first time in her life.

"Till then you will remain in my dreams"

Xian blushes with a seductive smile and says nothing; she has got a dose of love that could last her for many moons to come. Neil winks at her and caresses her chin, holding in the other hand the piece of paper, the name is tattooed on his brain and there are no chances for him to forget it.

"As of now... unfinished business! What are you gonna do with the brute in there?"

"Neil what am I supposed to do? I'll go home and change and when tomorrow he'll come to the bar asking for more or claiming that I was lap dancing for him in one of the zebra tents my father's men will send him back to his boss in a small box!"

"Oh, so that's how you settle things huh? I feel I should change the watering hole, now that I know daddy's princess tactic..."

"Yeah nice try sexy boy, ours is the only pub in Pokhara, possibly in the whole of Nepal that has your rum... and the sexiest bartender that you can't resist even if you were a monk ...See you soon...Cris Columbus!"

"Xian..."

"Yessss?"

Xian gives him a parting look, this time it's piercing, sharp enough to melt a mountain.

"You are amazing as amazing can get... maybe some other world, some other lifetime, I am in crazy love with you!"

"Try Me".

Chapter 23

A woman inches on planks, a makeshift rope bridge, with a river flowing hundreds of metres below her, though distant she can hear the sound of the water galloping between the rocks and flowing downstream. The bridge is old, the wooden planks beneath her feet creak with her every movement and she's scared, but she's half way now, she needs to move on.

Her hands hold tight onto the ropes at the sides of the bridge, she can feel that her sweaty palms tend to slide over the rope but her nails claw into it, sharpened by fear. She's young, she wears a white shirt that right now is glued to her back due to her profuse sweating: the weather is hot and humid and the sun on this very spot is merciless: it shines upon her making her very skin evaporate.

She stops to look at the beautiful scenery, if her life wasn't in danger right now this would be the perfect spot for breath-taking shots of the surroundings: around her are the two cliffs end in an intense red wall of clay and the red is made even more powerful by the contrast with the greenery above it. It looks like the jungle has been cut into two by a very sharp knife and the trees are indulging at the very end of the cut, a relishing red cake with green glazing that, in the heat, is starting to melt.

Suddenly her hand softens the grip and the sweat between the skin and the rope makes it glide, panic strikes her and makes her hurry to the end of the bridge, her camera, hanging from her neck, feels so heavy she can barely move and at once she misplaces her foot, one wrong step and her life is hanging from a rope bridge. Amusingly enough she feels more pain for a bleeding scratch on her elbow than fear for the fall that is bound to happen soon. She's hanging by her hands, like a sinister monkey, hundreds of metres above an enraged river.

But when her hands can't keep the grip anymore and slide away slowly but relentlessly she feels life abandoning her little by little, until a strong hand, a man's hand, fresh and powerful, comes to her rescue and pulls her up as if she were weightless. She takes a breath of relief. Life saver!

Shyla wakes up screaming, in a pool of sweat, in her room. She's alone except a cat has entered from a window she had forgotten open and rested on the bed until she woke him up with her scream. She opens her eyes to find the room gently bathed in the pink sunlight of the dawn, it's early morning, and it was a dream, a nightmare, rather. A premonition?

She pulls herself up and sits on the bed, drinking a glass of water she had left on the coffee table the night before, it takes her a few minutes to regains control over herself.

This dream has brought up many memories, as if these were events that she lived herself and memories that her mind constructed about her mother, a toxic fusion. She hardly remembers her but sometimes she feels like she's her reincarnation. Shyla know it's not possible but some of the things she heard Father Thomas, say about her mother felt to her as if she herself was going through them. Ofcourse she has read about the recent scientific discovery of memory genes passing from one generation to the other, but can it be so pronounced.

Even the other night with Neil, that strange phantasm... was it a dream? It was a feeling, as if what was happening then had already happened before, as if she was following a pattern.

Where would this pattern take her? And most of all, was this pattern bound to finally give her insight on her life? The latent mind never projects any apparitions without a meaning, a message to decipher she learnt in her psychology class. Since she has heard Thomas's last words she has been pensive. Rather Anxious. About the precise words of the truth that threw her life out of balance. The revelation that she has a rapist father, a rebel leader, a mortal militant in the very jungles on which she is investigating for her report, gives her recurrent nightmares even in broad daylight. But her fear, the cloud of gloom is overlapped by a sense of identity crisis. The issue of identity never felt stronger than now: who is she? Who was she until ten days ago? Where does she go from here in the coming days, as the plot of her life gets thicker?

A tornado of shrill thoughts have haunted her since she left Cape Town: she took a small bag, the one she uses for field visits although she had the strong impression she may not return. Did all her life fit in the small suitcase?

Maybe it did. Only when she will stumble on her roots of hell will she be able to climb her paradise of solace. But if she was to stay here to discover her roots, what could she do here? This was a rural area she had no business in, she's a town girl, a westerner of sorts... Besides, she hasn't even had time to think if she really wants to pursue: things have happened so fast, so many faces and voices overlap and the photos in her camera –just a fraction of the things she really saw- could be enough to last a normal person a lifetime.

What is she after? Truth? And provided that she finds it, will she be strong enough to handle it, no matter what comes out of it? With this question in mind she closes her eyes and slips back into sleep. Disturbed and Distorted.

At the same time while Shyla is struggling with her inner demons, other demons, more tangible ones and surely as dangerous, are testing a new weapon in the depth of the heart of this brutalized jungles of Dantewada in the south of Bastar.

Kedar Sing gets stirred up in the middle of the night with an idea; he woke Debraj up to help him put it into practice.

Too many of their men have died recently and something must be done or there will be no Turu Dalam left in a few months.

Kedar walks out in the faint light of pre-dawn, to find a wild cat in his porch, the cat comes here at night because Kedar always leaves him something to eat. They are both wild, they are both predators, and over time this tubby wild cat, that would scare anyone else in the world, has become somewhat domesticated. Kedar pours some milk in a plastic bowl and the cat drinks it as if he really was a pet. While Kedar plays with his dangerous toy -once again- Debraj is working on something, sitting on one of the benches outside and looking at both the wild animals with a certain apprehension. Debraj has mixed feelings about Kedar, he does think he is on the right side but at the same time doesn't approve of his abuse of violence. Everything for Kedar is measured in how much blood is spilled and Debraj, probably because of his past as scholar, would prefer a different approach. Sometimes he manages to talk him into it and sometimes he doesn't and when this happens, and dozens of people die Debraj can see a terrifying spark in Kedar's eye, like a hungry wolf more interested in hunting for the brutality of it then just to satisfy hunger.

As the cat is enjoying the cuddles of his master Debraj passes Kedar a red Velcro collar, like a dog collar with a small device attached to it. Kedar puts it around the neck of his friend, possibly his only friend, and reaches for a mousetrap under one of the benches. The prey is a rather large rat, brown and with the enquiring little eyes of all wild animals trapped in a box.

Kedar extracts it, pulling it out of the cage from its long tail and lets it run.

The whiskers of the cat vibrate with anxiety, he has been domesticated enough to wait until his master allows him to eat, or hunt in this case, but he is still a wild animal and his instinct tells him that this rat is fat enough to make a good meal.

The rat squats around the porch unsure where to go, inside the house there is food but the tough luck already forced it into a cage once, better not try again. It finally heads for the forest, the rat darts into the wilderness. Kedar gives it a little advantage and then pats the cat on the back: free to go. Hunting games.

He doesn't have to give him a second pat as the animal has already snapped into the forest with a long jump and he's after his succulent meal. The forest goes back to its white noise like it was time for Nature to meditate.

A few seconds pass before Debraj and Kedar hear a blast, the explosion was so strong it made a couple of young trees fall, a piece of furry flesh lands at Kedar's feet, on the porch. His wild cat.

Debraj looks at him because he knows that this war forces them to make decisions that affect their lives profoundly, it makes them grow fond of places, animals and small things as if they were people to befriend.

Kedar has sacrificed his pet to a greater cause, and he is likely to bring this scar on him for a very long time, thinks Debraj.

But Debraj thinks like a human being, with a brain and a heart, and although he has done many bad things in life he still knows the difference between good and bad, he can use his rationale, Kedar is beyond that, he is the incarnation of evil, by evil, for evil.

In fact, he smells the bleeding piece of flesh with relish and looks at the burning patch in the jungle with a satisfied air.

"Well, at least we are sure it works now! Make ten more and try and make them more powerful!"

Neil presses on the motorbike accelerator, the Rpm reading hits the red. With his mission achieved and with a hot potato to deliver right into Anand's hands Neil crosses the border again, rides through the desolate no man's land, same scene: he stops briefly, hands some cash to a Zamindaar who smiles happily flashing his bright golden tooth to the world. This is one of the security cracks of the Border security force. Neil is accustomed with these fragmented in-routes to enter India and to and fro.

Neil takes a deep breath, releases his tension, and uplifts his spirits with self-affirmation thoughts. He is back in India, back home, he has never felt so Indian like he does today, the road he has travelled a million times before and always found dull is now a welcoming path to his glorious return. He notices the small things and loves all of them. He is high on the adrenaline released into him by Gao Yee and on the excitement for what could possibly be a final round of this bloody war. They have a strong advantage, two in fact: they know whom to look for and they can also act undisturbed, as the Turu Dalam doesn't know that they are onto them.

As soon as he arrives in Chhattisgarh he knows exactly where to go, he parks his motorbike in a rather empty parking lot and saunters a short distance to the black SUV parked in the corner.

He ducks in, the smell of clean leather and with a comfortable seat under him for the first time in days he takes a concentrated breath, as soon as he focuses though he notices Shyla's camera.

She's here, she has been here, has she told Anand about them? Does she even care about them? What is "them" anyway? Was it just a one-night stand for her? What else could it be… he is the one who pushed her away pointing a gun to her neck? Idiot, idiot, idiot!

"I see she's befriended you as well..." he drops it casually, trying to master his voice.

Anand doesn't understand at first, then he sees Shyla's camera and understands.

"Oh that! Yes, great girl, isn't she? The friendly kind. Lots of passion. She definitely knows her shit, right?"

Neil laughs. The word passion rings in his mind with a stereo effect. He looks for something in the car that might become the next object of the conversation. He looks around until he sees a passport photo of Raghav.

"How's your boy? I forgot his name"

"Raghav, yeah, he's doing well... getting a bit cheeky about Shyla.

"Life is such..."

"Oh we got a philosopher fresh from Nepal... What's this talk about life? What you got for me today?

"A hell of a lot"

Anand gets a call on his cell that interrupts the conversation, it's not work, notices Neil, and otherwise he wouldn't be smiling at the name of the screen.

"Yes, Shyla. Yes, you left it in my car. I can drop it off... Actually why don't you join Raghav and me for a film tonight? Sure, we'll pick you up… we can do the tea later"

Anand's voice is slightly unstable, he's not stammering and master's pretty well the conversation, but a thought just crossed his mind. Shyla and Neil. He's on duty, what he's supposed to do is be professional, but his cranium seems to be filling with a liquid that numbs his brain, slowly but inevitably. *Shyla and Neil, of course, she's brilliant, he's an Indian Indiana Jones, and how could I be so naive to think that she might be interested in a kid, a garden and a dog in the heart of a Maoist ridden state of India? She wants to travel, take a bike and not follow a map, she wants to feel the wind in her hair and the taste of different foods, wake up on a mountain and go to sleep on a beach, and I am dedicated to my duty, what could I ever offer her?*

What he doesn't know, and at this point can't even expect, is that Shyla is genuinely debated, unsure which road to take. As a matter of fact the confusion stems from the fact that she is not prepared to be in a relationship with any man as of now. She has some personal digging to do, and only that can bring her liberation and make her feel complete. The irony is- does Shyla read her own inner thoughts! What she doesn't know is that her dilemma stems from the fact that her unconscious mind is desperately-seeking revenge. She is being manipulated by the longing to confront her rapist father. But first she needs to find him. So where do these two men stand in the midst of a battle that she is covertly nursing, nowhere, till she meets her summit of redemption.

On the other hand Anand feels that the car is consumed with male hormones, of course they are well-behaved, professional men, but deep down, their instincts would push them to establish here and now who the alpha dog is. Neil is rigid at once: he pretends to be listening, distracted by something that interests him outside, but deep down he's burning. This job is the most important thing he has: it's his chance to quench his thirst for justice that has haunted him for years, he has sacrificed everything to pursue it and he can't let anything, or anyone, stand between him and his revenge. Payback, rather. Right now Anand is his best friend and his worst enemy, he'll have to make do and postpone any conflict to whenever the mission is over. In the crucial times of vengeance, love can wait.

Anand hangs up and looks at Neil with an inquiring look as if nothing happened, Neil tries to keep calm and not look jealous -jealous of what?- but he's lost in his thought and Anand has to encourage him. "Sorry, you were saying?" Two men distracted by the same woman, need to focus on a larger goal. Many lives are at stake; the future of this district will be fairly dependant on these two men with a serious responsibility.

Neil explains what he has heard and what he has seen, who he has seen in particular, as this Gao Yee is someone new but not as powerful, considering that Xian's father can kick his ass if he wants to. Anand notices a spark of animosity when Neil mentions the name of Turu Dalam and its mastermind Debraj Roy. The plan is not clear but they have enough elements to work on something, first and foremost: where are they exactly located, to ambush them in the dense jungle is an impossibility, so how can they be pulled out from their comfort zones!

Anand listens in silence and nods whenever Neil comes up with a reflection of his own.

When Neil is done and has told everything he knows and could possibly think of to Anand, Anand doesn't look as worried as Neil thought he should be, he simply says: "Ok, I have a plan".

As he leaves the car, opening the door with a clack, Neil indulges on Shyla's camera, only a second, and his heart skips a beat. He can almost smell her scent lingering on the car seats.

"I wonder..."

"I'm sorry?" Asks Anand, unnerved with Neil's curiosity.

"I wonder, why we keep killing each other internally, why not unite against a common enemy, across the border, if there is one..."

"It's a tough question..."

"... to which you don't have an answer right?"

"Well I'm kind of late and you come up with philosophical questions..."

"Leave it, go to your date..."

"Neil look..."

"No it's ok, I have a reason for engaging in this war, a motivation, a cause to fight for, and for you it's a job. Depending on who your boss is you'll obey one or the other as soon as the wind changes. If you really wanted to catch the Naxals you would have a long time ago, there's evidently someone ordering you not to do what you guys should do, there is a hidden agenda by political forces, internal or external"

"I think this conversation is slipping out of hand and we should part to do our separate duties"

"Of course, I'll keep you posted"

"Neil..."

"Yes boss?"

"I'm not your boss Neil. You know why I'm doing it, you know where Raghav comes from, you know it all, so please don't let anger or jealousy cloud your vision. We are two professionals, two of the few honest ones in this country, if you have something to say, say it"

"No, it's ok... I'll see you around"

Neil leaves the car and walks away with his hands deep down in his pockets while Anand looks at him, debating if he should confront him straight away or pretend he doesn't know what Neil was talking about. He knows only too well, but he's running late: Raghav is waiting and together they'll have to go pick up Shyla and cross town to make it to the movies. But there are new developments on the work front and they can't be ignored. A lot is at stake but he will have to wait for Neil to execute his bit. Stick to the original plan- his rationale mind guides him. Get more intelligence.

He starts the engine and speeds, leaving behind a cloud of speckle.

CHAPTER 24

Neil enters the secret base of Turu Dalam. He looks at the thick trees that surround the area so well that even the sharpest of American satellite cameras won't be able to detect this hideout. He wonders how far are the landmines and how do these guys map it. Two recruits come and hold him tight as he alights the motorbike that he was brought on. His is frisked once more. They remove his blindfold and escort him to Debraj's den. Neil is more determined than ever to get a clue, a hint of Turu Dalam's plan of action. He looks around with hawk eyes but fails to gather any useful observation. The only beneficial inspection is that of Gopal's presence. Gopal an old recruit shares camaraderie with Neil. At one point of time Gopal used to escort Neil on the motorbike and they got friendly over Kishore Kumar songs. Gopal ignores Neil this time cause he and his teammates are being instructed by Kedar to service some Chinese guns. Kedar shoots a few rounds in the air to check their mechanisms. As the leaves get dented, sunlight pours in.

Neil enters a closed room. His eyes take a while to get used the dim light: an old radio set, green like the moss that seems to be growing all around them, is on the table, spitting out rocky sounds. The table itself has been taken from a school, or a pillaged office, after a more careful look Neil realizes that everything in this place has been taken from elsewhere. A left over furniture, something no one has chosen and is only functional to the purpose of storing things. "If you have interior decoration advice I'd be glad to take it..."

Taken aback Neil takes a second too long to answer and, as he turns to Debraj he realizes he looked around for a minute too long: Debraj was looking at him this whole time. His shoes creak on the floor, which crumbles like dry bread under each one of his steps, from the broken windowpane a strange breeze fights its way in. The room is frugal, more frugal than he had expected, and still a massive box styled TV screen camps right in the middle of a brown wall with red flairs, remains of *paan*, and some sketchy drawing pinned on one wall. Neil spends an extra second to notice the sketch of a concrete structure that looks like some government institution. His memory fails him to recognise the rectangular, single story building. The sketch in dried charcoal makes it more difficult to pinpoint. Neil pretends to look uninterested in the trappings of the workplace. The room smells of chai, incense and cigarette smoke. Debraj is sitting lavishly on a wooden armchair, his red scarf around his neck, as always, and a young prospect sitting tidily next to him with a big book and a pen in front of him. He has several piles of money on the desk and Neil notices how this young and skinny guy looks so different, so much better, than the old fox on the armchair.

Of course Neil doesn't approve of any kind of terrorism, but he has always been particularly gutted by the fact that these people were so greedy and disgusting to turn what started like an idealistic revolution into a horrifying carnival.

People like Debraj, educated, with ideas, different from his own, ok, but who has deliberated about them and decided what road to take, turned out to be just like any ruffian, sitting down on what they could make by smuggling and robbing and forgetting all they had wished to fight for.

Money can turn into a bad thing, it adulterates your soul and the more you have the more you want. But where to put the full stop is a quest, a choice that changes fate. Neil ponders.

Neil opens the package with the assortment of precious gemstones roll on the table before Debraj's eyes, they are quickly lit by a spark. Neil lifts one and gapes at it against the light: the reflections are bright that Debraj can't contain his excitement. But he does his best to do so, this is a negotiation, by not displaying any feelings he might bring the price down.

"Hey Professor, you must have seen plenty of these huh?"

"You could say so..." his voice trembles, he has given himself away.

"Even the big one?"

Debraj doesn't answer.

"You know, the 50 carat- the famous colour changing Alexandrite? I heard it has been found. Perhaps it's somewhere here..."

"I like your attitude but I don't approve of your curiosity. Curiosity killed the cat, as they say" retorts Debraj trying to regain his position of predominance. He sips his tea slowly, looking at Neil as a lion looks at the gazelle drinking from the river.

"In any case, I don't fight this battle for personal vanity, I trade in gemstones and diamonds for funds, if I find it and you have a buyer I will call you first... You know why I allow you to come here, right? Because some day... Time will make you come to your senses and you will enrol in our mission..."

"Time is a mystical abstract, Dai. It runs out if you don't live in the moment... Now is all I have… I'm not a long-term-commitment kind of guy, in fact, to answer your question about my taste for design, I don't even have a house"

Neil stands up ready to go, having cashed his money. He didn't want to risk his life by probing into Debraj's affairs. Debraj gestures to his guard. The armed guard who stood by the door snaps towards him and before he can open the door ties the blindfold around his head.

"Never forget: time gives you an opportunity to finish the unfinished"

"And you don't forget my young friend, it's Debraj who controls time... tick tock, tick tock..."

Debraj continues "and now it's time for you go Neil. But be careful in the forest, I have heard that some deadly pack of wolves are on the prowl so stay silent". Neil gets the hint and assures Debraj, the touch of dollars is all he needs to survive. Neil is escorted on the motorbike with blindfold intact. Debraj picks up his phone after making sure that nobody is around.

Purba inside her den chants a verse in front of a tribal deity by the name of Kaali. The inconspicuous hideout is part of a mud capped, circular bunker scooped out of the red soil. The roof is aptly camouflaged with shrubbery. Purba wrapped in a transparent loincloth is all by herself, with Chinese lanterns for company. Her comrades are waiting on the outside of the small stone temple where she had locked herself to perform the daily ritual. Every evening a goat is sacrificed in front of the blackstone deity and the meat is cooked and served as a meal to all her gang members. She has been taught the ancient Mantra by a tantric guru who resides in a cave on the other end of the forest. Back then Purba was just a new recruit anointed by Debraj. She was poor yet power hungry. In order to pay her fees known as *'Guru dakshina'*, she seduced the tantric all night. The tantric gave in to the dark rustic beauty. After the series of orgasms, the tantric warned her of any misuse of the powers that he has taught her to gain strength. Purba shot back at him with a smirk "I will seduce death if it comes for me, I am the demon, that even angels will dread". That day she improvised on her attitude. That day she seduced the devil in the confines of her own mind. Since then there was no looking back. Debraj recognised her daredevilry and thus Purba grew in notoriety as the merciless militant, more daring than the male gang members. Today she stands tall in front of the devil goddess. The red lanterns that illuminate her lean and precise body, cast a shadow on the walls that represent a serpent. Purba's prayers are interrupted by the vibrations of her cell phone parked on the muddy floor. Purba's irritation subsides when she sees 'Sir D' as the name flashing on the screen. Debraj is standing on an elevated watchtower from where he can keep a hawk's eye on his camp. He is quick to enquire about the Alexandrite, a task that he has assigned to his most favoured leader. Purba is caught off guard but being a cold, sharp woman she does not lose her composure. In a confident tone that echoes inside the temple cubicle she responds, "Like a hungry jackal, I am gunning for the 50 carat beauty and very soon I will nail the guy who is apparently sitting on it. I have my informers working tirelessly. But you have to stick to your side of the promise once I find it." Debraj has locked his eyes on Kedar who is secretly snorting some dope behind a bush. He replies nonchalantly "As soon as you find the 50 carat lottery ticket I will make plans for the two of us to escape to Bangkok. We can operate from there. We will play the bigger, sophisticated game. I guess I have found my fall guy. He is currently making love to some wild bushes". Purba's hormonal levels shoot up and she replies "It gets lonely staying with women all the time". She further lures Debraj in a husky tone "it's been a while". Debraj tries to maintain restraint but his voice gives in "yeah it's been a while" and he hangs up abruptly. Purba holds on to the precious 'Alexandrite' wrapped inside the jute bag, tagged on her naked body. She rubs it against her chest seductively and whispers to the dead stone "idiot, he thinks I will betray you for him". She kisses the hard rock with real passion "Honey I will make sure I die with you resting on my breasts, I have yet to find a man worthy of you, perhaps" Strangely a flash of Neil's face comes to her evil mind. She brushes off this hidden feminine side- "no friggin way".

At nine sharp Anand's black SUV pulls over in front of the Victorian building, which is the cinema hall. A banner of a Bollywood film hangs with the poster of Shahrukh Khan as 'Don 2'. Next to brightly bulb lit façade, the hazy signboard of the cinema reads as 'Jeet talkies'. Shyla gets off and tries to help Raghav who is profoundly offended.

"I'm seven, you think I can't jump out of the car?"

"I just thought... I mean it's so high! I have trouble getting on and off myself!"

"Yeah yeah, because you are a woman!"

"Raghav, what did we talk about last time?" interrupts Anand with a strong tone.

"Ok, I'm sorry, you are a lady, but I will be a policeman you see... I need to train and be agile!"

Shyla laughs as Raghav runs towards the theatre, Anand gets closer to her and whispers "Teaching manners to a seven year old boy who lives in Chhattisgarh is no easy task, I'm telling you!"

"Haha, I guess..."

The trio enters the cinema, with Raghav hurrying them, he doesn't want to miss even one minute of the action movie!

Anand goes to buy pop-corn and when he comes back they all take their places, Raghav sits in the middle with the huge paper bucket on his lap, and the movie starts while three hands dig in the white fluffy pop-corn.

At the same time Neil reaches home. It's an old concrete villa with no paint. He lied to Debraj, but it was only half a lie, this place belongs to him, true, but he has never done anything to make it his place: despite seeing how run down it is he has never thought of renovating it. Whenever he thinks of settling down the old memory of his brother comes up: if he will ever love again the person he loves might die. Neil is haunted by this curse.

As he enters the house two shadows approach. Two members of the Turu Dalam. One of them is Gopal.

Gopal thanks Neil for calling him home for drinks after a long day's work. Working under Kedar's direct supervision is a daunting task for all recruits. Gopal and his colleague trust Neil cause they have seen him doing business with their leader-Debraj. Infact they know that whenever Neil invites them over, it's their only opportunity to taste some scotch. A generous helping of scotch to men who barely get to drink country liquor is more than just a tempting offer. On a festive day a glass of Sulphi also known as Bastar Beer is what puts their grief to rest. Momentarily.

Neil lets them in as if they were friends; in the end they are just two lost souls like him. But this time Neil has an agenda. The house is dark and damp, a two story building that he has rented, which he had planned to redecorate for his brother's visit a few years back, but now has decayed with the callous Neil attitude. Weeds outside have grown so high to almost hide the house from the street, the perfect hide out if anyone was ever after him, but also a great way to disappear when he doesn't want to be found.

He turns the lights on and sees the faces of the two guys, young and starved, the future of the Turu Dalam is not twenty yet and has a swollen belly for having filled it with too much cheap alcohol and too little food. Depressing. Neil looks away, leaves his backpack in the hall without even thinking of emptying it -not tonight- and walks straight to the kitchen, opens the old fridge and discovers that most of the stuff has gone bad. He decides to go for the chicken and strange-smelling rice, which he mixes with a lot of spices to disguise the taste.

But if the food is scarce the drinks are poured generously, everything is washed down with a fair amount of imported scotch.

“Sorry guys, this is all I have in the house...”

“No worries, it’s far more than we are used to!” they both answer while digging into their chicken and ripping the bones clean. Neil refills their plastic glasses with double pegs of scotch.

“So I hear one of the big shots in Delhi will get his brain blown off one of these days...” he drops.

The two stop eating and exchange a glance. Their faces glow in the dim light as in the urge of filling their empty stomachs they have smeared the grease of the chicken all over their cheeks.

“Brother, all we know is that you reap what you sow. The so called ‘authorities’ sow the wrong seeds so they will have to pay for it... enough of taking this region for granted, they will know our might brother, this one’s gonna be a supernova, and from now on maybe they will take us more seriously”

The two-gang members raise their glass in jubilation and Neil forces himself to join them.

“When?”

“Tomorrow...”

“Shut up, Gopal!”

“Oops... I speak too much when I drink... where’s the loo?”

Gopal walks away and the other guy stays silent but Neil can see that talking about the attack has excited him so much he can hardly contain it. He only needs a spark to blow.

“What’s happening tomorrow, come on you can tell me, what if you need an extra hand?” asks Neil with a more paternal tone. He lifts his wallet and keeps it on the table. A few dollars slide out.

The young guy cannot hold it anymore and smiles broadly as he simply answers "Boom..." gesturing with his hands a great explosion.

Neil takes out a wad of cash from his wallet, *funny*, he thinks, *I took it from them a couple of hours ago and I'm giving it back to them now. And Debraj will never know.* The guy looks at the green dollar notes with greed in the midst of the whiskey smelling room. The notes seem to look bigger than what they are.

"Where?" the guy looks scared as he hears Gopal flush the toilet but at the same time his eyes shine in the dark and the sound all those banknotes make in Neil's hand. That same sound could come up of his very own palm...

"CRPF... don't ask me which cop station... I don't know" says the youth as he pockets the cash with grace, he takes it into his hand and makes it literally disappear up his sleeve.

Neil watches his movements, precise, spotless, and can't help thinking that this innocent looking guy must have already practiced a lot. This is definitely not the first time he sells information...

Gopal comes back from the toilet singing a Kishore Kumar song in Chhattisgarhi accent, the young guy joins in pretending to be a little more merry than he actually is, and Neil watches them as he walks towards the bathroom himself.

As soon as he's locked in he tries to call Anand.

In the movie theatre Anand feels the phone vibrate in his pocket, but there is no display of the name or the number. He looks at his cell phone's display but there's no network coverage in the theatre so he wonders whether he should try it outside.

"They shield places like this so that phones don't go off during the movie!" whispers Shyla in his ear.

Anand looks at her with his polite smile and nods. *In South Africa, maybe, but this in India...*

Shyla gives a warm pat on Anands shoulder. Anand feels the touch of a woman's gentle hands. His mind gets diverted to Shyla. The presence of a pretty woman sitting at a close proximity gives him a testosterone rush. He switches his mobile phone off.

Neil can't chase out of his head Anand's voice, soft and not strategizing, for once, "Why don't you join us?" join us where huh? Scenes of Anand and Shyla keep being generated by his imagination, he can't help it but everytime he thinks of him, even for work, the thought of her comes up, almost like a tsunami. He tries once again but Anand's phone is evidently not working, then he tries Shyla.

If they are together I can totally call her. I mean, it's for work, it's shouldn't get awkward. Yes it is awkward, but on the other hand what am I supposed to do, I'm trying to save lives here! But all his thinking is muted by the message on Shyla's phone "Sorry, the number you have dialled is currently unavailable". Neil is frustrated and by this point also concerned, there's no time to waste. Not a minute. He flushes the toilet and goes back to the room where the two-gang members are preparing to leave while still singing that song in a terrible tone.

Gopal is drunk; he takes the bottle with him, wraps the leftover chicken in a piece of paper and shoves it deep into his pocket. He looks at Neil with a strange look, as if to say "I know you don't mind if we take this for the road... How could you mind?"

The younger guy is singing, he's apparently drunk too, but Neil knows that he can't have gotten drunk so fast, he has only been in the bathroom a few minutes and the guy was very lucid when he made the money disappear inside his sleeve.

Out of the movie theatre Anand, Raghav and Shyla look like any other family, the sadness on Anand's face has faded out, for the first time since Shyla met him, he looks relaxed. Out of sheer joy, he even attempts to whistle a tune from the movie. They get in the car and Raghav can't stop talking about all the action, he jumps on the backseat. *"Don ko pakadna mushkil hee nahi namumkin hain"* Raghav quotes Shahrukh Khan from the movie.

"The movie was really fun, huh champ?" asks Shyla

"Yeah makes you forget all the bad times!"

Anand remembers that his phone rang once within bad network and takes it out of his pocket to check who called.

"Oh great, network is back"

There are six missed call alerts from Neil, this can only mean bad news.

Anand calls him back immediately but at the other end Neil is snoring on his bed, still dressed and with the bottle he keeps "for the bad times" hanging from his hand. One thing led to the other and without even realizing it, Neil was drunk, alone and in his shabby house, trying to remember the exact colour of Shyla's eyes.

Chapter 25

The rays of the sun land on Neil's face like blades and the twittering of birds reaches his ears with the power of a bomb exploding next to a glass window: fragments of the otherwise cheerful sound of birds in a glorious morning penetrate his skull like splinters.

"I will never drink again" he promises to himself as he gets up to jump into the shower, praying that there is some coffee left and maybe, but that's really farfetched, a carton of orange juice.

In Anand's car there's the fresh smell of a new day: Anand's breath smells of freshly brewed coffee and Raghav's school uniform of soap, the two drive merrily to school as Raghav finishes a drawing he had started the day before: it's a huge tiger which he has coloured in orange and black, giving it sharp and menacing teeth.

He writes "To Shyla. With love, Raghav and Anand" and then looks at it while he listens to his dada whistling the tune from last night's movie. They are really happy, both of them, and not happy like when they need to be, just naturally, genuinely, happy. Raghav looks at his dad and hopes that Shyla and him could find each other attractive and really make a family for him. He can then draw their sketches as a couple and fly kites together. Anand deserves Shyla, Raghav strongly believes.

Anand on his part is lost in his thoughts: he has always wanted to marry and have a family of his own, he loves Raghav like he was his own son but a child needs a mother, he does his best but he can't be both parents. Besides, he really likes Shyla, her sense of humour, her way of understanding things without him having to explain them to her, her interest in the development of the backward region, everything about her is magical and she seems like an angel who fell from heaven onto his life. He can never get anybody better with the life that he has. Anand stops the car in front of the police station, gets out and goes to Raghav's window to shuffle his hair.

"Listen champ, I have to go in here for a minute, wait in the car, close the window and lock the doors, don't open unless it's me. Understand? Good! See you in a jiffy!"

He walks into the police station.

At the same time Neil, fallen back into a deep yet troubled sleep after having discovered that there was no coffee and the orange juice had gone bad a long time ago, is woken up by the phone ringing. *Oh good God! What is it with noises today? This friggin phone... Here, much better...* and he hides the phone under a pillow, it keeps ringing but he can't hear it anymore.

He falls back into sleep, unwilling to hear anyone's voice, or troubles or plans or whatnot.

On the other side of town Shyla is in her room, sipping a strong coffee that should bring all her ideas into place, she takes her phone and calls Allan.

"This is Allan Fonseca's voice mail, please leave a message"

"Hi Boss, I have some great stuff to report but still need to put a few things in order. Anyway, I just wanted to say hi and that everything is going according to plan, no need to worry about me! Call me back!"

Anand is checking out some files that he needs to send to his superiors, when the morning routine of the police station is interrupted by a terrifying scream. It's a woman, she's outside. Anand's mind immediately goes to Raghav and he rushes out with a few policemen in tow.

As the policemen step out, a brown jeep speeds by leaving behind only the sound of bullets shooting through the air, Anand looks around him, something has hit his face, something warm and soft, creamy nearly. He touches it and is horrified to discover a piece of brain on his fingers. He looks around, he miraculously survived the attack but there's a maze of five or six dead bodies at his feet. Young men who were here to serve their country are butchered mercilessly instead.

A few more uniformed policemen come out shooting but another jeep speeds by from the rear side and with a battery of guns tears down more bodies, there is no escape. Anand wonders how many jeeps they still have. This attack was planned carefully, making sure to ambush as many cops as possible. His men in uniform have sworn to serve the country at the cost of their lives but what about their families, they are under no pledge. They want to live a normal life, be happy, and fulfil their dreams like any other family in any part of the world.

Anand feels something warm on his body but this time it's coming from him. He presses his hand on his stomach and watches blood pour down from it. He immediately looks at his car; Raghav is petrified but protected, still safely sealed inside it. He sees him scream, muted by the thick windows, and punch the window with his tiny hands. *He will be shocked for a long long time, but at least he's safe*, thinks Anand with what life is left inside him. *He's the son of a cop, and someone will take good care of him. Somebody will feed him and fly him a kite.*

But as he says so to himself Raghav seems to remember that he can open the car from the inside and, struck by this idea, storms out of the car running towards his dying father.

"Dada.... dada...."

The kid is terrified: Anand is his only family left and he can't die. He simply can't.

The drawing he had prepared with so much love and care for Shyla falls onto the ground and is quickly drenched in blood. The tiger has caught its prey. Or it is dying. Whichever the case maybe the sketch of the animal is now covered in blood, Anand's blood.

Anand feels the last bit of life slip away from him, he would like to say something to Raghav, depart with his son for this lifetime with something meaningful but his hands have already gone cold, breathing has become so hard he might as well stop trying. A white flash hits him and his vision blanks out. He finds himself standing in a large auditorium that looks similar to his school hall. He is overwhelmed with recollection of all his prime memories being projected around the walls of the dark, empty auditorium. His first day at school, his first love- a science teacher, his strict father also a cop, his doting mother, his mischievous elder sister, his best friend- a cricketer who he spent half of his childhood with, his first crush in college- a nerdy looking girl, all of them appear in this final moment of his destiny. Strangely they all have a big smile on their faces with their bodies in the form of white mist. They share a sense of pride for Anand for his self-sacrifice, for making a choice of becoming a martyr in the line of fire. Anand asks one last question to himself… what if I had not chosen this terror stricken region for my posting, maybe I would have had a family, a regular life, friends for company, but then I wouldn't have had Raghav. Instead Raghav would probably be a part of the militant camp where they recruit orphans and other underprivileged children. And some day this 'Raghav the militant' would kill more informers, cops, innocent civilians, and give rise to more of Militants. And one dooms day the world is ruled by Terrorists. Anand's face has an expression of a dying man who is torn between his duty and his compassion for a helpless orphan. In this lifetime he thinks, he probably failed on both counts. However his last breath is profound with gratification, he is thankful to his nation- a sense of finality. In the distance the first ambulances can be heard, useless now, after the massacre.

The tyres of a third jeep stationed in the alley creak on the road, the last jeep. The car approaches fast and no one around knows why: a pile of bodies is already on the ground, unless they are suicide bombers coming inside the police station there is no reason for them to come closer... They will surely get caught... And there are no cops left alive.

But Debraj and Kedar had a different plan: annihilation must be complete and thorough; no job can be left unfinished.

The woman who had attracted them all out with her request for help, emerges from the bushes, jumps in the car, without even letting the car stop, and she sticks her arms out to catch Raghav by the collar, nearly strangling him. Anand extends his arms as to protect him but the flame of life has abandoned him. Raghav screams for mercy but no one can do anything right now. By the time more help arrives, they are gone and the boy's voice is lost in the golden morning sunshine.

By the time ambulances arrive the pool of blood in front of the police station looks more like a sinister lake, bodies lie in unnatural positions with their faces deformed by the pain and surprise of a sudden death falling over their young age as a dark cloak.

Together with paramedics arrive journalists, photographers and any possible media, to feast on this bloodshed like flies on a pile of rubbish. More than twenty dead cops fill the headlines on the breaking news!

Who did it? What happened to the local intelligence? Who can ever stop these attacks? What will the CM say? Will he keep his iron fist even when he sees what these people are capable of or will he let go, like everyone before him? Will there be retaliation? There are also talks of a child being kidnapped: this is probably the juiciest news of all. The son of a chief policeman kidnapped by the Turu Dalam!

Neil, his head still pounding, sits on the couch and turns on the TV. Breaking News. The voice of a woman news reporter accompanies him to a place only too familiar: the police station.

There has been an attack. Words like "red terror strikes…shootout in broad daylight at Bastar Police station…twenty deaths, mostly policemen…one of the police chief being killed…his seven year old son kidnapped" spin in his head and make him physically sick. It all happened so soon. He couldn't pass on the most vital information he has ever managed to fish out. This has happened because of him. He will never forgive himself for it. This is the biggest mistake of his life. Neil tries to reach for the bathroom but the sight of blood, so mercilessly and so profusely spilt, together with the knowledge that if he had warned Anand this might have not happened don't allow him to get there in time and he throws up on the floor.

He cleans as well as he can, wears some clean clothes and gets on his bike as fast as he can to reach the police station. His hands tremble like never before and his bike moves like a drunken snake.

When he gets there the sight before his eyes is terrifying: looks like more bullets that could ever be produced in Chhattisgarh have been shot and the smell of gunpowder is still in the air along with the sweet and nauseating smell of death. People have gathered from the all over the neighbourhood, some to help, some just to watch, and some bodies already lie on the ground, sealed in black corpse bags. Some bodies, waiting to be recognized, lie on the ground face up. Neil is gutted at their sight: some have received so many bullets that their whole front has disappeared into a rotting mash of flesh. His head spins and right now he doesn't know what to do or who to talk to, he is as lost as a toddler in a battlefield.

He sits on the ground, on the other side of the street, facing the police station, to recover and breathe in some fresh air. The entire scenario appears blurred intermittently.

The front entrance of the building has a number of broken windows and bullet holes all across it. Debraj did a very capillary job this time: the face of the police will be mutilated by these bullet holes, cracked paint and broken windows for a long time, as to remind them that the Maoists win, always and no matter what.

A three-wheeler pulls over and Shyla emerges from it, dumbfounded and scared, trying to understand what is going on, trying to spot Anand in the crowd. She sees Neil instead, sitting on a green patch, lost in himself, with an expression of shock and horror she has never seen him. Is this Neil?

She goes next to him, she's standing right in front of him but he is looking somewhere in the empty space, his eyes are blank, his body is shaking and Shyla knows he hasn't even realized it. He is as lost as she is and this scares her a lot: Neil is always the one making fun of people's fears and broadcasting his fierce approach to life. Seeing him so defenceless confuses her, things might be even worse than they seem. And this is the scariest part because, just from what she can see, the world has changed for the worse, she can't even think of something scarier than this. This is reality written in blood and gore. She grabs his shoulder with her petite hands, he is dragged out of his confusion and takes about a minute to realize who she is.

They hadn't met since their fight on the riverbank and although it only happened a few days ago, they both seem to find each other again after an entire life of wandering. As if destiny had chosen this macabre episode to force them to meet again. Cruel.

Neil hugs her without saying a word and weeps, sobs that make his body shake. Shyla feels his muscled body softening, releasing all the pressure in his nerves against her frail and scented body, their skins touch and their sweats melt together. She's a safe port, the first one he has found in years and right now Neil is ready to let all his defences down, he has no choice.

"It's my fault... all my fault, Shyla, Anand's gone... His son is gone... and it's all because of me..."

"Neil, please... Of course it's not your fault..."

"It is... I knew they were going to strike. I didn't know when though...I tried calling him but..."

"Sshh... calm down, you can't blame yourself for everything"

In the background a reporter has grabbed an eyewitness and is asking him a number of questions, confusing the man and misinterpreting his answers.

Neil and Shyla look at him and take a while before registering his words.

"They took the little boy"

"Where? Where did they take him?"

The man looks at Neil blankly, he doesn't know, he was just standing there when a jeep took him... The local is just enjoying his ten minutes of fame!

Neil runs towards Anand's car, where the door is still open, he finds Raghav's school stuff and desperately looks for a clue.

Shyla follows him and picks up the drawing of the tiger scattered near the car.

"Neil..." she only manages to say before breaking into tears.

"Bastards!"

Neil is disoriented, no one seems to have a clue about anything they are just hungry for a scoop, anything goes: what the boy was wearing, what was his name, who his mother was, did he have his breakfast before the kidnapping, anything that can sell more copies of newspapers or increase the audience of a NEWS Channel.

Suddenly Neil sees in the crowd a face he recognizes. He can't make out where he has seen this otherwise ordinary man but as he tries, staring at him, the man notices Neil's look and tries to run away. People who don't have anything to hide don't run.

And in a split second Neil is over him.

Chapter 26

"I know you!" screams Neil at the man he is holding from the collar of the shirt.

The man, thin and wrinkly, not old but with a long history of skipped meals behind him, looks at Neil with big and liquid eyes, he looks like he is about to cry and for a moment Neil is taken aback, unsure if he is after the right person.

Ganpath remains silent, to let the sense of uncertainty and guilt sink into Neil and then slides away from his grab and walks away, getting lost in the crowd.

Neil is frustrated and his head is still killing him, he looks at Ganpath walk away and screams, kicking the nearest object. He knows he has seen him but can't remember where and with the little scene he just put up he might have blown his cover, if the man is affiliated with the gang and has recognized him he'll go and tell them he wants revenge for his friend. Not just a friend, a cop friend.

He must act before that scumbag finds Debraj, the only way of finding Raghav, alive, is to get to Debraj before Ganpath and not blow his cover. Now more than ever Neil must centre his emotions because the boy's life is at stake.

He stops a teenager who is passing by with his cycle, hands him a roll of cash and takes the bicycle, Shyla jumps on the back, just before he can pedal away. She feels he had forgotten that she was there and puts a hand on his shoulder.

"You said before that you wanted to warn Anand, maybe your source knows where Raghav is..." She has brought the issue up because finding Raghav now is the only thing that matters but a part of her is afraid that by bringing up Neil's source she might throw him back into the spiral of guilt he was in before. The last thing she wants now is for Neil to feel responsible for what happened. He strokes the slender hand and whispers softly "Gopal! I know where to find him!"

In Debraj's den Raghav's watch is being modified by Kedar. Raghav is strapped to an old wooden chair, he is afraid but doesn't want to show it and uses the only means to prove is by screaming- that they'll pay for this, that his dada had influential friends and that they will all be dead by evening. Raghav is afraid but, as his dada taught him, he tries to relax and register all the details around him, in order to be able to lead the police here -if he ever gets out, of course. The walls are dirty and of an indefinite colour, yellow? White? The room is dark and empty with no windows; there are a few chairs and a table with a radio set and a TV. A small bunk bed on the side. At once Raghav misses his home, his fresh laundry, his toys... his fruit bowl and ofcourse his father figure-Anand. He would want to cry but he'd never do it in front of these thugs. Of all the things that Anand taught him, the most important was as Anand would quote- "never lose your self-respect" remembers Raghav. And today Raghav realises that all these souls like him have turned cruel cause somewhere down the line they lost their self-respect when they must have been victimised, and now they are searching for it in absolutely wrong place. This way they will never get out of the vicious circle. Raghav just turns much older than he is. Poetic Justice.

Debraj and Kedar look at each other and smile a wicked smile. All the brainwash and the malice that they have applied to others have now accumulated like a mountain in their own minds, waiting to erupt as volcanoes of pure evil. Their intellects are running parallel to each other's with the same stream of wickedness. This is the going to be a historic day for politics in India. From here onwards the Turu Dalam will take over all the major operations of insurgency. They will reign over Chhattisgarh and then take over the entire of central India. Power to destroy is power to rule. Kedar straps the Mickey Mouse watch back onto Raghav's tiny wrist. He is happy to have it back, it was his father's present, but he notices that it's heavier and that there is something coming out of it, not too big, the size of a nut.

Raghav doesn't know yet but Debraj has modified the explosive to be as effective as the one he used on Kedar's wildcat but a lot smaller. The boy is their new bait, and a juicy one this time. Debraj has used a miniature Chinese explosive made of C 4 plastic. This is the future of terrorism he swears when he stares at Raghav with the attitude of a creator admiring at his brilliant innovation. He proudly remembers his words to Kedar "Its never about the explosive, it's always about how you use it and how much of damage it can cause." Debraj has hit the bull's eye with his machinations.

Neil and Shyla have reached the marijuana fields, the farms are minimal in size, deep into the jungle the trees clear and, out of nowhere, entire hills appear as green tea plantations. They are covered with marijuana plants instead and the local tribes are forced to work under the threat of death from the gang. The field is secured by guards who walk up and down with their radio buzzing and their rifles on their shoulders, ready to shoot at the first sign of insubordination from any one of the pickers. Human life is cheaper than marijuana in this lesser part of the world.

Neil guides Shyla through the high plants, the smell of cannabis is inebriating and reminds Shyla of the smell of her dorm at university. Students at the time smoked pot everywhere, even though it was illegal, and she always looked at them as losers who wasted their lives on drugs. She never tried it and now she's a little afraid that breathing in so much pot might get her high and not be able to think straight.

She's lost in her thoughts when a big snake crawls over her from a nearby tree. She doesn't see it at first, only feels something heavy on her shirt and assumes is Neil's hand. Then she registers and is left terror-stricken by the sight of this giant green animal sliding over her and stroking her neck with its hard scales. Neil turns around and sees the scene, he's onto her and before she can open her mouth to scream he presses his palm against it and looks at her in the eyes.

Her breathing is fast, her eyes full of tears, he looks at her reassuringly and when her breathing has slowed down he lifts the snake gently and throws it far away in the bushes.

The snake lands on a low branch and, untouched by the flight and the fall, goes back to wandering in the jungle in search of a rat to eat. Shyla is dumbfounded. She could have been dead if the snake was poisonous. Neil takes charge and pacifies her. "Just focus on the tiger that is inside you, the gut that brings you to these lethal hunting grounds".

Neil spots Gopal a few metres away, with a feline jump he is over him and, as Shyla twists his arm behind his back, he shoves a gun in his mouth, so deep Gopal's breath jaunts between his teeth.

"Today you decide if you live or die. I don't have time to waste with you, where is the boy?"

"Ngg nggg..." Neil pulls the gun back but keeps it in Gopal's mouth just in case he decides to scream.

"I don't know brother, I swear..."

"Well I'm sorry, because people who "don't know" in the gang die. And today it's your turn my dear friend"

"No... Neil... no..."

"I'm good at heart, that's my weakness and my strength, I'll count to three to see if your memory comes back to you, ok? Isn't it generous of me? Debraj would have shot you without a word..."

"One... Two..."

At the precise moment Gopal's radio coughs out some words.

"Gopal? Copy... Gopal for God's sake, do you copy?" Gopal looks at Neil, he can't speak with a gun in his mouth and if Neil doesn't want to attract attention and,

God forbid, have the jungle invaded by gang members looking for him, he might want to let him talk.

"Lal Salaam. Gopal here, copy"

"Report to base. Tell the others to be alert. Binod is taking the device in twenty minutes. Time to fry some big brains. Be prepared for the recoil, copy"

"Roger"

"Good job, traitor! Betraying me, betraying them, not bad, not bad at all... But you do know what happens to traitor's right? They die. And your time was nearly over if I remember correctly... Three!" Neil removes the safety catch from the gun and places his forefinger on the trigger.

"No, brother, wait..." his eyes ooze panic. Neil knows now that Gopal is ready to say anything because he can see death before his very eyes. He removes the gun from Gopal's mouth.

"It's Anand's boy who is being turned into a ticking human bomb..."

"What the hell? When? Where?"

"I swear I don't know... where and why? You know we are never told about these things..."

"Then let's go to your comrades and find some answers... Maybe blow some big brains too... Move!"

Inside Debraj's den Raghav has gone quiet, he wetted his pants when he saw what was being strapped to his wrist and now that he knows his father is dead he knows that by the time they will come look for him he is going to be blown in little pieces. They will never find him.

He cries in silence, his eyes sting from the many tears he has shed but not a sound has come out of his mouth. All the pain in a couple of days is too much to emote. But unlike a grown up, child has no remorse, no guilt, no unfinished business, he is not in this shaky situation because he had not harmed anybody ever, so Raghav is ready to accept his fate much more willingly. No real desires no real dread.

Debraj sits in front of him and with a paternalistic face feeds him biscuits dipped in milk. Raghav is suddenly hungry but fights against Debraj for a minute, turning his head to the other side. "Come on boy, you haven't had food since this morning, it's just a glass of milk... trust me, everything will seem a lot better after you drink it, it's hot, you need to rehydrate"

Raghav is only convinced because Debraj has used the exact same words that Anand used every morning "Don't forget to drink or you'll dehydrate".

He drinks the milk and once the glass is finished he smiles at Debraj with his sincere eyes and a nice white moustache on his upper lip.

Debraj grins and puts the glass on the table behind the boy, where the milk carton lies half empty next to a bottle of sleeping pills. Debraj contemplates the situation, he's haunted by the feeling that they are doing something wrong, killing a child is never a good thing but for this event there's all this planning... it's wrong at so many levels, even Rebels have a limit or they don't, maybe this will take their mission further. Raghav is that goat that one has to sacrifice for a greater good- Debraj manipulates his own intellect. Besides, looking at Raghav falling asleep, slowly, he indulges for a moment in thinking what his life could have been like if only he had a child, a family even... would he feel differently than the livid rush of anxiety that has walloped his mind. Would he be governed by peace instead of pressure! What he does not know is that peace is not a bullet, which you can load, and shoot into your mind. To understand peace takes a lifetime and maybe another one to experience it. But right then Kedar comes in, his mad eyes are glaring as he holds a little radio, which he turns on loudspeaker for Debraj to hear.

"Dai, tower blast successful, over"

Kedar turns the radio off, he has heard all he needed to hear and he can't contain his joy.

"Professor you are a genius!!! Advancement of India my foot, it's in the jungle that India advances... Look at this!!! Yeah baby! Tower down, no mobile phone network, entire district crippled... what a damn idea sir ji!"

Debraj shoots a wicked smile and pats Raghav's shoulder gently as he tries to say something but his little head hangs on the side, in a mild slumber and with a drop of milk still sliding down his cheek.

In the depth of the jungle Neil and Shyla walk behind Gopal, his hands have been tied behind his back so that he can't reach the radio or a gun. He has been instructed to lead them to where Raghav is but Neil has the feeling that he is just ambling away to waste their time.

Raghav will be killed in less than twenty minutes, they have to hurry!

Suddenly Shyla lets out a short cry and without even realizing how she is hanging upside down from a branch. A jungle trap. This is what Gopal was looking for: a diversion.

In fact, as Neil tries to check if she has hit her head or if she's hurt, Gopal runs, his hands tied behind his back, towards a clearing.

"Gopal you son of a bitch, come back!" screams Neil, knowing that there's little he can do to bring him back. He cuts the rope tying Shyla to the branch.

"Help me out of this trap, he was just wasting our time, we will follow him as soon as I get down... We are faster than him and..."

But just as she was finishing her sentence they hear a "click", it's about thirty metres far but they both hear it.

Gopal hears it too, with his hands sill tied behind his back he turns around, looks at them as to apologize for being a traitor and takes a step back.

As soon as his foot moves from the button buried in the ground the blast knocks Neil and Shyla to the ground and turns Gopal into shreds of flesh.

A landmine.

Was Gopal looking for it? Was he going to kill himself to attract the attention of the Turu Dalam? Shyla doesn't think so, she has always believed there's something good in each and every one and is almost sure that Gopal didn't know about this minefield, he was just trying to run, maybe to alert the rest of the gang or maybe just to run and not be identified as the one who brought them to the boss' den. They will never know.

What they do know is that the gang places landmines around strategic places, like their headquarters, so that they can be alerted of someone tries to come too close from the wrong side. There is one entrance, all around the camp there are mines except for the one path they use to enter and exit, they must find that path but the good news is that they can't be too far. A few miles away.

She turns around to Neil, with the feeling of having shared her thoughts aloud, but as she turns, she find Neil's body lying on the ground, the breathing is hard, he's alive but unconscious. The mine blew up while he had just cut her rope so she was already on the ground and wasn't hit by anything, but Neil was standing, a branch must have hit him and knocked him out. But the clock is ticking; several innocent lives are at stake, there is not time to lose. *Time earns meaning when death stares at it. Ironically the same applies to life.*

Chapter 27

Shyla pours some water on Neil's face as he is wounded and confused. Neil digs his hands into the soil. He stares at the sky and absorbs the energy floating around him. Neil has mostly been an atheist but today he knows that if there is a God it definitely resides in the palette of nature. Neil has always treated nature with love and affection, the mountains, the valley, the rivers, the trees, that is how he grew up- in the caring hands of Mother Nature and once again she is put to test this very moment. And from nowhere, his brothers profound words come and jolt him- *"The very next breath that you take is filled with the greatest gift of life, experience it"*

Shyla takes her scarf off and ties it around Neil's half burnt hand while he bears the pain bravely, she thinks that only a couple of nights ago, like... few hours ago, she was sitting in a movie theatre digging her hand in the popcorn bucket and sharing her touch with Raghav's and Anand's while doing so.

Now Anand is dead, and already he looks like a fading character from a different story far away in time and history, and Raghav is about to die, if they don't hurry. The situations in life can often get out of control, but what can be in your control is how you react to it. That's the share of fate that you have created for yourself. The more drastic the changes outside the more centred should be the mind inside. Shyla extracts and controls her racing breath.

Neil breathes heavily; the blast hit him harder than he wants to let her to know. Shyla can judge from the way he breathes, with his mouth open and the coughing every now and then, that the mere action of breathing is hard on him right now, let alone walk. But they must find Raghav as everything else comes later. Raghav is just a boy who has now most everything. And if they don't save him, or at least try, Faith will die with him. They don't need to remind themselves at this point that faith is why the human civilization is alive. Perhaps Faith is that collective force that wards out the evil floating in the energy fields. *Without faith there would be only one big war, man (the entire human race) against nature. In other words devil against divine.*

Besides for the personal reasons, Shyla knows that by now, judging by the number of journalists there were in front of the police station, everyone knows that Raghav has been kidnapped. He has become a symbol and he must stay alive to give everyone hope. *Hope will underwrite that Faith is the Truth.*

It's the first time for Shyla that she thinks of her life as less important compared to that of someone else. This is the beginning of her beginning. The creation of creation. The chi of chi. She is prepared to sacrifice her life for Raghav's and now for the first time she really understands Father Thomas's words when he spoke about a bigger cause, and his preaching about how the supreme power sacrificed his own son on the cross for a greater intent. Father Thomas used to tell Shyla *"To find a purpose that is higher than the self is the purpose of finding a purpose"*. The cryptic phrase now takes shape into such a simple message that Father Thomas was trying to emulate.

Of course Shyla doesn't dream of comparing herself to Jesus but she understands now the importance of a symbol, a living paradigm, of something to believe in despite of all hell around us.

She stretches her arm to help Neil when he falls, he follows her sheepishly, all his anger, all his energy, has now winded down. He doesn't know how much time they have left, for all he knows Raghav might be already dead. Neil walks in a semi trance, accompanied by all the spirits who left this world before him: his parents, his brother, Anand, they all seem to have come for him, to take him and walk him to a better life. And this woman so alive, so solid in her flesh and bones, so earthly, is doing all she can to pull him back on the ground, in a life that he never chose and certainly never loved after his brother's death. Is this the space between life and death?

There have been good times, yes, but now the battle is over. Not the war. But just let go.

"Neil, you punk warrior! You can't leave me in this forest on my own!!! We still have some time; we must at least try to save the boy! Remember Shakespeare, the amphitheatre, the dark rum, the cosmos dancing on earth, the first time we made love? I want all that back, don't you dare die on me!""

Shyla's voice has woken him from a sleep that was likely to turn into a long journey. They have time, not all is lost then. She kisses him on his lips and looks him in the eye.

"...This is the kiss that made infinity look like a joke that wiped out all my memories, like this is my entire existence... nothing before, nothing beyond."

Neil feels the souls of those he longed to see again slipping away from him, like when you wake up from a pleasant dream and you try to still hang on to it for a minute. Anand, Anil, don't abandon him, though.

They become a solid presence, as if their spirit all entered his body at once to give him the strength he has lost. Is it just his imagination or actually a connection with the departed souls? It doesn't matter as long as it works- Neil reaffirms his faith in the dear departed.

Suddenly he feels more powerful than ever and walks Shyla to the top of a cliff overlooking the valley: from there they will have a clearer idea of which road to take.

Shyla is revitalized, seeing Neil taking charge as he always does.

Even before getting on top of the cliff they hear a noise, it's a creaking sound, like a rusty chain... a bicycle! They look down and in fact they do see a bike crossing the fields. The man on it seems to have all the time in the world and to be enjoying his ride. In the distance Neil and Shyla see an old van. Ganpath, who was at the blast site! His face comes back to Neil, the Turu Dalam delivery guy, that's where he has seen him before: at the camp. He is the only one who knows how to reach it, except for the gang members, because he has to go daily to deliver food and medicines. His minivan is half a kilometre from where he is now, evaluates Neil, so if they run down they will get him before he can drive away. He doesn't know they are on him and he seems to be taking his time, it's not going to be hard to catch him.

Neil races and Shyla doesn't need to ask if she has to follow him, they run until they have no more air in their lungs and reach the rusty van before Ganpath arrives, and they hide.

When Ganpath finally arrives on his creaky bike he puts the bike in the trunk of the vehicle and goes towards the front to hop on. But before he knows it Neil is on him and this time his watery eyes don't spare him a punch in the stomach.

"Where, son of a bitch, where???" screams Neil. Ganpath looks at him with his small eyes, challenging him. Neil is clearly losing his temper whereas Ganpath is still as calm as when he arrived, unaware that they were waiting for him. As long as he can conceal his feelings he is in a position of power. And Ganpath has heard a lot of screaming and shouting and has seen too many guns to lose his temper before Neil, a terribly nice guy. Neil takes out his gun and Ganpath smiles, this drives Neil crazy but Ganpath doesn't stop smiling.

Shyla looks at the scene in silence. She's a woman and as such more prone to reading between the lines. Ganpath is not afraid to die, a part of him can't wait to end this painful life but he's not able to end it himself. Threatening him will not take anywhere because at some point Neil will lose his patience and shoot and when that happens Ganpath is going to die in silence. No breakthrough for Raghav.

From small things Shyla has understood that Ganpath is not a victim of this war, a part of him believed, at some point, that the Maoist revolution was the way forward for

India but then he was betrayed by it, by people like Kedar and Debraj and he lost hope.

Hidden somewhere in that bony chest of his there is a heart and Shyla has one shot to touch the right vein, if she misses Raghav is dead.

"I know you are not afraid to die" she starts with a soft voice that seems to come from another world.

"You might also think that if Neil presses the trigger all your problems, your rusty three-wheeler, your empty house, your empty life, will disappear with the shot. But I promise you, you will die with the voice of a seven years old boy echoing in your ears. You have been long enough in this region to understand what a seven-year-old boy's scream, with death dancing in his mouth, might sound like. It's not a threat Ganpath, I'm just letting you know so that you know what awaits you if Neil loses his temper and shoots. Shyla continues "*The journey to hell can be more hellish than hell.*"

At this point a sad smile appears on Ganpath's face and he moves Shyla to the side and gets on his van nearly as if he hasn't heard what Shyla just said or, worse, simply didn't care.

Panic.

Shyla and Neil stare into each other's eyes and Shyla remembers the story Anand told her about Neil- *He is reckless because he has nothing to lose: when his parents died he completely relied on his older brother, but then the Turu Dalam blew him up and since then Neil is a lonely tiger. He trades with them, ripping them off when he can, and selling their secrets to us.*

Ganpath is clearly not an informer -or does he want to make sure he doesn't blow his cover?- but there is something about him that points Shyla in the direction of loss-driven recklessness and, since he already ignited the engine of his vehicle this is her last card.

She looks at Neil, nearly as to say sorry for what she is about to bring up.

"Ganpath you can stop them from doing to Raghav what they did to you" the three-wheeler stops but Ganpath stays on it, looking at Shyla from the rear mirror, waiting for her to say something else and decide which side to take for the final battle. Shyla looks at Neil who encourages her to keep talking. "I don't know what happened to you, but I can see you are a young man, you look older because life has been unfair to you. I'm sure that in your house there are still some green glass bracelets and some family owned jewellery. You could have sold it, but you preferred to keep it as a memory, right?

Is there also a tin train? A toy car? A school uniform maybe? I don't know what happened to you, but I know that many people who have been stripped of their most loved ones by the Turu Dalam often live in a limbo between life and death.

Judging from your loyalty to Debraj, not telling us where the child is, I guess at some point in your life you believed in the Maoist ideal of a fair revolution to give the people back what the Government had taken from them.

I have only been in India for a few days but I have seen enough to say that, although I loathe violence, I can understand the frustration of bouncing against a corrupt government that takes everything you have and gives you nothing back. I do see how people like Debraj and Kedar have so many followers and I don't condemn you for having believed in them. Then I don't know what happened, I guess you stood up to them and told them that they had adulterated the idea of reforms with greed, and they punished you by taking away all you had. They rendered you useless by chopping out all the emotions that you once treasured. They made you numb. A Dead man walking.

And Ganpath trust me when I say that I know what it means to find yourself from having it all to being left with nothing in just one day, losing your world in just one day, losing yourself in just one day, you keep on living because taking your life would require such a huge effort that you think you can't make it.

You kept doing what you had always done, delivering groceries and medicines and bringing the news and after years it seems normal to you, but I see a flame in the bottom of your eyes. I even see it now from the rear view mirror, the rage, the frustration, the pain is still there. Pretending it had vanished didn't erase it, the wound never healed. The scars in the unconscious are threatening you with remorse every time you go to bed or when your mind is passive.

Help us find the boy and you will find consolation, it will be your redemption for years of slavery to the people who had taken everything from you. A clean conscious is the best pillow you can ever have under you head. From hell to heaven in just one move. Check and Mate.

Help us and you will help yourself, trust me, we have a few minutes left to save a boy's life and make sure someone uses that toy train again..."

Shyla is breathless, her throat is dry and this speech brought up everything she ever wanted to say to herself, to Neil, to Anand, it was as hard for her to deliver it as it was for Neil to hear it. She has no clue where it came from but it was definitely not premeditated. She looks depleted of all physical energy. She looks in Neil's direction and sees him crouching by the minivan, alienated from time and space, looking into the emptiness of the grass and mud as if all the answers were right there, engraved in the dry mud, in the fallen leaves and in the shape of a rusty van's tread marks. Deliverance.

She turns around, to look into the small rear view mirror and check if Ganpath's face has at least changed expression. If she has hit the right spot and managed to pull a string of his soul then she can keep on talking for as long as it takes for Ganpath to melt and comply. She feels a strange strength she has never experienced before. The sense of truth and justice helps to replenish her spirits. She's on a mission. And nothing can stop her. Like an arrow that has left the bow, too late for her own mind to change course.

In the rear view mirror she is surprised not to find Ganpath's face but his head instead, all she can see is his thin but still black hair because he has let his head fall, his chin onto his chest.

As he lifts his head, noticing for the first time after a few seconds that Shyla has stopped talking, she sees his face completely transformed: a shiny mask covers the lower part of his face, from his cheeks to his chin. Tears. Ganpath's is drenched in tears and his expression has changed as all his muscles have moulded into a mask of pain and regret.

He doesn't say a word but gestures Shyla to jump on the back of the van, where he has previously stored his bike.

Shyla hops on and helps Neil, who is happy she managed to convince him but mostly lost in himself. Her speech brought out so many memories and explained so many things that were right before his eyes and yet he had never been lucid enough to see. Was that Shyla or was it his own voice!

The minivan coughs a cloud of black smoke produced by the rusty and noisy engine, but it starts and, although slowed down by the weight of three people, it grinds on the road and with every metre they travel they are a metre closer to Raghav. Now they can see the light. They are inside the tunnel.

Funny thinks Shyla we made such a huge effort so far to get closer to the camp without having to get noticed and now the only way we have to enter it is by riding this old crock that can be heard from another state!

Chapter 28

The ground in front of the newly built school is cluttered with buses, vans, motorbikes, bicycles and people who have come to drop the children to school. The crowd gathered is also in anticipation to get a glimpse of their leader, hoping to be able to listen to his speech and ask him questions. Everybody knows that this is just a facade trip. The CM well educated, wants to look like American leaders, visit schools, promise big things, deliver heart-breaking speeches, but in practice he has done very little so far and the people notice and complain about it. His job is to be present among his people, of course, but also take definite actions in this desperate situation. He seems however to care more for the first part than for the second and with the tragedy that just took place yesterday, he won't be able to hide behind a finger anymore. He won't be able to bring out misinterpretations, blame the system and justify budget cuts: twenty cops have died, a child has been kidnapped – though the news is not confirmed yet-, he will have to promise something he can deliver and then act on it.

People have brought their children to school, but most of them are still afraid that the CM himself may be the next target and, as everyone could see the previous day, the Naxals don't exactly refrain from killing anybody if the situation requires it. Turu Dalam is on the rise. However, their apprehensions are put to rest when a cluster of white jeeps line up at the gates of the red stone laden, school rampart. The middle aged CM- Shekhar Singh is attacked by a barrage of press reporters. His crease-free, pleasant face looks undisturbed as he refuses to take the questions. A bespectacled young lady reporter dressed in worn out denim trousers instigates him: "Sir there was a blast yesterday morning, with about twenty cops left dead, some might think you didn't say a word about that as soon as it happened because your people honestly don't have any answers. Now I feel the Chhattisgarhi citizens deserve to know what happens in their State, isn't it? Are you here to explain or to cut a ribbon and be flown to an expensive restaurant in Delhi?" CM Singh fumes with rage, he turns back to reply. His security entourage stops him to react but determined Singh asks them to step aside. He goes close to the lady reporter and replies with a voice tainted with fear and rage "The CM of Chhattisgarh going to a public event like this one, in spite of insurgencies, is the exact answer I want to give to all the anti-democratic organizations. You attack the innocent or the men doing their duty and we will not shy away from our responsibilities. We will be there vigilantly looking out for these anti-national scavengers and hunt them out of their dens. We mean business and what better way to affirm that than being here at the opening of this school meant to educate the children of this very region? We will fight back with vengeance and we will pull them out from their snake holes very soon under my personal supervision". The press reporters are left speechless. Did he hire Obama's speechwriter? The crowd is impressed. The goods are delivered. The CM walks with a body language that speaks of grit more than ever.

When young Shekhar Singh was to decide what to do with his life, as a literature student uninvolved in politics, a group of students raided the campus looking for the few female students to torment every night. There were rumours of rape, but the girls had always been too afraid to report it both for the shame and for fear of retaliation. Shekhar was a very close friend of one of the girls and when she told him he went straight to the dean to report what had happened.

The Dean was more casual than a roadside Romeo.

"Son, girls in India are involved every day in some kind of sexual activity, you know... who knows what they were wearing or what they said to make the guys want them, maybe it was money?"

"So you are telling me you are not going to do anything as girls are being raped on your campus?"

"Well you see, the parents of the boys you are talking about, without a hint of proof of what you heard from some anonymous source, are very influential..."

"And that's why their spoilt brats can't be touched, right?"

"Putting it like this makes it sound like we are covering a crime, which we aren't... We are just being careful with accusations on such a dreadful crime. Now forget about it and get to studies"

What the dean didn't know was that, at that time Shekhar's mother was also very influential, being the head of the physics department of the University of Raipur. He went to her and not only told them about the rape cases but also about the dean trying to clean the mess and convince him his information was unreliable.

It took her a full morning and about a dozen phone calls but at the end of her operation the dean had lost his job, the kids were kicked out of the university and Shekhar had found what he wanted to do in life: protect people. He tried to get into the Government and his educational background and family records took him far in a short time. Before he knew it he was the CM of Chhattisgarh, determined more than ever not to resign to the pleasures of corruption. In his heart, he always carried his late mother's words "Being the son of a teacher is a privilege, a passport to Abundance, don't ever misuse it"

Inside the school campus, children are rehearsing the National Anthem for the last time when the CM's entourage arrives and barges into the school with no hesitation whatsoever.

Children and teachers had to go through a series of metal detectors from the early morning; the entire school has been checked during the night by sniffer dogs and special task force for bomb threats. The security arrangements are nail-proof and there's police everywhere. The school is a fortress and whoever tries to cross the gate without permission will be taken down, the CM's life is under no sorts of threat.

A dairy van parks nearby, a woman gets off and takes her child down, a police officer patrolling the area looks in, the child, a seven year old boy, seems very sleepy.

"All good ma'am?"

"Yes, yes... getting him out of bed after a nap is always so hard, but today the CM is here, it's totally worth it! When will he ever get the chance to meet such an inspiring man? Now, wake up honey!"

"Huh... you tell me, my boy is the same... he rushed into the school today, have a good day, lady!"

"And a good day to you officer!" *Bastard*, she whispers silently as he walks away.

Raghav is woken up but it will take him a few minutes before he fully recovers, he has enough time to amble into the school and do his job.

Purba walks him to the gate and begs the officer to let him in.

"I'm so sorry but he wouldn't wake up and I need to rush to work..."

She can't get anywhere closer to the metal detector or it will go off, for safety she always carries a gun. She makes sure the micro-bomb watch is well strapped on Raghav's bony hand.

"Ok, ok, I'll take care of him, now go away, only teachers and children are allowed on the school premises!"

She walks away into the bushes and whispers into her Chinese pocket radio "Package delivered. Back to the den, over". She jumps on her dairy van driving away with a triumphant smile on her face. Her ears are on alert waiting to hear the sweet noise of a bomb explode. Poetry in massacre!

In the general commotion for the visit of the CM and after what happened on the day prior, no one expects to see Raghav and therefore they don't see him when he strides by. He is still heavily under the effect of drugs and under preconscious instructions that Debraj hypnotised him with his calm dictation, against a swinging pendulum.

Raghav doesn't say hello to anybody but just goes to sit quietly on a chair very close to the podium where the CM will sit in a few seconds.

The Anthem starts, all the children stand up and recite while flapping their small paper flags, in the background the rusty noise of a three-wheeler is heard but the voices cover it. During the short trip Ganpath explained Neil and Shyla how he knows the Turu Dalam's plan: he wasn't part of it, but the other day, as he delivered rice, he had to take a pause as the rice bag was too heavy and overheard the conversation. Ganpath knew the exact time of delivery of the package-the mission was codenamed 'Mickey Mouse'. They weren't sure of who the carrier boy would be but they knew they would be able to kidnap one easily. Children are easier to procure than carrots in this part of the paradise. Raghav just fell into their lap or rather trap. And being the dead cop's son, now he is the new symbol of complete failure of Governance.

As Ganpath gets out of the car he takes Neil's hand and tells him "It's in the watch, don't waste a minute!"

Neil and Shyla see the huge crowd gathered and a heavy dispatch of security guards. They get instantaneously jittery. Their minds discharges arrows of anxiety at each other. A mountain of doubts piles up clogging their brains. How would they get past the tight security, what if they get caught up in the process, time is ticking and soon the sounds of children cheering will turn into a chaotic cacophony. Shyla's eyes fall on the mob that has gathered. Men and women of various demographic profiles, many of them are parents of the children that have come to witness the inaugural ceremony from far. Shyla knows that in a split second the hopes of so many people can get blown away to smithereens. Within the nanosecond she fires a very powerful thought into the universe. The instinctive prayer darts out of her head propelled by a generous stock of pent up emotions. A passing cloud clears off the sun above to let a ray of hope strike her glowing forehead.

Neil equally exhausted and disheartened enters a state of chimera, a figment of his deadly imagination. He hears a thunderous blast followed by a humungous cloud of fire and smoke that has enveloped the skies. Through the hell of the black gases he observes, disfigured bodies of innocent children. Raghav is just one of them. A chain of explosions trigger off violently albeit in the precincts of his mind. His reverie looks real to him because he recollects the self-animated memories of his own brother Anil and of his dear friend Anand's charred bodies floating in the smoky monstrous cloud. Neil witness's hell or something worst, a chocking hallucination that sucks out all his salts and freezes him with total numbness. The deafening sound of a bunch of brass trumpets brings him back from a flash-forward to his present senses. The CM is given a royal salute through the synchronized instruments that boast of the traditional fanfare. Shyla too gets an emotional jolt by the exchange of the nervous energies. She snaps to reality in a split second and taps Neil on his shoulder with extreme concern. Neil gathers himself, clenches his fists and is back on the operation with gusto. He has that to identify Raghav in the current time and space before the milestone-event gets tragically written in blood on the pages of history.

Neil realizes that he can't go inside the school without explaining and validating his claim. Even the press reporters are not allowed to enter the manned gates. Neil finds a uniformed cop refreshing inside a makeshift toilet van. He shadows him and knocks him unconscious. Then he steals his uniform, wears it and tries to enter the school premises pretending to be a curious cop, just willing to see the CM from a closer spot. Without difficulty, he manages to fool the entrance security guards but he is unable to spot Raghav amongst the hordes of young kids. The chief minister is lighting a lamp on stage amidst a lot of jubilation. Finally Neil spots the back of a boy who is incessantly falling off his chair without anybody paying heed.

All of a sudden, out of nowhere, Neil appears and is projected onto Raghav, who is still half asleep, without a look to the CM or his body guards he just jumps and takes the wristwatch off Raghav's arm. The children are dumbstruck. The security guards spring into action. They chase Neil who is darting away like a bullet. His agile body navigates through the throng of people like an automated missile. Neil leaps to the river flowing near the school and throws the watch, as far as he can. His shoulder almost flies out of the sockets. The velocity with which Neil manages to chuck the watch is unreal. It was like a few hands coming together to give it momentum. The reflection of the hand in the flowing water looked like a mythological character coming to life. *Like Vishnu throwing the Sudarshan chakra.* Just the hand seen in a motion blur.

The watch lands into the flowing stream with fateful silence. Like a transition between two different cosmos. And then the waters burst out. The blast is deafening. The birds in the vicinity break into a violent discord.

Water is splashed onto bystanders and only after the explosion the bodyguards realize what just happened and, fearing for another detonation, push the CM under the table. Everybody is brought back to reality from reality. And that's when they realise that however flashy it was not a daydream.

Shyla runs after Neil and goes to hug Raghav who is in the process of waking up and looks around himself, confused and afraid, finding himself among his school friends and with the far away memory of his father's death, as if it had only been a dream.

As soon as the commotion is over four policemen are on Neil and handcuff him while he lies on the floor. His leather jacket is torn, his once-white singlet is now grey and his face brings the scars of sleepless nights and days spent trying to save lives, beginning with his own.

"There is a mistake, I saved him... Let me go!"

"Yeah... as always, now you come with us and answer a few questions and THEN we'll solve the mistake!"

A few minutes' later reporters have gathered around the school. Today and yesterday have been two very intense days: started with the shooting at the police station and now with the CM at the school, it was supposed to be just something to report on, maybe some nice words of peace and reassurance but this... This changes everything. What next the Prime Minister?

The CM is visibly shaken. But then he remembers his day at college when he confronted the Dean and his mother and everything changed. Courage is the game. He calls for an immediate press meet since the media is right at his doorstep. If he runs away from this emergency its over for him. On the contrary if he faces the media with responsibility, he can turn the tables and become a Hero.

"An innocent child being used as a human bomb! Enough! We are not going to waste any more time. The

Red Terror must be eradicated. Immediate action will be taken!"

His opening press statement is filled with reassurance. Though his knees have turned white.

"What about Neil who saved you from the bomb blast? We hear his intervention was providential and that without him we may not be here now, asking you questions..."

"This is true indeed, but because we don't know which side does he belong to originally, if he played a role in some way in this bombing, since he knew something that we don't, Neil is with us for questioning as we speak"

In the dark interrogation room, with only a lamp hanging from the ceiling Neil sits in front of a senior police officer. It's been dark two days for them, a lot of their men have been killed and they need to hold someone responsible for it, the sooner the killer has a face the sooner they'll be able to metabolize and move on.

"Look, sir, I understand very well your reasons, I have almost been in your position once, but now is not the time God Damn it!"

"You are a smuggler of sorts. You knew exactly where the bomb was. Now, you can tell me whatever you want but you understand that I am likely to believe that you know more than that... You obviously know a lot about these bastards' plans, so hit the nail"

Just then a younger policeman walks in with a big file with a stamp on it "Confidential" and whispers something into the senior police officer's ear. Neil can only hear "Anand Sharma" and "informer" but this should be enough to get him out of here, for now at least.

"Ok, so you are clean. But you are still an informer, you know something we don't and you have to co-operate, or I have here a dozen of crimes that await justice...your lawyer will get confused"

"I would have done it anyway, SIR... Now if we can sort out this handcuff problem..."

"Of course of course..." and the senior cop gestures one of the guards to take the handcuffs off of Neil's wrists.

Just then, as the door opens to let a younger officer in, Shyla storms in and goes to hug Neil. Everyone looks puzzled but she doesn't give them time to tell her anything as she attacks first.

"Always barking up the wrong tree, are we gentlemen?"

The policemen in the room look at each other, bewildered. Who is this woman, what is she doing here? The younger police officer comes in their help though.

"Actually Ma'am... it was a misunderstanding. But it's all cleared. Now the CM has also given Neil a green chit and support to his effort alongwith the staff's full co-operation in order to nab the real culprits"

"Neil you are free to go but you need to help us" says the older cop.

"SKYNEWS is asking for exclusive byte. They want to know if we've finally captured a Turu Dalam big shot" interrupts the youngest.

"Tell them it's a mix-up, just routine stuff..."

"No wait... don't do that..." nearly screams Shyla "If the Turu Dalam assume that you think you have the man you were looking for, they won't be worried, they won't expect a smack down instantly and most of all they'll think they got rid of Neil, who is an outsider to them. They will regroup and reinstate after failure. Let them be lenient and lost and that's how we attack them. We can't lose this opportunity"

Meanwhile, in Debraj's den, Debraj is sitting in front of the TV screen, fuming. Kedar is doing the only thing he's able to do when situations like this occur: behave like a madman. His eyes are injected with blood and his stability is so fragile that at any given point he could snap and kill someone, Debraj himself if required. Right now he is sitting in a corner with a packet of matches in front of him and lights one after the other, possibly trying to set his own tongue on fire. The tip of it is already half burnt and he has another full packet to go.

Debraj looks at him and shakes his head, its times like these that he fully understands Kedar's psychosis and he questions whether this was a cause worth fighting for.

Other soldiers are squatting in front of the TV, pretending not to see Kedar. Over the years they have grown used to his lunatic behaviour and probably look at him as a progressive genius rather than as what he really is. A psychotic. A militant is bad enough and now there is a psychotic militant.

"Hey Dai, what if he talks?"

"Neil isn't stupid, he will not talk, and he never wanted to get into the Turu Dalam, why would he want to be part of it now that shit hit the fan? Sure he's not one of you scumbags, I know any of you would talk before even being asked a question, but not him. He is a player.

The real question is who the hell told him about the plan?"

Back in the interrogating room in the school laboratory, which has by now become the new headquarters of the covert operation to bust the Turu Dalam, Neil and Shyla strategize on what to do. The coordination between them is perfect and the senior officer lets them talk and interrupts seldom.

"She's right, I know how to get to them. It's now or never"

"Well what are we waiting for? Wire him" orders the senior cop.

"Neil, you can't. The jungle's too dense. You've been there. You'll be lost..." interrupts Shyla without finishing her sentence.

"Or killed. We will have to take one step at the time. I know who to start with…"

And then to the pool of cops that have gathered in the room come closer

"The first target is Ganpath!"

"Ganpath the grocer, but?"

"Yes, who are you?"

"My name is Ali, Neil, Sir, Ganpath has been reported dead half an hour ago. Someone went to his store and found him lying in a pool of blood, they thought it was a robbery, today there's not much police around and it might have looked like a good day for..."

"No, it was them, they know he could be the one who led us there... they are smart enough to cut all ropes that lead to them in times of active war. They are always one step ahead. Ok, plan B. Purba, the woman lead…"

"That bitch will smell you from a mile away, Neil..."

At once Shyla emerges from the corner of the lab, as if a light had suddenly been cast over her.

"I'll go"

Everyone seems struck by this simple yet so effective and selfless offer, but Neil, too scared to lose the only soul left in the world he cares for, snaps at her.

"Are you nuts? She's not your ordinary woman"

"Even better. I'll blend right in"

“Shyla look, I appreciate your effort to help, really. But this is not your war, you are not one of us, you...”

“I, Neil, less than a couple of days ago I was watching a movie at the movie theatre around the corner from this police station with new found friends- Anand and Raghav. In less than Forty-eight hours Anand died and Raghav was drugged and got almost killed with a bomb strapped to his wrist. Even yours and my lives are a bonus after the landmine blast and the school-bombing attempt. I know you are from here and I barely speak Hindi, but if you don’t mind sharing this is my war too. It’s a little late for me to call myself an outsider. Come on, wire me up!”

“Great. Wire her up. We’ll keep track of you, don’t worry!” Cuts in the senior officer from the special task force, he knows that if they want to act they need to do it fast before the gang finds out about their little stratagem. The Prime minster is on them.

Neil tries one last time to protest and change her mind “But Purba’s hideout is different from Kedar Singh’s...” but Shyla is determined and right now nothing can stop her, her destiny is waiting for her in that bloody jungle and it’s her time now to go and face it. This is not just a war it’s a personal score.

“We can get them first and use them to take us to the headquarter hideout”

“Wait a minute, wait a minute, every Thursday she takes a truckload of guns and grenades to Debraj”

“Brilliant Timing. Tomorrow is Thursday. We’ve gotta move now.”

“But first we need some makeover, they wear saris to blend in and camouflage the weaponry”

In a minute two female police officers are over her with makeup and hair products to turn her into someone who could go to the Turu Dalam... for real. Her hair is tied, and the old sari is layered with sand and dry mud. Her face is darkened and creases of poverty are etched out on her face with charcoal. A lady constable walks the walk and talks the talk to emulate the Chhattisgarhi women folk. But with the given deadline Shyla can't pick up much. Her biggest asset is going to be her confidence and her power of observation that she is going to use to merge with the women militants. Neil stares at her helplessly as his stream of thoughts juggle around- *"I thought I was daringly crazy, and here we have a Anglo-Indian girl who lands up from nowhere and is willing to brave the fanatic rebels...is she as fanatic or does she have a personal agenda... just like me"*

Meanwhile in Debraj's den, Kedar Singh is flaming quite literally, there is no stopping him and seeing Debraj relatively calm irritates him even more. Kedar is holding his hand over a thick candle to burn it in order to distract his tormenting mind.

Debraj gets nostalgic. He is cutting a newspaper article for his corkboard collection, in the distance he looks at it and smiles with satisfaction, from where he is he can see the article that, many years ago, was written about him, the headlines is faded but he can still read "Political Science Professor Debraj Roy Abducted by Red Terror Militants".

"That bastard! I could smell he was a traitor!" snaps Kedar, furious at Debraj's calm.

"Ganpath has been taken care of. Rampal will deliver the supplies now, there's no need to worry."

"I'm talking about your Rayban Boy! He's still out there. I want his head for breakfast with mustard sauce!"

"Neil is in police custody, Dai"

Kedar doesn't want to hear this story, he's mad but not stupid, he knows as well as Debraj that Neil is a born survivor, if he has to rat on them, to get out of jail, he damn will. Kedar hates not being the master of the situation, not knowing when or how his camp will be attacked.

"Bullshit! BULL-Frigging-SHIT! I want the CM's head and that bastard Neil's head NOW! I've lost face, Debraj, thanks to you. I am also being held accountable; I have responsibilities to some people, higher than me in the hierarchy. Do you have any idea how your failure to get rid of the CM will affect our trade now? What is our standing...? Who will support us? And when I lose face, Debraj, ugly things come out, my friend, real ugly things."

"Kedar you know that the failure of the CM bombing is not my fault, everything was perfect and we couldn't suspect Ganpath until that very moment... Things can't get any uglier than this. I know it and you know it too"

"What's your point?"

"My point is that WE have strayed from the ideal. I joined you because I saw a purpose in what we did. But now it's just a power hungry, money making game"

"Debraj, when I enrolled you with us, you were a nobody, a young professor from a small university in a little state. Today you are powerful thanks to me. So watch your mouth or else..."

"Or else what? It's not too late to remind yourself why you got into this in the first place. Wake up to it, Dai. There's still time to transform you back from the monster you've become..."

Kedar is fuming, he pulls out his gun and points it at Debraj, and he snaps from where he is standing and in a split second he is over Debraj, pointing the gun right at his neck. Debraj stretches his hand to reach for the scissors he was using a minute before but decides not to retaliate. He talks with the coolest tone he can find within himself.

"This is exactly what I mean"

The radio coughs out some words that Debraj can't make out, but he hears only too well Kedar's response:

"Then don't lose him... Kill him!"

Chapter 29

When Shyla is finally ready a small GPS is strapped onto her, under her clothes that she has hidden under a sari.

"Huuu it's hot in here!" Neil smiles. A smile similar to that of Anand's, a sad one. But Neil is also engrossed, *which leaves room for triumph, thinks Shyla, sad is just sad, as if there's nothing we can do about it, but anxious... there is a silver lining. But what is bothering him? Is he worried for me or he too is heading to redeem a dark secret that has tainted his soul.*

Both, at the hint of twilight, get dropped off where the jungle begins and from then on they are on their own. Nightvision glares highlights the path. Neil checks on his set of hunting knives and blades. He adjusts the radio. The weather is not turbulent and the signals are clear. A GPS screen shows him where they are roughly standing but it is all too dense and expansive to pinpoint any landmark. Neil pulls out a map sketched in his notepad and a small torch and skims down his memory: they don't have time as the Turu Dalam is certainly patrolling the area, especially night times, they have to keep moving and pay attention to any little sound. In the jungle the auditory skills need to be the sharpest.

To protect the camps, they are strategically positioned a few kilometres away on the circumference. Suddenly a big torch pierces through their backs, projecting their shadows in front of them, on the mist that the tropical forest produces after a long day in the heat. They stop.

"They certainly have radios, if we run they will call the others, if we stay they'll come closer to see who we are..."

"Come closer Neil? They are armed!"

"Yes I know baby but if they are close there's something I can do, let me handle ok babes?"

The two men's steps are right behind them when Shyla turns around abruptly and sprays on their faces her pepper spray; Neil looks at her in disbelief.

"What? I'm from South Africa, very dangerous country! And please don't call me babes when we work..."

Neil stares at her, puzzled and with an idiotic smile on his face. The patrolling rebels are yelling in gruelling pain. Neil lifts one of the rifles, strikes the side of their heads and knocks the two of them comatose. Neil reverts "and I am from India...verryyy wild country". They keep marching through the Bamboo density until they hit a camp, buzzing with torchlight. There is movement galore in pin drop silence like a pool of snakes getting ready for an attack. Armed women dressed in ethnic saris and Muhar Mala (a garland made with coins) are loading a truck. In the moonshine they can spot Purba uneasy in her red sari, which she too has to wear in case they come across the police, shouting orders. But her hunting shoes are a giveaway.

"Anand told me that your brother was killed by the Turu Dalam..."

"Yes, and now it's payback time. I have been working for this all my life since Anil died. Opportunity is nothing but correct timing backed by resources, and this is why I had to do a lot of things I'm not proud of. But I had a cause to fight for, my own. Although I despise how these radicals fight their cause, I must say that after so many years determined to kill the desperado who killed my brother, sharing meals with him to gain his confidence and looking at him in the eye, I feel stronger thanks to the chase in my mind. Anybody can bite into a cooked fish served on his place but when you go in the midst of a tornado to catch your own fish and then come back and eat it, you have achieved. In the garb of forest trade, I was hunting for my own treasure trove filled with revenge that I had buried deep inside me. When you live in self-belief, you are invincible, there's nothing that can stop you. It's time for that revenge now: blood for brothers' blood"

"I guess then we have something in common..."

They look at each other in silence, a silence that seems to last forever and which is devoid with words or thoughts, only emotions. They have to move and yet those eyes can't break the spell that keeps them stuck together.

"Ok babe... Shyla, you are on your own now, I'll go back to the station and follow you from there, don't lose the GPS or we are pretty screwed, and you are too. All clear?"

"All clear!"

"And please, as a personal favour... don't get killed coz I lo... anyway, don't, when an informer dies there's a hell of a lot of paperwork to be done and if I get you killed they'll make me do it..."

"Sure, heartless Neil, sure... Go now!"

Shyla crawls to the truck, taking advantage of the dark patches, she leaps in, blends in, helping the other women, in silence, to load the truck with the wooden handicraft that they need to cover the real load, which is now lying beneath her feet: enough ammunition to drive a revolution across the whole country.

The truck finally plies and the women militants are as quite as a pack of wolves heading for a midnight manhunt. Shyla's thoughts roll out in the eerie silence of very dangerous women now rubbing shoulders with her. *"Life is full of accidents and discoveries. Like stray asteroids, the situations crop up accidentally and then we make choices only to discover who we really are"* Shyla is not sure about the rest of the women in the truck but it begins to dawn on her that she is getting close to finding out her true self. Maybe!

She leans on the side; a part of her has gone to sleep because she hasn't slept in days. She is exhausted and also because by sleeping she can avoid speaking, the other part of her is afraid that if she falls asleep she might uncover her face fully and they will find out that she's not one of them. She dozes off; her ears ready to pick any sound. The truck navigates through the thick of forest, at times almost turning upside down. But the driver knows these topsy-turvy roads like they were etched on her palms.

Back at the police station Shyla is only a red dot on the screen and Neil can't take a full breath until the truck has reached a spot where it stops. Debraj's headquarters is more like a medieval village than a camp: there are tents, mud cubicles but also stone constructions, flat structures that seem to have seen better times; one was probably a stone temple that the jungle, or the gang, reclaimed. The ruins have ancient pillars and some tablets with carvings lying around. The irony being that these stone relics could be national treasure but the wolves can't feel any poetry in the song of the hummingbird. Everyone seems busy with logistics, a sense of guerrilla warfare prevails and Shyla guesses that they know the special police force are onto them. They are getting ready for an oncoming attack. Strangely there is no fear on their faces. Militancy is all about brainwashing till the extent of destroying the very fabric of the human soul. These killer recruits were innocent toddlers at one point of time and now they have lost all traces of their original being.

She needs to get out of the truck and disappear in the jungle until Neil arrives. She helps the women unload the truck and then leaves, gesturing that she needs the toilet, but as she steps down she misplaces a foot and trips, nothing serious, except for the fear of being discovered, but she doesn't notice that a small black device is blinking its red eye under one of the benches inside the truck.

Shyla hurries towards the forest where she takes off her orange sari like the others already have, and is left in jeans and camouflage shirt, this way it's harder to spot her and she might get a slight advantage should she be chased.

She takes off a small camera from her pocket and clicks pictures of the offloading of ammo and at people's faces, thinking that once at the police station is going to be easier to recognize and classify them. Soon a lot of militants at work get registered on the chip of the camera. But this is on the surface. The actual face that Shyla is looking for is a shadow that is lurking in her nightmares. Like a serpent it stings her out of her sleep.

The accumulated poison has to vent out. But Shyla has no clue, how? Is there a sign somewhere!

Purba shouts her orders in a dry voice, she's evidently in a hurry to leave the camp and Shyla wonders if this has anything to do with that lump under her shirt. Neil hasn't mentioned any medical device, and he has seen her up close, so she's definitely hiding something, but what? Cyanide? Purba seems very careful about how she moves so that her shirt doesn't expose anything. At the beginning Shyla thought she did it out of decency but looking at how she treats the men and shouts orders at those who have a lower grade than her, it's definitely not the case.

"Hey you, little one, keep your pants zipped or I'll chop your little willy off, ok? My women cannot be touched unless they want to, am I making myself clear?"

The boy looks at her, she nods without saying a word and he rushes off like a rat. Everybody knows that Purba is a cold-hearted bitch more of a trigger-happy maniac. She has killed for a lot less and her complete devotion goes to her women, they would die for her only because they know she would do the same for them.

The truck sets off and the red light moves again.

"Something's wrong. She's in trouble. Shit, I should never have let her do this! You guys follow the truck, she might have had to stay on it, and I'll go to Debraj's den, when you clear the truck come to Debraj's and we'll have our little party there..." Neil smiles as he tries to make a joke, no one laughs, as they know Shyla could be in a lot of trouble. Neil is armed with self-confidence. Now he has a woman on his side, rather in his heart, his *Shakti*. The lore of the land (Shiva and Shakti) has taught him that every man like Shiva needs the Shakti- the strength of a woman in his heart; earlier it was nature- 'the eternal beauty' and now its Shyla. But first he needs to rescue her. As soon as he's done talking they storm off like target missiles. Back in the jungle Shyla has noticed there is something missing and touches herself to check where the GPS might be, she's horrified to find out that it's not on her and, worse, nowhere around her. She remembers tripping on the truck, she might have lost it there, but this means that no one is coming for her. Neil and his team will get misdirected leading to chaos and boomerang. Now she is on her own straight in the lion's den. She closes her eyes to fight back a panic attack that is about to strike but she doesn't have time to take a first deep breath as a strong and rough hand catches her from the back. She closes her eyes, overwhelmed by fear, and passes out.

Neil has set off for the jungle; he has followed the route that Shyla's GPS tracker traced on the marker. In no time, he comes across a gang member patrolling the area and in a split second he is over him.

"Now you take me to Debraj, I know we are very close, come on, good boy, if you think you can screw with me you are wrong, and if you try to escape or call your friends, I blow your brains out, understand?" Neil's voice is absolutely flat, calm, and his face is smiling. The poor guy is terrified, unable to speak, he nods and marches towards the camp.

The headquarters is shrouded in the shadows of the Sal trees with Militants scanning the area hovering on treetops. Kedar is pacing up and down his room, furious and also deeply afraid of what is about to go down, he knows something big is bound to happen and this is the time for him to make a decision, it's his call since he doesn't feel comfortable trusting Debraj anymore. *That geeky idiot, couldn't he wait until tomorrow to wake up his conscience? Screw him...* A gang member walks in with news.

"An informer just radioed in. CRPF is gearing up big time, what do we do?"

"Shit Shit Shit! I could see this coming. Get everyone on red alert! Radio them. Alert Purba right away, and tell her to return to the headquarters, we need her". Another senior gang member walks in, he fears Kedar, and it's easy to see his psychosis and more so tonight. "We... I think... We have a visitor..." Kedar incinerates him with his look.

A few metres away, in Debraj's room, Shyla, tied up and unable to move, wakes up. Her eyes can't quite make out where she is and her vision is still blurred but the place is dark and not too small, there are dark corners where anyone could be hiding. She thinks she is alone, but is she?

From a corner Debraj emerges, she recognises him from his eyes. The shadow in her nightmare was similar to Debraj's frame. The coloured eyes are ditto, straight out of her jagged dream. What was it, genetic memory passed down? Yet from a different corner Kedar intrudes, he looks at her, touches her, she kicks but can't move her arms and there's not much she can do. She is prepared for the worst. It's funny how she had expected this to happen differently, she would have confronted Debraj, alone, and killed him. From the very day that Father Thomas told her about her being a daughter of a rapist and that too a militant leader, she was partially destroyed from within. The hatred inside her was growing at a rapid pace, oblivious to her conscious mind. She suppressed her angst but the desire for revenge spread within her like a cancer. Her fears are dwindling as she faces the man who was responsible for her undesired birth and then her emotional affliction. The suffering that comes with knowing who you are, and hating it all the way to the core of your soul, is a deeply painful agony that can last for many lifetimes.

Now Shyla is tied to a pole and is likely to be raped by the whole gang... It's sad enough when plans don't work out, it's tragic when revenge awaited, that seems like a lifetime doesn't work out.

As she's trying to think what her options are the radio buzzes and Kedar is onto it in a second, a Nepalese voice comes out of the scratchy device and Kedar snaps like a good soldier. Leaving the room he gestures Debraj to slice her throat, he covers the microphone of the radio and whispers "The cops are onto us, we are getting ready for an attack, she's not bad but you'll have to give her up for today. Kill her and we'll find you someone else, God Promise!"

Debraj sits down like a cobra; Shyla looks at him with her soft, almond shaped eyes. Surprisingly her hatred has turned into lust, but is it intentional?

"Who sent you?

She coughs, looking at the jug on the table, he releases her from the rope that was cutting through her wrists and hands her the jug. She drinks and pours the rest on her head, wetting her shirt that adheres to her body catching Debraj's attention.

"I asked you a question..."

"I'm a photographer... I was looking for tigers and unfortunately ended up here"

"Ha Ha... well then I hate people who invade my territory, maybe you can take a photo of me..."

"Oh well, I said tigers... not bastards… Besides, invade your territory? Have you got something against wildlife journalists?"

Debraj looks at her, the eyes are very familiar…to his. She reminds him of someone but can't quite tell who, her shirts highlights all her curves and now she's standing with her hands behind her head, leaving nothing to imagine...

Shyla leads him on- "Frisk me if you want. I'm a harmless National Geographic journalist..."

Meanwhile Neil has reached the camp, he hears Kedar's voice on the radio, and the sound comes from a log hut not far from where he is. This voice must have also ordered the blast where his brother was killed. The jarring voice is brimming with wickedness. He enters the hut but Kedar doesn't see him as he has his back to the door. *Fool*, thinks Neil as he approaches. Neil clenches his fist like a tiger about to catch its prey.

Debraj keeps looking at Shyla, it was a long time since such a beautiful woman offered herself to him. He wonders what's with him, such a charming girl is luring him, there must be something!

All of his repressed sexual drive comes to surface and drown him in lust. The storm raging outside has subsided in his mind as the dopamine rush kicks in like a wild waterfall. Pure sex would be a good warm up to face the looming tempest. She's in the same position as before, hasn't moved, she is pulling him like a magnet and he gets up and goes closer, feels her arms, her stomach, her breasts, her wet skin. The beast in him gets ferocious; he is transported to his younger days instantaneously. She stays like a rock but keeps her eyes on him, she's not afraid, he would have preferred that, but it's ok, she's young, she's pretty, she looks like a women from a long time ago, a different life... *What was it? Thirty years ago? Mara? Mira! Mira Sarkar!* He briefly wonders how she might be doing nowadays but soon moves on: he is holding Shyla's neck and licking it, his mouth goes down to her breasts and she tries to resist but he's too strong. He bites her. Shyla panics: in her head she was going to seduce him and then overpower him, she hadn't taken into consideration that a man who lives and fights against the jungle everyday is bound to be a lot stronger that her.

With her arms still up the Trishul tattoo is exposed, Shyla looks at it and feels her mother's presence closer than it has ever been, she hears a whisper, can't tell where it's coming from, probably her own head giving words to her mum's feeling- *"Kill the demons inside you and make room for angels... Angels and demons reside within us... It's heaven or hell in every moment you live. The choice is yours. Choose wisely"*

Debraj overwhelmed with this opportunity of a lifetime is now turning into a lusty monster that was hiding inside his unconscious. He looks at Shyla but sees Mira, her moist lips part as they get closer to his ear to whisper something. Debraj is so turned on and can't wait to hear that voice again. The husky voice is pumping in more adrenalin into his craving.

"Is this how you raped Mira Sarkar?"

Suddenly the image of Mira has faded away and before his eyes is a flaming Shyla, her voice, the heat of her body, her look, all burn with revenge, she's seeking it, has been all her life, and she'll get it. Tonight. He sees a blazing sun in her face that is dying to turn him into ashes. Debraj steps away, realizing for the first time that he should have not untied her...

"Who the hell are you?"

"I don't know, PAPAAA, you tell me! Mira Sarkar was here for a wildlife photo shoot, you said you'd help her around and took advantage of her instead. You raped her and inserted her with your evil hormones. She was a good Hindu, also a believer in Christ, and kept the fruit of that brutality. She would have given me a lot of love, nurtured me with care, if she had time, but unfortunately she died. Now you were trying to rape me as well, your own daughter, you sick bastard?"

Debraj is still drenched in desire. With a pounding heartbeat, he chases Shyla. She manages to escape, grabs a bottle from the table, breaks it and turns to him threatening him with the sharp glass that reflects the last rays of the dying moon.

Shaken to the toes, she trips, she falls and cuts herself, it's a superficial cut but as she sees blood oozing from it she loses sight of Debraj who, in a moment is over her.

"I didn't rape her, she wanted me..."

"That's not what I heard" she holds the half bottle to the neck and points the broken glass to his jugular "It's a good time to tell the truth now, or else you die..."

But Debraj is already lost in a reverie that brings him back to many years before when he accidentally met a woman, a South African photographer and had helped her find tigers and pot. They had spent time together, they have smoked together and then, when he had tried to take all the kissing to the next level she had turned him down. He had thought it was ungrateful of her and had eased the process; he was helping her enjoy and definitely didn't deserve to get his throat cut for it...

Rape is a bad word, a bad action from bad people, he definitely wasn't a rapist. When Mira said "No!" it was pretty clear that she was teasing him, she really wanted to say yes but didn't want to sound easy, he helped her feel more comfortable with herself. Besides both of them were intoxicated. He imagined she was desperate to have him inside her."

She started bleeding. He didn't know she was a virgin. She was in pain. He was a born sadist. He was ecstatic. His childhood memories came tumbling down. He had heard his own father lay over his mother. She was in pain too, all the time. Back in the woods, Debraj thrusts his muscles onto Mira with velocity. Then the beating, well yeah, he could have not gone so hard on her but she has used a glass to hurt him, he could have died... He remembers beating her. She went unconscious. But he felt it was not too hard but from what this girl says it was enough for her to drag her feet through the pregnancy and let herself die straight afterwards...

Is he a rapist? *Am I a rapist?*

Chapter 30

The police chopper is frantically flying over the forest, trying to locate the coordinates transmitted by Neil, they wait for his signal to land but the people on it are getting impatient, in the end Neil is not a cop, what if he dies and they miss this miraculous chance of getting all of the Turu Dalam at once?

But Neil is driven by the same fire, which brought Shyla across the world to kill the man who raped her mother, and Neil is not going to die. Or at least not before he has finished the job. Neil experiences the darkness that had nested inside him creeping up to his alert mind. The darkness of his brother's ashes had made him a detached personality. The darkness of the wood that burned with the brother's body had perpetuated a steely resolve inside a man who was actually a die-hard romantic and a college buffoon. The darkness of the noise of the bomb blast had resonated a misleading purpose in a young man who had zilch ambition otherwise. Neil today faces the devils that he had planted inside the deeper layers of his mind. The devil inside him is on a bloody date with the devil in front of him. He enters Kedar's control room after having scared away the guard at the entrance, most of the Turu Dalam men were abducted, and were taken away from their families, unlike Purba's women who had voluntarily enrolled. The forced militants of the Turu Dalam will fight until someone threatens to kill their wives and children but as soon as things turn sour their loyalty goes down the drain, *getting rid of guards is always a joke, they are hollow as Bamboo,* thinks Neil.

Kedar has his back to the door but hears Neil enter the room: his footsteps are heavier than those of his men, he is not afraid to be heard, his body language spells control, maybe Debraj was right, maybe they did need a man like him in the gang...

"Kedar Singh... This is it... My brother Anil taught me that evil could survive but only for a while... But how can you remember my brother after all the people you've killed run into hundreds. Well, let me remind you: DSP Anil Mahajan, got killed in the MP Sahu car blast many years ago, remember now?"

"Interesting story, but I blow up several cars a year it's a full time job you know... I don't bother learning the names of the dead, they are dead... gone... like birds" Kedar spits out his arrogance.

Neil collects all his strength like gathering an army of a billion cells inside his muscles- In a flash all his passion ignites the strings vibrating inside every atom of his guts. An energy burst is what Neil feels in the precincts of his mind with memories of love and brotherhood spitting out like a bull blown supernova. Is this the power of emotions;

is this the orb of chi that his brother left for him before he left? Is this what your dear ones leave behind for you once they are dead and departed? "Well, it's payback time now, and I will do you the favour of reminding you each and every significant man you've butchered before I kill you. Anil Mahajan, Anand Sharma, Ganpath..."

Right then two gang members, probably alerted by Kedar's guard, run in with guns in their hands, Neil armed with one of their weapons, shoots them down but in the time he took to turn around, a minute, Kedar has ducked under the table and ran outside. Neil is on him, he jumps out of the window and glass is scattered all over the place, he is hurt, but no pain can stand the energy rush of finally having his brother's murderer in his hands. Kedar scoots like a hyena. Neil runs after him and meanwhile gives out the signal: the dark sky is bathed in the red light at once, red smoke emerges from the top of the trees and the whole police force of Chhattisgarh finally know where to land. The hunt is open.

While the world as they know is altering right outside their door Debraj and Shyla rehearse they personal drama. The air on the room is filled with lust and reparation. Shyla's scent is all over the room. Debraj is almost hypnotised.

"She provoked me, it wasn't my fault... Look, she attacked me..." and he shows her the cut under the scarf.

Shyla is shivering with anger but at once she's brought back to the red lit gipsy room where she got her tattoo made, even that she never remembered until now -she was barely a few years old- but which was extensively told to her by Father Thomas.

She stops with the half bottle in her hand as if she could hear now what her mother, from a different world, had whispered into her ear that fateful day: *Use the invisible weapon of Shiva to kill the demons inside you... Use the three spiked 'Trishul' for the war within... Forgive, Forget, Further... There is a whole new wonderful world waiting for you right at this doorstep... there is a beautiful universe out there that loves you more than you can imagine... don't waste your existence on revenge or regret... Step out of this illusion and feel the presence of the real force that is holding you in its lap like a mother holds her child. Make the right choice. Now.*

The action outside is furious, the battle is brutal, its do or die, corpses fall on the red soil, flesh looks like a generous spray of street art, blood seems to have lost its worth, the rain of bullets and grenades is nonstop. Purba and her women are at the front. They were under fire as soon as they arrived back. Purba secures her treasure hanging on her chest, chants her Guru Mantra and retaliates with a river of bullets. She stands for all the torment the women of the region have been bearing. But Shyla is just awaken from her reverie by the smashing of the door opening under the weight of Neil and Kedar fighting like two wild animals. Debraj takes out his gun and points it at Neil, Shyla kicks him and he drops it but Kedar tries to reach for it, as this chain of events happens before they can even realize it, from the chopper comes the voice of the senior officer who offers surrender as the only way to stay alive. They are surrounded and will be targeted with more grenades if they don't surrender.

Kedar grins: the orders are clear -never surrender, die fighting! From the window he sees the human shields being brought out endlessly. They are unarmed -should they decide to turn against the Turu Dalam- their faces are deformed by fear. The Militant in command makes them run around so that the police think it's them and shoot them down. When they are tired and run out of ammo the gang members will come out and have their own war.

Kedar takes advantage of the commotion triggered by the human shields to grab Shyla and point a gun at her head.

"You might want to add her name to the list as well... this bitch" he says with a impish grin looking at Neil. He twists her neck and locks his finger on the trigger. But he can't finish the sentence as a precise shot pierces through his head leaving only a drop of blood on the back of his collar. Debraj has shot him. Debraj is stunned at his own spontaneous decision. He doesn't know which Debraj pressed the trigger. The Debraj that was tormented and forced into taking up militancy, or the Debraj that wanted to steer the Maoist movement in the right direction to not let it get swallowed by the madness of Kedar, or Debraj the father who felt the need to redeem himself before he is shot dead by the cops. All his educated mind can comprehend is that humans under tremendous pressure get split into multiple personalities otherwise hidden below the subconscious and in the tick of an epiphany one of them breasts' the tape first.

Just then Shyla sees Neil leaning against a wall and leaving a thick red mark as he moves. A chance bullet from outside has hit him and he is bleeding profusely on his thigh. Shyla runs out to look for help and Neil can hear her voice screaming amidst the whistling of bullets. Neil feels partly redeemed. Kedar is dead. Debraj will be in police custody soon. Given the intensity and the number of crimes that he has committed, he would be dealt with the toughest of punishment as per the law. The

Turu Dalam will be erased for good. But what about him, is this his finale, the moment of a white light at the end of a tunnel. Will he now enter the gates of heaven or hell, well whichever is more of an adventure!

Purba breaks into the room. She is terribly wounded. She sees Kedar on the floor and with her last breath addresses Debraj.

"Don't die, Dai. Surrender, Chung San Lee will get you out of this shit but if you die it's over..." She falls into his arms; releasing the pressure of her hands from her stomach a rivulet of blood oozes out, draining life from the inside. She didn't know which bullet hit her, was it from the guns of the raiding police force or a stray bullet from one of her own rebels. For a change her entire life doesn't flash in front of her eyes. But what she hallucinates is about the alexandrite as she dives into a well of greed? Debraj holds her as he sees his entire world come crashing down in just the last few minutes. The end is near he senses. Purba lies there motionless, her head on his lap and her eyes half open, and that's how the cops find them when they barge into the room. Debraj sees the end of an era. One battle that he was fighting from his childhood, the other battle of finding purpose, and then the third battle of deciding whether being a Militant leader was the right choice and now he has found his answer. Something went wrong in the way he saw things when he was younger. He was blinded by his predisposition. But he still has a choice. He can confess and be a witness by submitting all the information that he has about other parallel outfits or wait for the parent militant sponsors to fish him out from the prison bars. Too much has happen too soon. He needs time and he needs to rethink about his actions, his karma, which now has a successor- his blood daughter. Maybe she is the only answer, the only way forward.

Neil is semi-conscious but his blurred vision and the copious loss of blood numb the world around him, he barely hears Purba murmuring his name with the last bit of her breath and Shyla getting back with a stretcher and screaming at him "Don't you die on me...I cant do this time and again, the battle is over" as she cries hysterically. The armed officers of the special task force arrest Debraj amidst tight security. They have descended at the right time and the right place for heaven's sake. The police officers would have to hide their faces when they would watch the local news with their family that highlighted helpless children and youth being dragged into militancy or become human shields. Similarly the wives of these brave cops would have sleepless nights when their husbands would be out patrolling this insurgent region. The country will finally salute these daring heroes for having captured one of the most dreaded red terror gangs' alongwith their leader alive. Debraj the mastermind would help them bust other militant outfits in the neighbouring states by spitting out classified information.

Neil perceives the situation is under control and that his revenge is accomplished: he can finally let go, he closes his eyes and is transported in a warm world where pain and horror don't exist, where he can play *Pachisi* in peace. Shyla's voice can still be heard but it seems so far away... Can he hold her caring hands for the last time, can he smell her once and for all. Can he freeze the reflection of the red sun, rising in his eyes, for eternity! As he feels strength leaving him, for good this time, he smiles "Everyone dies but only a few die after having lived a life of pure passion, this is eternity".

Chapter 31

Three months after the day she has decided to settle in India, Shyla is back in her office, setting everything up in the conference room for the presentation of the data collected during her fieldtrip. This is her last ones as an employee, the final day after serving her notice period. The last couple of months have been like the coda chapter to her South African life. Shyla has great memories of this office and the café across the street, and the bar just around the corner, and the bookshop a block away but then people and places are transitory, experience is immortal. She has packed all her experiences in a brand-new suitcase and thrown it into her mind-space. Now it's proprietary. Only she has the key to the locker of her memories. Some of them she is going to share today with a distinguished audience that is keen to learn the truth behind Shyla's Buddha smile that has never left her face from the day she resigned from the organisation to settle in India. India calling it is!

Everyone sits down, Charles with the usual, chauvinist lack of attention and Shyla can shoot. Two hours fly with her projecting data and photographs on the wall and telling the real story of what she has seen with her own eyes, what she has lived through, scars of the soul that will never heal and she had to endure for a few weeks, whereas people living in Chhattisgarh are faced with them every day. Her deepest upheaval of a lifetime is just another day in the lives of these mortals of a lesser earth. She closes her presentation with the video of the pregnant girl in the refugee camp. She is knitting a jute blanket. That is all she can promise the child in her womb. The village belle has 'gang-raped' written all over her face. Her eyes are evident of the innocence that was snatched away from her mercilessly. However she wears the most pristine smile that speaks volumes of a woman's endurance. That she is also a soul like anybody else going through a human experience, a little nasty though, unlike many others within the comfort of their electronic gadgets, wine tasting, fast cars, and flying jets. Ironically we are blissfully ignorant of the impermanence of life and nature. Shyla adds passion to her velvet voice. "So her name is Anjali who has been raped, the child in her womb has no father and she will have no one to lean on- to raise the infant: not only everyone in her family has been killed but all the young men were kidnapped and used as human shields, I've seen this happening myself" Shyla's eyes are watery but her speech is still resilient.

"And here are the victims, those who could do nothing but witness the madness and who are now in refugee camps hoping one day to return home. Rather to simply own a piece of shelter. Their food is watery and their water is brown in colour. The eyes are worn out but their souls swear of strength. Though the boundaries between heaven and hell have blurred in this bloody war even most of the perpetrators were victims. So what do we do? Do we stand aside and watch? Do we spend more time in research and data collection? Do we discuss this over lunch at a fancy café? Well this is a good time to act, the Turu Dalam gang has been beheaded and before they reform in a new and deadlier shape we can help the people and possibly save them, but we need to be committed. We can bring them home. We can sleep peacefully once they sleep in solace. We can save their souls and ours. Are we interested?"

For once Shyla's words were not heard. They were felt. She so brilliantly translated her experience to the poignant energy floating in the room. No one was spared by the Truth. The commotion in the office is palpable and Allan, despite his long career and the many things he has seen, has to take a sip of water before the closing statement. Allan has made many tough decisions and sanctioned several grants. But this powerful presentation by her favourite employee of Indian origin has managed to stir his soul. All of a sudden he feels that all his labour uptill this hour was superficial compared to the experience that Shyla has been enlightened with- in the very Jungles of India. Like the rays of the sun in different regions of the world every experience hits the human consciousness with varied intensity. Like the camera aperture, the human soul takes in different volumes of light. And to Allan this dramatic episode has been of intense exposure. His hand shivers a bit before he can put the sparkling-water bottle back in the tray.

"Well Thomas, a spotless job as always. It is evident that the affected provinces require immediate assistance, both financially and through capacity building. As you rightly concluded, we need to support this rehabilitation programme with human resources as well as with funds in order to re-establish a valid education system, rehabilitation of the refugees and reformation of infrastructure. As we all know money alone does very little. We need to feel their pain. We need to redeem our phony attitude. We need to put our hearts on the line"

Charles grunts heavily "this is bullshit, we are not in a classroom" Charles ego takes the better of him. Shyla, who was unsure whether to use this card until the last minute is now very sure it's the right move.

"Well, Allan, if you don't mind I have one last source I would like to introduce, I understand that mine is a report so I also brought live evidence of the data I have collected"

She taps a few keys on her computer and suddenly a gigantic version of Raghav's face appears on the white screen on the wall. The Wi-Fi router blinks a live feed.

"Hi Raghav, these people would like to hear from you what you think about our 'Action Against poverty'- project"

"Namaste! My name is Raghav Sharma. My father was a local police informer who was killed by the Red Militants when I was a baby. A police officer adopted me and I was happy but then the Turu Dalam killed him too. Despite the tragedies I had to go through I have been very lucky, as God has sent me a new godfather – Neil. In my country there are millions of Raghavs' who are not as blessed as I am. They need help. My grandmother taught me- stay connected with the Supreme Being and he will protect you. And that's what I did in times of despair. We are Indians and we keep our heads up. We only need an opportunity, a chance to get back on our feet. Choices to go to school, to cross bombed bridges and not see dead bodies along the way, to survive and live freely. To have the liberty see the same sun rise, to breathe the same air as you do, without the burning smell of gunpowder.

But I shall choose to live in Faith. With Faith we can build more schools, we will walk across broken bridges, with Faith we can heal tormented hearts, and rebuild our future. With Faith one day, you and I will be the same in every respect. Like here and like there. Neil dada, do you think they heard me?"

Neil appears in the picture, his wounded arm still wrapped around his body, he looks into the camera to check if the sound was on but Shyla has to interrupt the conversation before she gets too emotional.

"Yes we heard you little angel!" says Shyla "I'll chat to you both later, ciao" and closes her laptop. The tumult in the room now is even more intense. The triumph of the human spirit can seldom be explained. It can only be felt. Just like the spirit divine- thinks Shyla with a warm smile simmering on her lips. She is electric from within.

Later, in Allan's office Shyla sits down with a cup of Columbian coffee, they are both silent as he reads the parting letter she has just handed him. She wanted to thank him in written words for all his professional and personal kindness offered. But the words though simple are not as effective as they were earlier in the conference room. Sometimes words are limited by the intensity of the intent.

"I'm going to miss you, kiddo. Are you sure this is the right thing for you, I mean look at you, you are young and pretty and can have the whole Capetown at your comfort?"

"Sure as sure can be, Boss. I've got my friends waiting for me. And now I can finally work for people who need me most, I've found my true calling, but I am going to miss my blind dates"

Allan smiles, he will miss her, her red nail varnish and her bad mood in the morning, her Columbian coffee odour and her arguments with Charles. He gets up and without a word goes to hug her. They stay like that, tight in a hug for a long time. The world takes a pause, the breeze skips a beat, and the sunlight goes soft on the windows. It's time for two friends to part, each one in a different direction, each one to a new life. The story of life!

"God bless you, child" whispers Allan as Shyla leaves the room, her mind already projected on the sky. The soulful silence between the two speaks volumes.

Shyla tiptoes with nimble feet into Father Thomas's room. It's well lit by the Oakwood French windows. The Victorian, eagle armchair with mustard velvet upholstery still reminds Shyla of the warmth that father Thomas carried in his aura. But this time she can only feel whiteness all around her. The gentle daylight that the high walls reflect gives the room a natural glow. However she fails to sense any spiritual presence around her: the air is quite flat and unattractive. The light is evenly settled and there is no particular halo in the room. Shyla tries hard to recall her mother's presence but there is zilch response to her stimuli. She desperately attempts to connect to Father Thomas but her mind is numb. All she can hear is the sound of a fan revolving in the adjoining corridor. Dejection prompts her to step out and leave for her destination- India. Her footsteps slow down as she feels a tingling sensation in her guts. A stream of energy flows through the flesh preceded by hormonal rush to her brains. Shyla for the first time gets a sensation of a strong spirit brimming inside her consciousness. The flow of blood gushes within her veins, where every drop effortlessly carries with it a promise of passion, fortitude and commitment. Her head rises towards the sky as she bids farewell to the blessed building. Likewise she whispers a poignant goodbye to a life that is gone with the wind, a life that no longer belongs to her, a life that will be part of her fairy tales when she would be a grandmother.

The airplane descends from the sky with a heavy heart. Coming from the tidy and spotless airport of Cape Town the airport of Delhi is a nightmare for tourists. They breathe in India with excitement and fear of the unknown, the air is filled with the smell of fried food and curry, of perspiring people and air freshener. Shyla looks at the foreign tourists and smiles, they remind her of herself when she first got here. Neil and Raghav are waiting for her outside. They came all the way to Delhi to meet her as soon as she set foot in India. Raghav is over the moon. He is holding a kite that reads "Welcome Shyla". The drive to Chhattisgarh is not as adventurous as it was the first time Shyla landed. At times- Lack of adventure is the best adventure- she ponders after her dramatic last few months. Back in Chhattisgarh, at night, as she tucks Raghav into bed, he smiles in his sleep and hugs the stuffed tiger she has brought him from South Africa. He feels secured. He breathes in love.

Neil is waiting for her outside, the sounds of cricket has its own symphony. Neil gets musical with his hands moving like a conductor. The contrast of the skies hides the limp on his leg that is yet to heal from the bullet wound. Neil had never imagined an evening that felt so young and fresh. A new start. A new life. His eyes sparkle with the moonbeam dancing in his iris. Shyla notices in the sky a set of stars that look just like her Trishul tattoo, wishful thinking, she smiles as she joins Neil on the stretcher chair. A cup of hot masala chai and an earthen vase of tiger orchids await for her on the little coffee table between the two chairs.

"So, this is your crib, huh?"

"Yeah, well, it needs some work but more or less it's gonna be our home..." Shyla shivers at the word "home" but for the first time it's not a shiver of fear or pain, at the idea of having to share the rest of her life with the same person. Strangely enough it's a shiver of pleasure. Home. That's it.

They kiss for a long time and for the first time not as they run from something but giving it all the time it deserves.

"Do you want to tell me something?"

"I know what you're thinking... You are thinking, "How the hell is Neil going to save tigers without a penny? Shyla I'm committed to this cause, honestly. The same commitment you have towards the development of Chhattisgarh and its tribes."

"Neil, it's not that I don't believe in your commitment, I'm just worried about..."

"The money?"

"Yeah well, it's not secondary and now I don't have my fancy South African salary anymore and we have Raghav... it's ironic but it's actually quite expensive to work for a cause"

"I have got that sorted... A tiger will save other tigers... Let me show you something..."

He opens his shirt and a huge gemstone appears underneath it, hung the way Purba would hang it, wrapped in a jute bag. Voila: The fifty carat magical Alexandrite, the tiger of gemstones. Neil takes it close to the candle and the stone changes colour so evidently, from blue to red, it's almost like a miracle.

"Where... Where did you get that?"

"Purba gave it to me before dying. She and I never had a story but there has always been something... special... not just basic instincts. An unspoken passion she had for me. She has never been my type, too crude, too driven to enact the revolution and too greedy for my taste, but she has always been very kind to me and when she understood she would have not lived to enjoy this treasure, she gave me the gem she had smuggled from God knows where"

"And what now?"

"I have an idea...my name is Neil"

The next day Neil leaves on his rusty motorbike to go to Nepal. He passes many towns and several forests. These lands remind him of the journeys that he has taken earlier. The route has always been long but Neil's brother had taught him in childhood days: that the journey is more important than the destination. Trekking on mountains, swimming across rivers, walking in the forest, at the age of ten, he planted the seeds of adventure, of life being an amazing journey. Thus Neil would seldom get excited reaching someplace, some destination, it was always about the trip, travelling through places and people that made him come alive. On every occasion that Neil would traverse distances on his motorbike, he would go back to his childhood experiences as a strong reminiscence for comfort. Neil would imagine himself as a ten-year old- Neil riding the second hand military bike that he bought from an auction in Nepal. Through the eyes of a ten year old Neil would be able to see the mundane in the most extraordinary way. *Through the eyes of wonder the world is a wonder.* The trees, the roads, the people, the animals, the hamlets and the textured sky all appeared as wonderful as a fairy tale. The road of a few hundred miles was like a fly, a mother holding on to the baby and gliding through earth with a sensation that would put paradise to shame. For Neil, it was never about the gems that he was smuggling, or the money or the sex that he indulged occasionally, it was always the moment. Neil is so involved in the present moment; he is perpetually making love to the marvellous woman called 'Now'. *Probably as a child, when he got lost in the clouds atop a mountain, the sky whispered to him in private "never leave the hands of 'lady now' and you will never ever feel lost".*

Today Neil stops for a short exercise. His back is sore this time. His wounded thigh is stiff. Perhaps the action at Debraj's den was something his body was not well prepared for. Neil bends a few times to touch his toes. He gets a familiar smell, a smell that gives him an orgasm virtually. A tiger is drinking water by the pond downhill. Neil clears his view and takes a peek at the marvel of nature. The morning sun gives the majestic cat, a furry corona that matches to none. The tiger on cue turns to face Neil standing on the edge of the hill. An enticing exchange of man and the man-eater takes place in the confines of Sundarban. The considerable distance between the two is what makes Neil feel unthreatened. But what Neil finds strange is that the Tiger is evenly poised. There is no fear or, excitement or anger on the tiger's face. The tiger seems to be in its Nirvana moods. Neil gets a hint when he stares directly into the tiger's eyes. The communication is clear. The tiger's eyes give a clarion call "we are not here for long, one day all of us tiger's will be extinct, so enjoy the tiger spotting while we last, soon we will be just plain pictures on the wall just like your ancestors" Neil eyes turn moist and so does the tigers'. The young tiger turns away and disappears in the Jungle soundlessly like two brothers part across the border of life and death. Neil ponders "do tigers have souls, no way, on second thoughts maybe, some cosmic connection"

Neil reaches Pokhara in the middle of the night. He checks into his usual lodge overlooking the lake. Next morning Neil meets Peter, the middleman from Bangkok. He avoids Xian's bar, he has never been good with goodbyes and he wants to leave her with the best possible recollection of him. But while passing by he sees Xian from a distance doing what she knows the best- playing the perfect host. She looks like a free spirit waiting for her love to walk through the door. Someday. Some world.

Neil meets Peter in a hostel for backpackers. They are confined in a rooftop balcony. Neil hands him a jute bag. Peter checks out the content against the bright sun. The colour changes. The Alexandrite looks genuine. Peter smiles in greed. He is too preoccupied in the future, all the monies he will make in this deal. Obviously he misses the beauty of the stone. He cannot fathom the light that changed the colour of the stone. So much so that he is already thinking about his next big deal.

"So, I've heard there's a ruby as big as my fist in Orissa, any news? I have a buyer who would pay..."

"I'm sorry man, I'm out of the game..."

"The game is never over Neil"

"Well every precious stone shines only after it is cut, till then it's only an ordinary piece of rock"

"Think about it Neil, I have several thousands of dollars waiting for you..."

"Yeah, you can keep them waiting, this is my last job, for now, I need to get going, I don't want to miss my son's first gardening class... that's the shine bit"

And he gets back on his motorbike riding away in the midday sun, leaving Peter with a huge gem in his pocket and several thousand dollars less in his bank account. Neil has smartly hidden the hundred dollar bills covered with a waterproof plastic wrapper, which is floating inside the petrol tank. The petrol tank has been modulated to open from the side too, attached with a palm-sized lid that looks like a patch of junk metal. Neil knows his routes, he has the Zamindars of the borderland that let him in, and even if he is stopped, he knows the trade secrets of the security staff. Everything is for sale. Except! Neil rides with his palms stretched out in air, on both the sides, balancing the motorbike with his muscular lower body. He shuts his eyes kissing his fate in a splinter of time. His dry palms vibrate with the whistling breeze. The energy around swallows him like the water swallows the fish. Once again, his brothers' profound mantra reverberates in his tranquil mind *"Never run behind life... never let life lag behind you... hold life in the grip of your palms and ride along with it like a butterfly"*

A few kilometres away, Shyla is at the Government High school in Bastar. The same school that was inaugurated by the chief minister- Shekhar Singh. The school is celebrating Dusshera, which the district of Bastar is famous for. Almost every household in this region awaits this festival. A humungous effigy of the biggest villain Ravana as per the Hindu myth is burnt to celebrate the victory of good over evil. Strangely the inhabitants of Bastar are still fighting the evil forces that are keeping their lives in constant turmoil. They are probably awaiting for a 'Ram- the true saviour', the ideal hero to come as the knight in shining armour. Unknown to them a few people (the true saviours) are trying their best to awaken the Ram that resides inside all humans. Shyla believes that Ram dwells inside the hearts of every human being and thus it needs to arise from within. There are two split characters in every human being-Ram and Ravana. In this subconscious battle within, the character that will win is the one who you feed the most. Today she initiates her pursuit of stirring an awakening with the children who are the most receptive. They don't use too much of their mind when they know that something is right. She is entertaining the school kids of Bastar with a puppet show. Two stuffed puppets that boast of the tribal art are being manipulated by her nimble hands. The puppets are made of shiny and colourful hand-woven fabrics and stuffed with cotton. The orange puppet seated on a golden horse represents Ram while the black one seated on a monster bull symbolises a Ravana on the prowl. Right above their heads, Shyla has hung some metal toys in the shape of the sun, the moon and the stars, that cumulatively create an illusion of a miniature galaxy. The kids get frightened of Ravana- the demon when they see some special lighting effects, which highlight its vampire teeth and bloodshot eyes. Raghav is helping Shyla on the lights. He is rotating a combination of some torchlights and a handy tube bulb. Shyla juggles the puppets with great momentum: a fierce battle between the two puppets keeps the kids glued. Their heads sway in perfect sync with the momentum of the raging puppets. They feel they are in the midst of the battle. Soon one of the stuffed toy- the Ravana drops dead. Shyla ends the show with the commentary in her hypnotizing voice "So in the fight of angels and demons, demons do look more powerful and win quite a few battles but the ultimate victory in this deadly war belongs to the angels. It is for this very reason that we are still alive and it is for this very reason, the universe will survive beyond our existence." The children are awed by the conviction in the gentle voice of their lady Puppeteer. For a moment they forget to blink. Shyla smiles in conquest. She has accomplished her hidden agenda- to plant a strong seed of nobility in these divine kids going through a human or rather a very sub-human experience. This is the very gratification she was in search for. The hunt for her rapist father was all a superficial endeavour. The militant father by blood had no direct connection with her existence whatsoever and will never have. If life is about meaning, she mulls, then heaven can be experienced on earth- she infers. From Capetown to an almost non-existent town in Chhattisgarh, Shyla wonders- how far has she travelled! The answer reverberates- "*She has travelled very far indeed. Far beyond her own expectations*"

Her soul speaks to her.

"Some places don't have an address"

It's her voice.

It's her true self that was shrouded behind all that sham.

It's a choice.

As Neil gets home, he hides the money Peter has given him at a secret place in the garden backyard. He has dug a covert trench, which is enclosed by thorny shrubbery. There is a metal casket planted inside the furrow. Neil also throws in the *Pachisi* dice that was always resting in his pocket. He has a last look at it and bids a heartfelt farewell. Anil would habitually win the *Pachisi* game. This would make Neil feel inferior as compared to his brother. Today Neil finds himself liberated of all self-doubts. He stands tall. He is self-assured. He shovels the earth back to its place. The shoulder length undergrowth ruffles his hair. The patch on the pit merges with the soil like a bird in the sky.

Neil joins Shyla and Raghav at the plant nursery. Shyla is taking Raghav through different types of plants with tenacity. Neil spots a nimbus around them. Is it Shyla, is it Raghav, or is it the spirit of Anand that surrounds them. Neil stands there still like he was a holographic image made of ice. A ray of light bursts open inside his mind. Neil has an epiphany. It's the glow in his very own eyes. He intervenes to steal her thunder. "You see, this is a lentil seed, we will put it in cotton and in a week it will sprout. And in two months... Daaaal" Shyla is not amused. Neil is too excited.

"Enough of science, people... time to play, time to be!" Neil opens the water sprinkler behind them getting all of them wet and laughing. The water molecules appear frozen in the path of time while Neil and Shyla are losing all their memories. They are suspended in this bizarre capsule of timelessness.

Fate cannot help take notice the exuberance of this ordinary moment. Fate innovates to create a dimension par eternity, freezes the very moment and captures the pristine fusion of two bodies but one soul.

When two soul mates unite with equal daredevilry, against cruel circumstances, and fight their inner demons only to discover their true calling, they are destined to be Tiger Mates.

Says who, says me.

And I am fate.

- -

The choice: Let it be love now, so it will be love then!

– Amrish Shah.

www.amrishshah.com